PHOENIX RISING

*

THE THIRD BOOK
OF THE FLOOD TRILOGY

PHOENIX RISING

By

MARGUERITE STEEN

COLLINS
ST JAMES'S PLACE, LONDON
1952

*The title of this book
in the United States of America
is " Jehovah Blues"*

PRINTED IN GREAT BRITAIN
COLLINS CLEAR-TYPE PRESS: LONDON AND GLASGOW

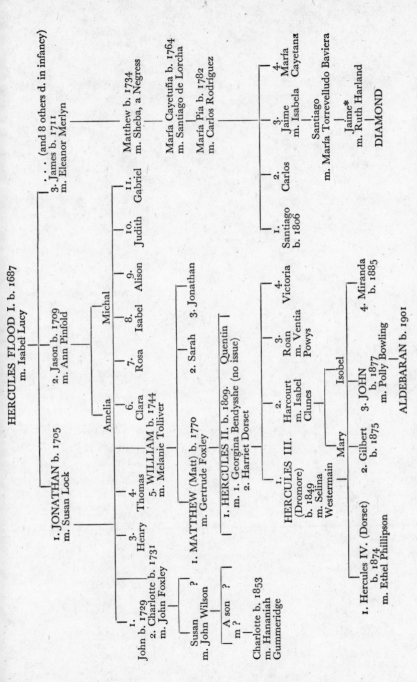

HERCULES FLOOD I. b. 1687
m. Isabel Lucy

1. JONATHAN b. 1705
m. Susan Lock

2. Jason b. 1709
m. Ann Pinfold

... (and 8 others d. in infancy)
3. James b. 1711
m. Eleanor Merlyn

Amelia   Michal

3. Henry   4. Thomas   5. WILLIAM b. 1744
m. Melanie Tolliver

6. Clara   7. Rosa   8. Isabel   9. Alison   10. Judith   11. Gabriel

1.
John b. 1729
m. Charlotte b. 1731
John Foxley

1. MATTHEW (Matt) b. 1770
m. Gertrude Foxley

2. Sarah   3. Jonathan

Matthew b. 1734
m. Sheba, a Negress

María Cayetuña b. 1764
m. Santiago de Lorcha

María Pia b. 1782
m. Carlos Rodriguez

Susan   ?
m. John Wilson

1. HERCULES II. b. 1809.
m. 1. Georgina Bendysshe (no issue)
2. Harriet Dorset

Quentin
(no issue)

2. Harcourt
m. Isabel Clunes

3. Roan
m. Ventia Powys

4. Victoria

1. Santiago b. 1806   2. Carlos   3. Jaime
m. Isabela

4. María Cayetana

A son   ?
m.   ?

HERCULES III.
(Dromore)
b. 1849
m. Selina Westermain

Mary   Isobel

Santiago
m. María Torrevelludo Baviera

Jaime*
m. Ruth Harland

DIAMOND

Charlotte b. 1853
m. Hananiah Gummeridge

1. Hercules IV. (Dorset)
b. 1874
m. Ethel Phillipson

2. Gilbert
b. 1875

3. JOHN
b. 1877
m. Polly Bowling

4. Miranda
b. 1885

ALDEBARAN b. 1901

*Santiago María Xavier Jaime Mateo de los Flujos Rodriguez y Torrevelludo Baviera. See Twilight on the Floods, p. 440.

Chapter One

I

"**B**EEN TO the Empire this week?"

"What—Polly Bowling?" The speaker chuckled tolerantly. "Getting a bit past it, isn't she? The Astaires are more in my line—Hi! look what you're doing!" he snapped as a big ebony ruler clapped down within an inch of his left hand, negligently disposed with a cigar between the first and second fingers, on the edge of the Board-room table.

"Fly," muttered Joe. "Can't stand the brutes."

He leaned back, folded his arms and lowered his heavy lids upon their chatter. The red mahogany table with the note-pads and agenda-sheets, the leather-seated Board-room furniture, the big plate-glass windows opening on the (to him) tasteless and squalid scene—all faded out, as he tried for a moment to imagine himself back in Queen Square, Bristol: in the long, panelled room with its shell-arched windows and doorways, its wine-dark Chippendale, its mellowness of tradition, and the old sand-boxes and quills which, still occupying their time-honoured position in front of the clerk's chair (no clerk was ever called a secretary under the Flood régime), rebuked the user of fountain pen and typewriter with their air of dignified leisure. There, from his Chairman's seat which he never occupied without a sense of humility and gratitude, he had looked out upon a delicate tracery of rigging, meshing the scene he had loved with passion since childhood: the soft lift of the land on the other side of Avon, the warm confusion of little tiled roofs topped by the Redcliff and the gentle horizon, moistly golden or grey. His heart sickened for Bristol each time he caught glimpses of sullen Mersey linking the uneven building line of the waterfront; of the Overhead shaking its soot down on the Back Goree as it

7

rattled along its out-dated track; and he pinched his nostrils against the stench of oranges and malt that thickens and poisons the air blowing from the Pier Head.

Perhaps, thought Joseph Prior, all that was beautiful, to Liverpool men; perhaps the crudely modern Liver and Dock Board Buildings embodied some sentiment—if it were only the bitter pride of a seaport trying hard to recover from the blows dealt to it by the 1914–18 war: that war to which Floods of Bristol was not the only one of the ancient shipping firms to fall casualty. That was how he, Joe Prior, chose to regard the enforced amalgamation. No longer Floods of Bristol—the Purcell–Flood Line, with headquarters in Water Street, Liverpool, monopolized the trade he had striven, for five heart-breaking years after the Armistice, to recover.

He had done his best to take it philosophically; to accept with good grace the position they offered the Chairman of Floods on the Purcell board; his main inducement being the hope that, by continuing to hold office, he might be able in some degree to safeguard the interests of those who, for the sake of their living, had been obliged to accept the new order. The Liverpool gentlemen had been courteous; had almost —not quite—succeeded in concealing their good-natured scorn of Joe Prior's old-fashioned methods, his distaste for modern hustle, his suspicion of sharp practice, his unvarying courtesy to inferiors. From the day he took his seat on the Board, there was none who did not accord respect, albeit unwilling, to the tall, burly figure, limping heavily on its stick as it entered the Board-room. "Good morning, gentlemen"; his greeting never varied, despite the casual "Hallo, Prior"-s, the "How do"-s of those reared in a less stringent school of courtesies. Sir Vincent Purcell ducked his head and fidgeted with his papers; a short, tub-fronted, over-dressy personage, with the ugly, "across-the-face" local accent smeared over his speech, he was the only one actively, though secretly, to resent Joe Prior.

Not that Joe put on airs. He lowered himself quietly into his armchair, saw that his stick and artificial leg (he had left the other in a South African field hospital) were in no one's way;

nodded gravely to his neighbours and picked up the agenda sheet to refresh his memory (unnecessarily) of the contents, which he already knew by heart, while the others gossiped, told Stock Exchange yarns and lit pipes or cigarettes. A heavy smoker, Joe never smoked at Board meetings; he could hardly have said why—save that authority had come to him too late and too hard for him to lay aside the small ceremonies which are authority's due.

Behind his closed lids he listened, now, to the idle chatter. There was important business on the agenda; one item—the first after the reading of the minutes—which had kept Joe awake through many nights. That it should stand there, in the first place, proving itself, in the compilers' estimation, too trifling to call for lengthy discussion, added to his inquietude. Could there conceivably have been a moment in the history of the firm of Flood when a matter concerning the lives of scores of human beings was treated by the Board as a bagatelle?

Sir Vincent brought a particularly smutty story to its conclusion in a roar of laughter, as two late-comers slipped into their seats. From the corner of his eye Joe noted that most of the laughter was forced; two men on the opposite side of the table were not even smiling, as they leaned together to compare the notes they had been making. But Sir Vincent had his syco-phants, and they kept up their tribute in muffled chuckles while the Chairman called for the minutes. During the reading of the minutes several continued to whisper and titter. There was a perfunctory show of hands. Sir Vincent scrawled his initials and passed the minute-book back to the secretary.

"Well, I take it we don't 'ave to waste much time over this first item"—his watery gaze ran round the table—avoiding Joe—as he thrust himself back to the utmost length of his short arms. The attitude was belligerent; Sir Vincent was accus-tomed to dominating his Board. "Last meeting, you'll re-member, we run over the pros an' cons, and we was most of us in agreement——"

The man opposite Joe lifted his head quickly.

" 'Ad you got something to say? " asked Sir Vincent suavely.

" As the minutes have just shown, I was unable to be present at the last meeting, and had no opportunity of taking part in the discussion." The speaker deliberately clipped a pair of pince-nez on his long and well-cut nose, and lifted the agenda. " This is my first intimation of the Board's proposal to pay off the British crew of the Purcell–Flood liner *Obango*——"

Sir Vincent lifted his hand and turned pettishly to one of his Yes-men.

" I thought you were fixin' that ? "

" I—we—we talked it over last night," stuttered the other, with a reproachful glance at the pince-nez. " I understood we'd come to an agreement——"

The owner of the pince-nez raised his eyebrows.

" A verbal report of the Board's discussion hardly covers the position, I think ! "

" If you don't turn up at meetings you can't expect the firm's business to stand still," said Sir Vincent rudely.

Joe leaned forward in his chair.

" If the Chairman will allow us to have the minutes again, Mr. Goring will see exactly where we got to in the argument."

The appropriate minute was read—in silence. Goring thanked the reader ironically.

" It would not appear that there was a discussion—in the exact sense of the term."

" There wasn't," grunted Joe. " The matter was raised less than ten minutes before the meeting closed, and there was no time except for the Chairman's statement——"

" With which, as I'd bin given reason to believe, the majority of those present was in agreement." Sir Vincent dispensed with the phraseology of his office and thumped his fist on the blotting pad before him. " Damn it—we got 'alf a day's work a'ead of us—and this *Obango* business is only a matter o' routine ! "

" It wouldn't be a matter of routine if somebody was to put you off the Board and take away your director's fees without giving you rhyme or reason—would it ? " said Joe Prior.

Sir Vincent held his breath until he appeared to be at bursting point, then half rose from his chair.

" Gentlemen—I—I'm sorry ! By heck I am ! But I must ask you to accept my resignation."

Amid an uproar, and shouts of " Sit down, Purcell ! " Joe tried to collect his thoughts. When at last there was silence, and a few faces were turned disapprovingly towards him, although the majority were concentrated in embarrassment on the agenda, Joe said slowly,

" I suppose I owe the Chairman an apology. I'd no business to say what I did. If there's to be any resigning, I'm the one to do it. But I've got something to say first."

" Excuse me," said a little dried-up person at the far end of the table. " On a point of order ?—Is Mr. Prior's resignation effective ? If so, I put it that he is not in order in addressing the meeting."

" Oh, shut up." The speaker grimaced at Joe. " Jabbering about resignation—like a schoolgirls' debating society ! Go on, Prior ; let's hear what you've got to say."

" It won't take long. The proposition before the Board is the paying-off of the crew of the *Obango* in favour of Asiatic labour. Gentlemen, I ask you." Joe looked slowly round the table ; several people uncomfortably avoided his gaze. " What mortal justification can we find, as Britishers, for an action that goes against every instinct of human decency ? "

There was a pause, before someone muttered that that was all very fine, but economic conditions brought about by the war obliged people to do a good many things that were against their normal principles.

" The *Obango's* the most costly ship of the line. She's never paid her way since her maiden trip. Passengers want luxury these days, and they don't expect to pay extra for it ! We're up against the competition of the bigger liners—half of 'em running on Goanese and Lascar labour, and we've got either to cut expenses or put fares up. If we put fares up we lose our trade to the White Star and Cunard, because we can't offer White Star amenities. I take the Chairman's view ; I don't see there's anything to discuss."

For all that, a ragged argument sprang up round the table.

Few of the Board were disposed, outright, to support a step whose repercussions would certainly go far and wide along the waterfronts but the majority felt that there was no other solution of a problem which was weighing heavily on every shipping firm in the country.

"We're bound to do it—on account of the shareholders. As it is, our balance sheet isn't going to make very pretty reading at the next shareholders' meeting."

"H'm—old Mildenhall's going to have something pretty drastic to say, when he gets his dividend sheet!" grimaced Joe's neighbour. Joe winced; he too was sensitive to the feelings of shareholders, and it had been against his advice that the Marquess of Mildenhall had increased his holdings in Purcell-Flood.

"Now look 'ere." The Chairman had recovered his equanimity, realizing that the meeting, if not morally, was effectively with him. "Figures talk—so 'ere's some figures for you. If we get rid of the chief cook we're savin' fifteen quid a month; a dago'll do the job for five. Same thing with the stewards——"

Goring's face was chalk-white, his thin hands, knotted before him, showed the knuckles staring through the flesh. Joe looked at him, and looked away.

"You may be right, Purcell. I—I can't support you. It's not men we're selling—it's a principle—for thirty pieces of silver," said Goring, almost in a whisper.

It was not often that Joe's old amputation hurt him, but for some reason, while still his heart lifted at Goring's words, a dart of such anguish went through the nerves of the stump that for very shock his senses almost left him. In the brief black-out, while he struggled to recover himself, it was as though a hand came on his shoulder: a small, hard hand whose touch, so long unfelt, so nearly forgotten, revived a love that once had governed his life. *Johnny!* Oh, Johnny Flood, how like you to come, in my most need, to comfort me!

"There's one point, gentlemen, we have all of us forgotten." It was so long since Joe had spoken that several of the listeners started. "Suppose we set aside, for now, consideration of what this step we're proposing to take will mean in misery to some people who have served us—served the line—well for a good many years. Suppose we don't think of the children who'll be running barefoot about our streets and the women who'll be driven to thieving—or worse—because there's nothing to eat in the house."

" Oh chuck it," muttered a voice on his left. " What do you think we are—a lot of bloodsuckers ? "

" I say—leave all that out ! " Joe's voice rose ; to more than one startled listener his voice was the voice of old Harcourt Flood ; incredible as it seemed, he even looked like " old Iron-guts " !—" We got something else to think of. What about the bitterness we're going to stir up ? What about the way every white man's going to hate every coloured man, when he watches his job, that he's dependent on for his living, put in a nigger's hands ? What do you expect'll happen here—down Park Road and round Herculaneum ?—and in Cardiff, along Bute Street and round Loudoun Square ? What about us in Bristol ? What about Hull, and Glasgow, and the southern ports ?

" You're going to start war, gentlemen—no less surely than the damned Germans started it in 1914 ; it may be a smaller war, but it'll be no less bitter, and cause no less sharp distress——"

" Gammon ! We aren't starting the war ; go and talk to Cunard, White Star, Brocklebank, Holt, Elder Dempster——"

" Does that make us any less guilty, if we take part in it ? Flood's a great name—and Purcell's a great name," he remembered to add. " More than two hundred years my old firm's stood for honest dealing and steady employment——"

" Ay—when you were slave-trading ? " jeered a graceless voice. The atmosphere froze ; even in 1930 reminders of this kind were not well received in Liverpool shipping circles.

" We wronged them plenty in the past ! " Pride swelled in him with the involuntary use of the pronoun " we." It was long, now, since he had doubted that he was the son of Harcourt Flood. " Maybe that's the reason I won't be party to any more wrong-doing so far as coloured people are concerned."

"But it's not the blacks that are being 'wronged,' as you put it," his *vis-à-vis* leaned over to say in a reasonable tone. "I thought that's what you'd just been saying? The fellow that's got the gripe is the white—poor devil; and there I agree with you. It's a bloody shame, but it's got to be; you must see that, Prior, for all your persuasiveness!"

"It's the coloured fellow who comes off worst," Joe persisted, "whether he's black, yellow or ginger. First, because he's exploited for wages a white chap won't accept——"

"You mean, that his union won't let him accept!" sneered Purcell.

"What's unions for? To see a man gets a living wage."

"The blacks' living standard's lower than the whites'; that's how they can afford to——"

"Why should it be lower?" Joe's hand smote the table with Harcourt's gesture. "That's not what we're here to argue about. The biggest wrong we're doing the coloured folk is setting the whites against them: fomenting hate between the races—hatred that'll work itself out in crime and violence. Hatred for which the coloured folk will pay—because when it comes to a showdown between black and white, white always wins."

A heated argument sprang up on the equity of British law —and was furiously interrupted by the Chairman.

"There's been enough gabbing on this bloody subject! It's time somebody proposed——"

He looked round; the wizened little man who had shown himself anxious to accept Joe's resignation bobbed to his feet and formally proposed "that the British crew of the Purcell-Flood liner *Obango* be paid off in favour of foreign labour." Another of Sir Vincent's toadies seconded it. The Chairman called for a show of hands. One or two went up with noticeable reluctance, but the call that followed for "those against" was a mere formula. Only Joe and Goring raised their hands. "Carried," said Sir Vincent, and accepted a light for his cigar.

"And now, p'r'aps, we can get down to business."

"Just a minute, if you please, Mr. Chairman." Joe struggled

to his feet. "It's my duty, now, to ask the Board to accept my resignation."

There was an uncomfortable silence, ended by Sir Vincent's mutterings,

"Well, if that's 'ow you feel—I suppose there's nothing more to be said."

"Nothing," agreed Joe, and took his weight on his stick. "So—I will wish you good day, gentlemen."

He walked to the door in a silence that made him sorry for them; it could not be good, to carry that load of guilt. At the door Goring overtook him, holding out his hand.

"Goodbye, Prior. I am more sorry than I can say——" He looked more than sorry; deep lines were drawn under his eyes and at the corners of his mouth. Why, wondered Joe, returning the grip of his hand—if he were as sorry as all that, did he not also resign?—and then reflected that it was as well, for Purcell-Flood, that one man of Goring's integrity should remain on its Board.

Down on street-level, he glanced at his watch: going on for half-past three, and his train did not leave until six. Two and a half empty hours to be filled—somehow. He rejected the idea of the club; too many he might meet there were aware that it was the day for the Purcell-Flood Board meeting, and his appearance at such an hour would start a spate of gossip. Take a taxi to the Adelphi and spend an hour with Polly? ("Getting a bit past it." Ignorant puppy! As though Polly did not dwarf her contemporaries as the name POLLY BOWLING dwarfed all others on the bills.) It shocked Joe a little, to discover that he felt for once unequal to Polly's robust good cheer.

He found himself limping down towards the Pier Head. The salt air and the sight of rolling water helped to restore him, although he felt a painful stab of the heart when he found himself under the towering lee of a Purcell-Flood liner, lifted by the tide, her Plimsoll high above his head. It was hard to realize he no longer had any concern with her.

He thought, I'll write to Aldebaran. It'll do me good to get this off my chest, to Deb.

II

A slow gratification puffed Biri's cheeks into mellow half-moons. At least a dozen of his customers were " in the news," and he liked it that way. There was a pleasant sprinkling of the younger aristocracy. The stage, for once, was represented only by a shy young leading lady, too recently arrived at glory to blare her presence from a table reserved by tradition for the famous. A pretty, modest creature, low-voiced and delicate-mannered ; Biri sighed in approving her. He did not care for actresses ; he knew from experience that this one would in a month or less be treating his restaurant as an extension of her stage, and his guests as her reluctant gallery.

Biri was making the first of his three routine appearances, that carried him down the centre aisle with a brief pause at each table. It was said one's status was determined by the length of Biri's pause.

When the door, revolving in its cage of glass, swung into the room a tall young woman in a dark grey tailor-made, Biri's, for a moment, held its breath—then let it out again. The white face framed in waves of cinnamon hair, the black line of the brows across a pair of yellow eyes and the stubborn scarlet mouth were known to most of Biri's customers. She was hatless, but her hands, stuck in the pockets of a coat that bore the stamp of *haute couture*, were gloved, and the gloves matched the bag thrust negligently under her arm. Her slim legs ended in a pair of narrow feet. Dressed for the paddock, rather than Biri's, " after the theatre," she stood there, with a youth's insouciance, indifferently scanning the tables, with a frown that suggested short-sightedness, and smoothed itself out when she found Biri bowing in front of her.

" Hallo, Biri. Is Lord Orlando anywhere around ? "

" His lordship has been waiting some time. Very pleased indeed to see you, Miss Flood ! Show Miss Flood to his lord-ship's table."

Conscious of the display of her immature shoulders, one of the débutantes leaned nearer to her companion.

" Isn't it rather *nerve*, to come to a place like this in a *suit* ? "

" Darling, don't be an ass. That's Aldebaran Flood."

" Aldebaran—you don't mean *Bells on her Fingers* ?—and all *that* ? " The speaker drew in a long breath. " Real " evening dress lost its glamour and youth its assurance. " Well . . . I suppose that's fame," said the deb, in a small, schoolroom voice of innocent envy.

" Sorry to be late." Aldebaran slid into her place on the banquette, told the waiter curtly, " Double Scotch—straight," and pushed aside the menu placed at her elbow. " Madly busy ! " She shot a quick smile at her companion.

" Madly hungry, I hope ! Darling, where've you been ? I'm ravenous ! "

" You order." She shrugged her shoulders. " I don't care what I eat." Still smiling, she propped her chin on her thin hands, looked round the tables, nodded vaguely here and there, pushed back the hair that curled about her long throat. Orlando said,

" I was starting to panic, for fear you would not come."

She turned her head slowly and gave him the look that stopped his heart. She might as well have uttered it : " Not come—when I gave you my word ? "

He thought, How quickly and faithfully she gives her word about little things ; jerked his head aside, and met the full-orbed gaze of four young women, whose expressions, if flattering to Orlando Sax, were uncomplimentary to their partners. Orlando, who held with playing the game, glared at his Martini.

People were given to staring at Orlando Sax. Apart from the fact that he was the heir to the Mildenhall marquisate, and— that curiously respectable thing in an age governed by the Divorce courts—a widower in his early thirties, his looks recommended him no less to men (suspicious of the spectacular) than to women. In any clothes or any company it was impossible to mistake him for anything but a gentleman. An inch over six feet in height, and—in spite of a war-wound (1916) that had taken him out of the Brigade of Guards and limited his athletics

B

—pleasantly muscular, his sober, Angevin type of good looks
derived from the maternal side. Mildenhalls, taking them by and
large, are more rakish, skinnier and even a little picturesque :
Georgians strayed out of their century. (The necessary exception
was the current Lord Mildenhall, Orlando's father, who more
closely resembled a prosperous pork butcher than a peer of the
realm.) Orlando had inherited his mother's long nose and long
pale face ; his sober grey eyes and small dust-coloured moustache
would have appeared reasonable through a gap in eleventh-
century armour. He had a slow, kind smile, and at least half
a dozen young women in Society were prepared, on the least
possible encouragement, to take upon themselves the task of
effacing the memory of the departed Vanessa, who (according
to history) had done Landy down right and left before she died
in the unsuccessful attempt to give birth to the child of one of
her reputedly innumerable lovers. These young women viewed
Aldebaran Flood without favour ; even famous novelists had
no business to come poaching their preserves.

"Darling," said Aldebaran, and yawned. "What-for are we
having supper here ? "

"I thought you liked it ? Last time——"

"When was 'last time' ? " She picked up the Scotch,
drained it, and smiled like an angel at Orlando. She was tight,
or tired, or both ; he longed to cherish her. And felt her
holding him at arm's length. "It's next time counts—isn't it ? "

He felt his face burn, and gave his attention to the menu.

"Smoked salmon—and be sharp with it——"

"Yes, my lord ! "

"——bécasse—and send the *sommelier*."

"Oh, darling ! " breathed Aldebaran. "You've brought
Laura ! " Under the table a damp nose nuzzled her ankle, a
dome of satin pressed itself into the curve of her hand. "*Sweetheart* ! " murmured Aldebaran ; the waiter, hurriedly removed
himself. "You brought her to say Goodbye to me—— ? "

"I thought it would take her mind off things."

"Is she terribly self-conscious ? "

"I fancy the others rather rub it in. I'm going to let her

get the business over in Portland Place ; she can go back when the gossip's died down."

" Don't forget you promised me one."

" What—a mongrel ? I'm not going to give you a mongrel ! "

" But Laura's pups are bound to be angels, anyhow. What are you going to do with them ? "

" We'll not go into that in front of Laura." Obeying her gesture, he gave her a light for her cigarette. " I'll find you a puppy—Paget has some ; his bitch is a half-sister of Laura's, as a matter of fact——"

" I'd rather wait and have one of Laura's."

" I'm afraid that's no good. I mean, from point of pedigree. Laura's lapse has cost her her character—too bad, old girl," muttered Orlando, as a shamefaced nose came up between his knees. " I know—it wasn't your fault. If I could get hold of the brute who let her out, I'd sack him on the spot," said Orlando, while his hands fondled Laura's ears. " My lovely little bitch —it's a dam' shame."

" Poor sweet ; she must just forget all about it and start a new life." Aldebaran curled a flake of salmon round the prongs of the fork and thrust it into her mouth. " After all, she's young enough to live this down——"

" You are positively the only woman I know who can talk becomingly with her mouth full. That's all very well," said Orlando seriously, " but it's a dead loss, from the breedin' angle. Most owners aren't keen on mating their dogs with a bitch that's had a slip—and I'm not sure, either, of the position with the Kennel Club. I'm awfully afraid she's a done-er, socially." He gloomily attacked his plate.

" It does sound too dreadfully Oscar Wilde," Aldebaran was beginning, when the lights dimmed suddenly. She blinked round the room. " What do you suppose this is in aid of ? "

" Probably some sort of floor show—it must be midnight. What a bind. I didn't know Biri went in for this kind of thing," he muttered discontentedly, as a sudden beam picked out the piano on the small dais at the end of the room. " Do you care ? "

" I can take it ; but how about Laura ? "

" I'll have to hold her jaws."

" I could take her up to the girls' room, if you like ? There's an awfully nice woman there, who often looks after dogs."

" She'd scream the place down," muttered Orlando. " She's been awfully neurotic since her pregnancy started——"

A young man in tails stepped through the curtains at the back of the dais ; his smile was a flash of nut-white across the honey-and-blackberry effect of a small-boned face ; his heavy lids allowed a glint of surfeit and assurance to escape ; it trailed like a sticky feather over the women in his audience. Clutching Laura's jaws, Orlando muttered, " What a repulsive type ! " and returned a blank stare to the glare of the débutante who, settling her elbows on the table, brooded with lips and eyes of rapture upon the " type."

" Ah'm going to play you-all a li'l thing of mah own, ah call ' Risin' Rivah.' "

A sigh of ecstasy went up from the stretched throats of his listeners.

" Do you like it ? " Orlando, who was hungry, risked letting go of Laura's jaws with one hand, to shovel some more smoked salmon into his mouth. Aldebaran was eating quickly, neatly, with her head bent far over her plate.

" It's good, of its sort."

" Do you know the dago ? Have you heard him before ? "

" Darling, don't be *silly*. It's *Gaff*."

She too ? He searched her face for the abandonment that was on the faces of the other women, but Aldebaran's was like a hard white mask, tired and a little cynical.

Laura appeared to be amenable to " Risin' Rivah "; gently removing her muzzle from her master's hand, she settled down with her chin across his feet. Even the applause did not disturb her.

" Mah next numbah is given by request ; ah guess ah don' need tell you-all——"

" Oh, *God*. He's going to do ' Jehovah Blues.' Now I shall *die*," announced the débutante, on a loud, flat note of emotional strangulation.

" Come on ; let's go."

Orlando's jaw dropped.

" But—I've ordered *bécasse* ! "

" Let's go," repeated Aldebaran. Her face had sharpened
into grey bone with a coral gash across it. She thrust the table
away. Laura, disturbed, gave a faint, ladylike yelp. People at
adjoining tables were glowering. The head waiter came anxiously
up to Orlando. " Is anything the matter, my lord ? " The
air was hot. The beat of the music was a slow dripping of
blood.

As Aldebaran strode towards the door, followed by Orlando,
a perilously pregnant young spaniel waddled slowly after them.
The head waiter averted his eyes. No dogs are allowed in
Biri's. As he took his coat from the cloakroom attendant,
Orlando, for once, was annoyed with Aldebaran—whom he
found waiting in a taxi. He fumbled with silver for the linkman
and clambered in ; then clambered out to shovel up Laura
—whimperingly protesting that, in her condition, she could not
be expected to negotiate the high step of an old-fashioned taxi.
Orlando flung himself in a corner, and, presently, found Aldebaran's hand seeking his . . .

III

" If this were the States, I'd have on a dainty apron and be
fixing you a soufflé in a Pyrex dish ; you'd be in a tuxedo and a
sanforized shirt, ogling me across a glass of milk. The ' set '
would be something between a model dairy and a cocktail bar "
—Aldebaran tipped the ash of her cigarette into a broken egg-
shell, scraped the remainder of the scrambled egg on to a plate
for Laura, who, stretched in front of the electric stove, was
obviously trying to pretend that she was on a tigerskin, before
the vast log fire of her master's library. She made a slight gesture
of acknowledgment, laid her head back on her left ear and
sighed. " Poor sweet ; she's awfully like Elsie the Borden
cow. It will be fun," said Aldebaran, continuing to make

conversation, "to find out if all those American advertisements are phoney, or whether life really is like that in the States——"

"Do you care for me at all, Aldebaran?"

"Oh—must you—tonight——?"

"You've left me no choice. You tell me you're 'full-up' tomorrow, and you're sailing on Saturday. You're going to be away four months. Why can't we be engaged before you go to the States?"

"Oh, Landy." She forced a laugh. "What an hour—what a place—for a proposal!"

"Don't let's be trivial. This is deadly important—for me, if not for you."

"I can't talk to you in the middle of this mess," she sighed. Suddenly the room was shameful: the litter she had made in her attempt at cooking; the soiled plates scattered on a table covered with oil cloth; the squalid cutlery, rattled haphazard out of a kitchen drawer. She had done it, in a way, deliberately, and now regretted it. Why, after all, should she present herself to him against this sordid background—giving him advantage and letting down her own side? She snapped at him, "Do you know it's nearly two o'clock?"

"I don't care about the time, or anything else." He had risen to face her. "What happened—at Biri's?"

She jerked her head aside.

"Oh—the noise. The heat. That piano! I was tired. I was tired!—and why'd I got to listen to somebody playing a piano?" She clashed a pan into the already crowded sink, turned on a tap viciously, and water spurted over the front of her suit. "Oh——!" She bit her lip.

"You hadn't got to do—anything. But we could have gone on somewhere else——"

"And had a decent meal. I know. I'm not domestic. If I break an egg, the yolk goes on the table. If I make toast, most of it gets burnt, and I'm more than likely to burn myself as well——"

"Then why——?" He could not resist smiling.

"Why did I bring you back here and make you a perfectly

revolting scrambled egg, when we might have had an ambrosial supper at the Ritz ? Oh hell, don't ask me why ! Unless it was to give you another reason for not marrying me—not," she added, with a lop-sided grin, " that I take it I'd be required to cook at Paragon ! "

" Shall we go in the drawingroom ? " suggested Orlando, after a pause. " I don't think we're at our best, either of us, among pots and pans."

When she switched on the lights, the drawingroom had a soft, sad, muffled look, a look of farewell. The vases were empty. " Agnes hadn't time to do the flowers this morning ; and anyhow, what was the good ? We've been packing all day, and all yesterday——

" Darling." She turned to him desperately. " You *can't* marry me. You can't make a mess of it all over again ! "

" That's the damnedest thing to say ! I——"

" Landy, you *must* use your commonsense. Your father would be furious. You've got to make a go of it next time, not only for your own sake but the family's."

" That's exactly what I'm proposing to do "—his mouth was stubborn—" with your co-operation."

" And your mother "—she floundered, knowing this was foolish, Lady Mildenhall having been dead several years—" you know she never liked me."

" That's nonsense ; you misunderstood her."

" No, I didn't ; I saw her point of view. She didn't approve of Cat's schoolgirl friendship with the daughter of Polly Bowling and one of those Floods who were rude to the Saxes in eighteen something-or-other——"

" We all thought it was rather comic "—his smile brushed " eighteen something-or-other " aside—" as all Cat's friends up to then had more or less followed a pattern "—it was his turn to flounder—" and you came along, and were so original, and—and different," he concluded.

" Darling, don't you see that's the answer ? Setting aside all the studbook business, can't you see I'm not the kind of person to make mistress of Paragon ? Even as a schoolgirl, when Cat took me home in the holidays, I felt it—the immense gulf between your world and mine : wonderful, and romantic, and—in some way—despairing ! Cat and I vowed to eternal friendship, yet something inside me warning me all along there could be no reality in a friendship between her and me : Cat, with her title and traditions, and me, with my background of stage doors and theatrical lodgings and Mother's appalling husbands, Bert, and Harry, and that awful little bounder, Tommy Snow ! You can't contemplate importing all that into Paragon ! "

" I don't—and we're getting off the subject. Do you love me ? " He looked down at her gravely, where she lay curled in a corner of the couch. Aldebaran wriggled.

" It's such a dam' silly question ! It's perfectly obvious that —that a person like me hasn't got time for love."

" I think," said Orlando slowly, " that is a lie."

Her eyes fell before his steady gaze.

" Oh darling, I don't mean to be brutal ; of course I love you. But there isn't room for love in my present life—not the sort of love you mean, the sort you deserve." She stopped to swallow something that had risen in her throat ; as though Orlando, with all his goodness and patience and loyalty, through his silence rebuked her. " Oh darling ! " She tried desperately to make a joke of it. " Why do you have to be such a terrible picker ? I'd be no more good to you than poor Vanessa—and you couldn't even divorce me ! It makes a man look too, too much of a fool, to admit jealousy of his wife's work."

" Do you remember our planning you should have the Burlington wing, and run it just as you run this house ? You'd have the Medallion room for your own study, and we'd fix up the Œil de Bœuf as an office for Agnes——"

" Pipe dreams." But her smile trembled as she laid her head against his hand.

" You mean—you were humouring me ? " His face stiffened.

" And myself ; oh Landy, and myself ! Do you think I——" Again she had to stop and swallow. " Some things are too good to be true. Me—sitting in the Medallion room—with a footman on guard—turning out best-sellers ! Can you see it ? " She gave a hysterical little laugh. " With Inigo Jones, and Soane, and John Wood the Elder, and all the Gainsboroughs and Law-rences lifting their eyebrows at me, and Capability Brown gaping through the windows ? All those fine ghosts—sneering at me and smothering me——? "

" Why should you take it that way ? " He spoke as though she had hurt him. " Why shouldn't they inspire you—as they've inspired innumerable creative artists, from their own to the present day ? "

" Because," said Aldebaran bitterly, " I'm not a creative artist ; I'm only a glorified hack, a cheap camera-man of my period——"

" Don't belittle yourself," he interrupted her.

" I won't ! " she flung back at him. " I'm a dam' good craftswoman and the best-paid short story writer in Europe ! "

" And you wrote *The Sad Dove*," said Orlando quietly.

She drew a quick breath.

" And who cares ? *The Sad Dove* didn't buy me this house, Landy, or pay Agnes's salary ! " But her smile was mirthless. " Let's forget about *The Sad Dove*——"

" You might begin to write poetry again, at Paragon."

" Never," she said harshly. " I've gone too far from all that. And I don't write beautiful, silken prose either, about fine, contemplative aristocrats living in Palladian mansions ! The things I write are hard and tough. I write about the kind of people I know, and if I lose touch with them I'm finished."

" I don't wish you to lose touch with anything. I also have my life—and since Father's health began to fail, and he leaves almost everything to me, it's a very full one."

" Then why do you want me ? " she cried.

" I've told you. Because I love you."

" Wouldn't it do," said Aldebaran after a silence, " if I were your mistress ? Darling, I didn't mean to—to insult you ! But isn't it the simplest solution ? Of course I know it's wretched for you, going on like this—I do care, Landy, I do care ! " Tears were streaming down her sad, sophisticated face ; she made him, as it were in compunction, this sacrifice of her pride.

"No," he said slowly. "From my point of view it wouldn't do. You see"—he knitted his brows in the search for words that would seem simple enough—"it would be like giving sugar to a person who is hungry for a square meal. If all I wanted was to sleep with you—well, I suppose I could find myself consolation of a sort. But I want you for my wife or nothing."

"How difficult you are." She sighed, pushing her hands up over her brow, straining back the listless wave of her cinnamon hair. "Why me? I can't think what you see in me, that fits into the pattern of your life."

"Do you mean—why do I love you?" The gravity of his face relaxed into a slow smile. "I thought we'd been over this before! Are you, like the rest of women, greedy for compliments? Well, listen: and, by heaven, this is the last time! I love you because you're brave and honest and full of integrity; you're as stubborn as a mule, you're gracious and insolent. Sometimes you're vulgar," the smile broadened into a grin— "but you're never cheap!"

"Thanks," said Aldebaran. "It's the first time I've heard vulgarity cited as a virtue." She spoke flippantly because his description of her touched her to the heart.

"Well—how much are your books part of you?"

"You've got something there," she admitted.

"There's something else I like about you," he told her unexpectedly. "You're well conditioned. Mentally, I mean. I like your hard, neat mind, that never turns in on itself——"

She almost let out a laugh, but managed to strangle it. Then the impulse towards laughter was washed out in pity. Poor Landy; how he, in his simplicity, had suffered from Vanessa— excusing all that she was, and wasn't, in catchwords from Freud and Havelock Ellis. The very names, in 1930, carried a kind of *pourriture*, led nowhere except into the thicket of amateurish dabbling where Vanessa and her crowd belonged; set the seal of pseudo-science on their departures from the old-fashioned moral norm to which Orlando and those like him still subscribed . . . and I, and I?

I believe in the whole of it, she asserted stubbornly, to her heart ; and yet, believing, I can't—I can't . . . But I'd have to, as Orlando's wife. Darling, you've got me wrong ; so utterly wrong. I'm only Vanessa—with a difference. That " neat, hard mind ! "—which is partly my Flood inheritance, partly illusion —*yours*. I've got my own private madness, which I don't exhibit ; that's the only difference between Vanessa and me. And if I were to reveal it to you, I'd break your heart——

"Tell me," he was saying, " what are you doing tomorrow ?" She was instantly on the defensive.

"I've told you : I'm full up, every minute. You can look for yourself." She let him see she was being patient as she got up and found an engagement pad on the small desk which was faintly powdered with dust. " Four appointments—all business —before lunch, then the hairdresser, and I'm snatching a sandwich at the club with Bob Winter "—her publisher ; that at least was convincing. " After lunch I've got a last fitting—and my broadcast's at three. Then I must tear down to Fleet Street to see an editor about a weekly column they want me to send from the States, and go on to my lawyers to fix the power of attorney I'm leaving with Uncle Joe. What's this ? Oh hell ; the young Lakes are giving me a sort of farewell cocktail ; I can't cut that. If you'd like to pick me up about six, at Clements Inn——"

"Right ; we can have dinner somewhere, after the cocktail."

"No, we can't. There's Mother. After all, you're driving me down to Southampton—— ! "

"You and Agnes, and Polly and Bob ! "

"Orlando," she sighed at last, " I *do* love you ! "

"I know." He returned to his point like a child who cannot argue, can only reiterate. " Why can't we be engaged before you go away ? "

She let the book fall on the lid of the desk, and lifted her hands to her head with the familiar gesture ; the unbuttoned jacket of her suit, splashed darkly by the water, fell loosely away from her breasts, her thin belted waist, her narrow hips. Apart from the light from a wall bracket which caught the wave of her hair, she stood etched in shadow against the pale Georgian walls, her palms pressed into the sockets of her eyes. Presently she dropped her hands ; they swung for a moment at her sides, before she thrust them fiercely into her pockets.

" All right. I'll tell you. This trip to America—there's more in it, for me, than a lecture tour. It's a sort of—a sort of test, of *me* : and that means of us as well, Landy. I can't put it any more clearly, you must try to understand.

" Perhaps it's only the old travel-fever that tormented my people—and sent us out to the Gold Coast and Barbados, and on the high seas, looking for something—for something——

" I don't know what I'm looking for." She had crossed to the empty hearth, where she stood, hands on hips, looking down at her foot, cocked on its brittle heel against the curb. Then she laid her arm along the mantelpiece ; her hand, blindly seeking, found a lump of jade—two kittens fighting over a bird —and fingered it absently. " Perhaps it's only myself. Until I've found it, I'm not whole, not complete. I'm—in a kind of way I'm fictitious, like the characters in my books."

Orlando sat patiently, his wrists drooping between his knees, the fingers clasped. He did not look at her. At long last he seemed to be getting past her resistance, past her evasions, past the trivial excuses she had brought up in falsification of their love. If he had loved her less, perhaps he would have been satisfied, would have accepted this explanation—nebulous as it was—of her obstinacy. But because he loved her in his very depths, he sat there waiting for truth to break through the tangled web of her words. As she continued in silence, he asked her,

" But—America ; why should you think you can find —whatever it is you are seeking—over there ? "

She opened her lips, closed them, and shrugged her shoulders.

" One has illusions about foreign places. Going to the States has always seemed to me like going into a hard clear, crystal light that shows up the worn-out patches in our own civilization ! "

She is making phrases, he thought sadly. As though his thought communicated itself to her, Aldebaran swung her head towards him ; her brows were knitted.

" Oh darling, there's nothing mysterious about it ! After all—it's only the tom-toms ; they're at it all the time, aren't they —in books, and movies, and music——? "

He shot at her,

" Do you mean—like tonight ? Like that half-caste, playing jazz ? "

As the notes of " Jehovah Blues " drummed in the air—inaudible, yet distinct to both—he felt her sharp withdrawal from him.

" All those things," she said with a cold vagueness. " All the infiltration of American creativity and American culture into our lives—all that feeling of immensity and violence and brand-new energy that pours from over there—I want to test myself against it ! I want," burst out Aldebaran, " to forget all this "—she flung out her arms in a gesture that embraced, he felt, her surroundings, her world, her life.

" And me ? " He dropped the words quietly into her pause.

" Oh, forget *me*—let's forget each other, only for four months ! " she implored him. " Let us, just for these four little months, be as free of one another as though we'd never met. Let's—"she flung herself down between his knees and her arms round his neck, and he could feel her body clinging to his as her hands clung about the back of his head—" let's *lose* these months, and never, never, either of us, speak of them again ! "

She could not realize, he thought, the immensity of what she was asking.

" Well, but to what end ? I've waited four years," said Orlando gently. " Four more months don't make much difference ; but how is it to be when you come back ? We can't go on like this ; we'll have—either to call it a day, or be engaged, when you come back." He felt her shrink from the finality in his voice.

" Do you want me to give you my word—now ? "

" I think," he said carefully, " it would be the fairest thing, to both of us." He felt her slight pull against the encirclement of his arms and let her go free, but he continued steadily with what he had to say. " For one thing, I don't want it to be a long engagement, so I'd like to prepare my father. He's getting old, and he's inclined to put up resistance to anything that is presented to him suddenly. Not that that would make any difference to us, but for everyone's sake I'd like things to go as smoothly as possible. I could let him know that, although we aren't engaged at present, we intend to be on your return, and the fact of its not being a *fait accompli* will dispose him more favourably to the idea than if it's just dropped on him, complete. Then I'd like to get my affairs organized, so that we can take as long as we like over the honeymoon——"

" I seem to have been wasting my breath," she sighed.

" You have, rather."

" What is the difference between being engaged now and waiting until I come back ? " she demanded petulantly.

" I was waiting for you to arrive at that conclusion," admitted Orlando, on a dangerous note of satisfaction.

She scrambled to her feet and went to the farther end of the room, where she loitered for a few moments, frowning, fingering shelves from which books had been removed, picking up and flinging down parcels which Agnes Chester, her secretary, had piled on the chairs.

" Well—I *can't* tell you tonight, Landy." Her voice was hard and matter-of-fact ; she pointed at the clock. " Look at the time ! It's after three in the morning. Nobody's in her right mind after two—— ! "

" I am not, on this occasion, asking for your mind," said Orlando. " I am asking for your heart."

" And my hand." She smiled reluctantly. " You're pure Keepsake sometimes, darling—and terribly sweet ! Trust a woman's brain ; it's more reliable than her heart."

" By God, you said that exactly like your old uncle, Harcourt Flood ! "

" Great-uncle," corrected Aldebaran mechanically. " Did I ? They called him Old Iron-Guts," she reflected. " According to accounts, the description might apply to a good many of us. I'm often aware of the streak of metal, here "—she tapped her breast. " Don't regret it." Her voice had softened unex-

pectedly. " The time might come when it would serve you well.
Good night, my dear." She held up her cheek to be kissed, and,
suddenly angered, he pulled her chin round so that her mouth
was at his mercy.

" What do you think you are—my spinster aunt ? "

She submitted—no more—to his kiss ; when it was over
they scowled at each other, in the eyes of each a smouldering
dissatisfaction.

" Six, then—at Clements Inn ? "

" No—it doesn't give me long enough to think," said
Aldebaran hurriedly. " I'll let you know on Saturday."

" That's kind of you ! " He toed Laura viciously from her
repose on the hearthrug ; she gave a slight, protestant whinny.

" So that's how you treat an expectant female ! " Indignantly
she clutched Laura to her bosom.

" I hardly touched her ! Come on, you neurotic bitch ! "

The ungrateful Laura floundered out of Aldebaran's arms to
her master's heel, her eyes raised in adoration, her tail vibrating
with ecstasy at the prospect of a walk.

" You'll ring up a cab ? She can't walk all the way back to
Portland Place ! "

" Exercise is good for the coming generation," retorted
Orlando.   " She's not a Victorian ! "

" Well, I hope you'll remember, if the occasion ever arises,
that I *am* ! " was her parting shot.

She stood on the step, listening to his crisp steps retreating
round the crescent. The starry silence, the green fringes of the
trees painted on the darkness by the street lamps, filled her with
a trembling loneliness. When she closed the door, the air of the
narrow hall felt heavy ; the servants had remembered, of course,
to close everything before going to bed.

Already she was detached from it all : from her little Regency
house whose acquisition had been the greatest material achievement of her working years. Agnes's absence—she was spending
a night of farewell with her family—completed the sense of
disassociation. She went down the hallway to the arch which
led to her workroom and Agnes's office—a modern excrescence

on the back of the house, overlooking the Regent's Canal. Agnes had been busy—the final clearing; the blank neatness of the big, flat-topped desks—one dedicated to journalism, the other to fiction—stabbed her with emptiness. Under the shaded lamps she had switched on from the door she found herself wandering like a *revenante* in search of her banished personality.

A tremulous uneasiness took possession of her, and as she stretched out her hand to the cigarette box she saw it was quivering. She struck a light viciously, and the match wavered in front of her half-closed eyes, of her lips dragged back from the teeth clenched on the end of the cigarette. As she tossed the dead match away, she was aware of the panic, shapeless and unreasonable, that sometimes descends on one, face to face with the unknown. In little more than twenty-four hours she was setting forth on an adventure different from any which had ever come her way; unsupported—save by Agnes—she was going to face the judgment, the criticism, perhaps the condemnation of a whole continent whose opinions and points of view she knew only through the treacherous pages of literature. She was Aldebaran Flood, the well-known author of the book from which Hollywood had made the film *Bells on her Fingers*; but she was also an unproven British lecturer, up against the toughest audiences in the world. . . .

Descendant as she was of generations of adventurers, it was not this prospect that infected her with a sense of weakness and shrinking—mingled with personal shame and a longing to hide from herself; to hide from the grey face she saw reflected in the glass.

> *Upon the mountain Jehovah spoke,*
> *Outa his mouf come fi-ah an' smoke.*

Hands beating on the piano, a foot beating out the time, hot heart beating to a hot rhythm. . . .

Chapter Two

I

WHEN THE hall porter came into the billiard room to say a lady was waiting to speak to him, Orlando's heart leapt into his mouth, he flung down the cue and took the stairs in a couple of bounds. It could only be Aldebaran; none of the other ladies he knew called for him at the club. His fond, foolish heart hammered with the hope that she had made up her mind and come to put him out of his uncertainty, then lapsed like cold wet jelly within the cavity of his bosom, for fear her answer should be No.

She was wearing a plain black suit and a blouse whose collar came up like petals of ice under her chin; it gave her the slick, efficient look of the career woman. He was too excited to notice her face, which was in shadow. The hall porter's presence damped down any ebullience of welcome.

" Hallo—this is a surprise ! "

" I'd like a word with you. Shall we go in the park ? "

They turned into St. James's Place. On account of the traffic and the narrow pavements, Orlando had to keep stepping off into the gutter. Conversation was impossible. Round the far corner they crossed over to the alley which links the Place with the Green Park. The long sweep of trees and grass offered refuge to lovers ; he took advantage of the privacy of the alley to catch her gloved hand, and was taken aback when she dragged it away.

" Is it true your father's got shares in Purcell-Flood ? "

" I'm dashed if I know," said Orlando, when he had recovered from his astonishment. " I shouldn't be surprised. Why ? "

" I thought you dealt with all his business."

" Well—nominally." His lips quirked involuntarily into a smile. " As a matter of fact—you know people of his age are inclined to be secretive. I suppose it's natural. As you get older, and feel your authority slipping——"

" Then you'd be surprised to hear that he's one of the biggest shareholders ? " she interrupted him. " So big, in fact, that he was offered a seat on the Board—— ? "

" Nothing would surprise me about Father," was the calm reply. " He's one of the most incalculable people I ever met. But, apart from the dear old fellow's being incapable of directing a perambulator over a street crossing, I can't see him going up to Liverpool once a month—or whatever it is—to attend directors' meetings."

" He wouldn't need to, if he had a stooge."

After a silence :

" I'm not quite clear what a stooge is, but I've always assumed it was something unpleasant."

" Even the Victorians had a phrase about ' pulling chestnuts out of the fire ' ! " she flung at him.

" If you're attributing anything dishonourable to my father, you're very much mistaken." His voice was cold and formal.

" Read that." She pushed Joe's letter towards Orlando, who, after a brief hesitation, took it and glanced at the first page.

" When did you get this ? "

" Today—on the first post. Go on ; read it."

Leaving him on the gravel, she went to stub her toe into the grass verge. Two puppies, rolling on the plantain, failed to draw her attention. Her hair swung forward in a short curtain at either side of her hard white face.

Presently Orlando crossed to join her. Without speaking, they turned, and began to trudge up the slope of the grass towards Piccadilly.

" I don't see why you associate this with Father. It certainly seems a bad business, but, according to what your uncle says, he resigned of his own accord."

" What else could he do—being Uncle Joe ? I suppose you've

heard of a packed meeting? Purcell and his toadies had the
whole thing fixed before it started."

"I still don't see how they could possibly tell it would bring
about Prior's resignation."

She gave a short, contemptuous laugh, and lifted her eyebrows
as though in deprecation of his naïveté.

"Anybody who knows Uncle Joe knows his opinions! He's
spoken his mind often enough in public; he's even had a
question asked in the House, about coloured seamen with
British papers getting the same payment as whites for the same
work. I've heard him blaze off when some fatuous ass has
been preening himself—and the British nation—about the
advantages Negroes enjoy here, in comparison with the States.
And I've been to Cardiff with him and seen the black quarter
—Bute Street and Loudoun Square. I suppose you'd say there's
no such thing as segregation in England? Go on: go to
Cardiff and see for yourself." She paused to draw breath.

"But—surely this means advantage—extra employment—for
the coloured seamen."

"It gives our whites a genuine grievance and brings racial
hatred—the thing that isn't supposed to exist in this country—
right on our doorstep. For the sake of your father's dividends!"

"I don't for a moment believe he knew anything about it,"
said Orlando at last.

"Don't be so dumb! You can bet your sweet life Purcell
keeps a shareholder as important as Lord Mildenhall briefed on
all the Board's up to."

"Listen," said Orlando quietly. "You don't know Father
—at least, you hardly know him. You've only met him socially,
and listened to him bumbling about architecture and the rise
in land values—on both of which he happens to be quite intelligent. But you must really accept my word that, even if Purcell
did tell, or write to him, about this business, he'd be most
unlikely to take it in. Definitely, he wouldn't contribute to
putting British-born seamen out of a job."

She hardly appeared to be listening.

"We—I mean Floods," she corrected herself, "have always treated our people decently. What's going to happen, now Uncle Joe's off the Board? This *Obango's* only the beginning; one by one it'll spread to the other ships, and the people who worked for us will be the first to get thrown out. Purcell may or may not look after his own lot; it's certain he won't give a damn for Bristol men, who only came in with the merger."

"It's a pity they did not put you on the Board." He was serious, but her face flamed with resentment.

"I'm not in a frame of mind for humour!"

"I wasn't joking. I wish to God I could be of use." He paused. "I must go and talk to Prior."

"What about?"

"I haven't a notion," he admitted simply. "But I've had a certain amount of experience with poor relief——"

Her lips twitched involuntarily into a smile.

"I wouldn't, if I were you, mention poor relief to Uncle Joe—just at present!"

"I wouldn't, naturally, presume to make suggestions—even if I had any! But the administration of an estate does give one a few practical ideas that may be useful in an emergency."

Aldebaran stood still to look at him; the smile which still lingered at the corners of her lips was less strained, and her voice less metallic, when she answered him.

"You mean, the administration of an estate like Paragon?"

"Even Paragon isn't without its complications, in these days," he reminded her.

"I don't suppose it is. It just happens to be a different kind of complication. The people you have to handle are traditionally disposed to accept the authority and the leadership of the lord of the manor. They touch their caps and remember to say ' my lord '——"

It was Orlando's face, now, that burned.

"What an utter ninny you think me! Do you think I was called ' my lord ' in the trenches?"

"You had your officer's uniform, hadn't you?" She made a simple statement of it, without bitterness. "I'm not belittling you, Landy; don't think that. I'm only trying to show that, ever since you and Cat were children, authority's been made easy for you; it's been handed to you, tied up with blue ribbon. I know you've made the best possible use of it. But it's not what you need in dealing with *our* people; even in dealing with a bunch of sharpers like Purcell and his Yes-boys." She gave a short little laugh and her hands bunched themselves inside the pockets of her coat. " If I could get off this goddam trip——"

" Well—if you could—— ? "

" Oh—nothing. Only—my name's Flood, and we talk the same language. I mean, the seamen and the dockers and the women and children that hang together with them. Uncle Joe's seen to that ! As a kid, in my holidays "—again her voice trailed away. Presently her head jerked towards him. " I didn't spend the *whole* of my holidays at Paragon ! "

" I know you didn't. Cat said you were in town."

" I was ; but most of the time I was with Uncle Joe. His idea was to bring me up as a Flood of Bristol ! My cousins never gave a damn for the town or the business : you know the Hampshire Floods—Uncle Dorset's sons ? Belgravia and county ! And I got side-tracked into writing."

They had reached the broad walk that runs parallel with Piccadilly before he spoke again.

" Darling, I give you my word, if Father has really got anything to do with this wretched *Obango* business, I'll work like a beaver to find out some way of making up for it."

He saw her chin quiver, the implacable lines of her face soften, against her will.

" Landy—why do you let me be so terrible to you ? I can't help being passionate about anything to do with the coloured people. I suppose it's blood guilt, working itself out ! "

She was mocking herself, but for a moment he saw in her, in the violence of her black brows and beautiful, stubborn mouth, those slave-trading forebears whose imprint was in her body and her character. He remembered a portrait in Paragon —accredited to a Mildenhall ancestor—of a dark and sullen beauty who had been responsible, according to legend, for a blood feud between brothers. Someone in his grandfather's day had labelled the portrait " La Incognita ": a face-saving device on the part of the family, who knew only too well that this sultry creature, descendant of a wandering Flood, had colour in her veins, and that with her began the long enmity between Saxes and Floods. He remembered, a little guiltily, his own relief, when a careful study of Flood genealogy established the fact that Aldebaran inherited no drop of that dubious blood, which had flowed away distantly into a branch far removed from her own.

" I'll go straight on to Bristol, after I've seen you off, and have a talk with Prior," he promised her.

" What could you do ? "—but she spoke almost tenderly ; her glittering eyes held a sad desperation. " And anyhow, how could you go to Bristol ? You'll have to take Mother and Bob back to town," she reminded him.

" Bob can drive the Bentley and I'll catch a train. I shan't be exactly companionable after saying Goodbye to you ! "

" It would be no end of a comfort to Uncle Joe ; if it hadn't been for this business he'd have come to Southampton to see me off." She smiled ruefully. " Under all that rough stuff he's an idiotic old sentimentalist."

" I'm another."

" Darling "—she brushed this aside—" I must fly. I'm late already for my fitting."

" Are you sure you've said—all you meant to say ? "

She flinched from the hopefulness in his eyes, and hardened again.

" For heaven's sake—— ! " Her voice crackled. " Won't anything convince you, Landy ? Just because we've got a biological urge for one another, do we have to behave like a couple of hysterical 'teen-agers and plunge into a relationship that can't come undone without a lot of mess and unpleasantness for everyone ? "

" If that's really what you feel—— " He was trying to be cool, to conceal his hurt. " If you're really thinking, even before we're engaged, of how you could escape from it—— "

" I'm trying to rationalize. I'm a person with a career ; a person whose whole life is planned and confined in schedules. You've never known the discipline of a time-table ; you've never been obliged to accept a ruling with which, in your innermost soul, you disagreed. You could always walk out on it——"

" You mean, I've never had to hold down a job."

She gulped, in the effort to accept this simplification.

" Yes—I think—perhaps—that's what I mean." She swallowed again. " I know, of course, that you had plenty of discipline in the Army—but—but—you were given your commission ; you didn't have to work for it. The discipline was part of the honour and glory of being a Guardsman—part of the fun—before the war. All I am—and my people were—we had to fight for, like hell. How can two people as different as you and I "—it was like an appeal—" really understand one another ? Your people always said, ' It shall be,' and it *was*. Mine had to struggle, and trick, and plan, to get it our way. We've grown up with a different vision, and we express ourselves in a different vocabulary. We have a different set of standards——"

" That, at least, is ridiculous," he interrupted her. " We both believe in the same human essentials ! "

" Big words. Don't you know it's the little things that make up a human relationship ? Don't you know it would be easier, for me, to think about marrying somebody who'd got to make himself, and me, a living—with no sort of backing but his own will and his character ? Somebody I could go along with, feeling him dependent on me, the same way I was dependent on him. Somebody whose outlook is of the same dimensions as mine——"

" You think I'm narrow-minded ? " Orlando knitted his brows to ask. She answered, after a pause,

" That you can imagine it shows how hopelessly distant we are from one another in our ways of thinking. It's a matter of different horizons, that's all. You can't help looking at everything from the angle of privilege, and I—what I want is *justifications*. Hell—when it comes down to it, I suppose I'm just proud! I can't accept what would come to me, as your wife, knowing I haven't earned it——"

"I don't know what to say: except you're so wrong. So utterly wrong. I can't understand anyone of your intelligence being so out of touch with the movement of life today," said Orlando clumsily. "I—you seem to me to have got the whole picture out of focus. You're looking at it from some remote, Victorian angle——"

"Georgian," corrected Aldebaran; she gave him a rueful little grin. "You've got something there. Well—let's face it: I'm still—part of me—an anachronism, a unicorn, if you like to put it that way, in modern society. People like me are always conscious of our roots, while yours—you've forgotten them. It's *we* who remember——"

"You're remembering ghosts," he answered harshly.

"All right. Perhaps I am. Perhaps all that's finished—outside of literature."

"Not *your* kind of literature," he could not forbear reminding her.

"Oh—me. My 'literature' doesn't get on to paper. Me—I'm a schizophrenic!" she jeered at him. "Me—I don't want anything, except the best of both worlds—and "—she broke away from him with a wild gesture—"that taxi! Catch it for me—there's a darling: I can't run in these unspeakable heels."

II

Polly Bowling looked across the room at her daughter, stretched flat on the divan that crossed a corner between the fireplace and a curtained window. Supper was over, and the secretary, Agnes Chester, had left them alone. Aldebaran, in an old grey peignoir, whose crinkled folds, drawn over her long thighs and poked into peaks by the tips of her slippers, flowed to the carpet on either side of the couch, resembled altogether too closely for Polly's peace of mind a carving on a medieval tomb. For almost ten minutes she had lain there without speaking, her arms folded on her breast, her eyes lifted to the ceiling—as though she had forgotten she was not alone.

Polly did not agree with people who called her daughter beautiful ; Deb was too long and thin, her face too bony and sharp in outline—and it was no use trying to make her put on " a little colour." Her mouth was the mouth made fashionable by a popular film star—the mouth every young woman who aspired to fashion was painting over her own. In Deb's case it was natural, and Polly, whose taste ran to the Cupid's bow, would have " improved " it with the lavender pink Aldebaran rejected for coral. And that funny-coloured hair, that made her eyebrows look as though she had been blacking them ! How pretty her hair had been as a child : rich auburn, with a haze of gold over it. It was when she came back that second time from Paris that it started to fade and fall out, and when it grew again it was this unfortunate colour that was neither brown, gold nor grey, but had something of all three in it, and turned almost to ginger in certain lights. Polly sighed, as she thought how little she really knew of her celebrated daughter.

" Indigestion, Mother ? " inquired Aldebaran crisply.

" No ; I was just feeling a bit ' down.' " Polly blew her nose vigorously, while Aldebaran hoisted herself on her elbow to reach for a cigarette. " So would you be ! " she asserted, " if you'd just been told you're an old has-been, and you might as well look out for a nice plot in Kensal Green."

" Who says that ? " Hardened to Polly's histrionics, Aldebaran gave herself a light.

" Jeff Cattley."

What, she wondered calmly, had Polly been up to ? The agent of a famous star of the music halls does not allow himself as much rope as that without provocation.

" Eleven dates since Christmas ! " burst out Polly. " ' Call yourself an agent ! ' I told him. Always whimpering about the movies and making out the halls are finished—any old excuse, I told him, for not delivering the goods—not," she mumbled, with a sidelong look at her daughter, " that he's not right, in a way. But I'm not going to be told so, by a little twirp that was call-boy at Daly's when I was at the top of the bill ! "

Sitting up, her elbows propped on her tilted knees, Aldebaran allowed several rings of smoke to escape into the luminous cone of the lampshade behind her head.

" Why don't you marry Uncle Joe ? "

A faint gasp shook itself from Polly's open lips; they remained open, while a slow crimson burned up the powder she had just renewed.

" It's time you made up your mind to take things easily, and run a comfortable home for yourself. Uncle Joe would be thankful to get you out of that dingy old flat—and I shouldn't have any more worry about the pair of you," concluded Aldebaran with a wry smile.

" A lot you worry, my girl ! And the dingy old flat, as you call it, 's been my home for the last twenty years—and poor Tommy loved it——"

" Oh poops. What are you blushing for like that ? " pursued Aldebaran. " Really, Mother ! You may as well come clean and tell me why you've stalled Uncle Joe off all these years, for all those awful Berts and Tommies——"

" There's no need to be rude about your stepfathers ! " Polly winked fiercely to keep back the moisture her burning cheeks had forced into her eyes. " I'm sure they were all very nice to you—stuck-up little beast that you were ! And I suppose it's my business, who I married——" She caught her lower lip in the still beautiful line of her teeth. " You liked Bert ; you know you did ! "

" Oh, for Jesus' sake ! "

" And I wish you wouldn't use such bloody awful language after all the money's been spent on your education," Polly recovered her spirit to retort, drawing a hysterical laugh from her daughter.

" You've not told me about Uncle Joe."

" If you want to know," muttered Polly, " once upon a time—before you were born—I played a mean trick on Joe."

Taken by surprise, Aldebaran looked at her curiously.

" Did you now ? Well, he doesn't seem to hold it against you."

" Joe's not the sort to bear a grudge. If he'd only let fly at me, and we'd had a good row, and some plain speaking, and —and a bit of a cry," sniffed Polly, " we might have got it straightened out. I know I was false, and wicked, and I'd have felt better if he'd told me so. But I couldn't have faced the prospect of living the rest of my life side by side with Joe's forgiveness !"

So that was it ? After a moment, Aldebaran rose and pressed her hand on her mother's shoulder. It was only half an admission —enough to rouse a curiosity that was not, for the present, to be satisfied.

" Have a drink, Mother. I didn't mean to make you cry."

" You're a good girl." The heartening sound of the syphon helped to stem the tide of Polly's tears. " You remind me of your poor father—God rest him. It's a pity he can't see you——"

" It's just as well he can't—having died in the happy conviction I was going to be a boy, the shock might be too much for him. Drink up."

" Thanks, dear—a little less soda, if you don't mind ; all that fizz doesn't agree with me." Aldebaran repressed a smile as she complied with the euphemism of Polly's request for more Scotch. " Thank you. You'd have loved him. I didn't know him very well," admitted Polly simply, " but he was a real gentleman. The best of them all. He'd have been proud of you : your work, and the name you've made for yourself, and—and the good girl you've been to me, and your Uncle Joe." Her eyes on the glass in her hand, she missed Aldebaran's movement of distaste. If there were only some way of avoiding these gushes of maternal sentiment. " He thought the world of Joe. There wasn't anything snobbish about your Father——" Aldebaran's silence penetrating her memories, she turned on her the singularly sweet smile that, through all the years when it had been her principal stock in trade, had never lost its simplicity. " I wish you weren't going off tomorrow, but it's been nice having this last time together. I got a notion it might be a party, till Agnes rang up and said not to dress."

She remembered regretting the foolish compunction which had prompted her to give up these last hours to Polly.

"I couldn't be bothered." Although the night was warm, she stretched out her hands to the fire and shivered a little.

"You're a fine one to talk about getting married!" Polly it was who now strove for lightness. "Twenty-nine last birthday—goodness, it makes me feel like an antiquarian. At your age I'd been widowed three times and I was just trying to make my mind up about poor Tommy——"

"I'll say you were."

Polly winced.

"I suppose I've not been much of a mother to you," she murmured humbly.

"Oh *Mother*." She caught back the words of impatience that rose to her lips. "You did the best you could," she muttered, hating herself for the ungracious sound of it.

"I sent you to that swell boarding school, where you made nice friends—you did like The Lodge, didn't you?" she heard Polly pleading. "You made friends with Catherine Sax and got all those invitations to Paragon."

"What's worrying you, Mother?" interrupted Aldebaran. She went back to sit on the divan, looking at the tumbler clasped in her hands between her knees. "Why do you have to sound as though you had something on your conscience? I haven't accused you of anything, have I?"

"It's all turned out so different from what I expected. I thought you'd have been married and had children of your own by now."

"It would be difficult to fit a family into my present circumstances, wouldn't it? I'm quite satisfied, the way things are."

"That's what upsets me. Why should you be satisfied?" said Polly, with a troubled glance. "The sort of life you're living isn't *natural*. No girl your age ought to be satisfied without she's got a man of her own."

" You're rather inclined to judge other people by yourself, aren't you ? "

" There was that boy you met when they made Paragon into a war hospital. What was his name ?—the one that played the piano."

" Lee Marion."

" That's it—Lee. It's funny, hearing that tune of his played all over the place : ' Jehovah Blues.' "

" They played it at Biri's last night."

" That number must have made him a packet. You've never heard from him since, have you ? "

(Since what ?) " No."

" I didn't take much of a fancy to that boy friend of yours. I never cared for red-haired boys anyhow—but there was something about him didn't seem quite *open*. It could be he was a foreigner," said Polly fairly, " but I've met plenty of Yankees since the war and none of them gave me that impression."

" Lee wasn't a Yankee. He came from the South."

" You wouldn't like to marry a Yank and settle down over there, would you ? " pursued Polly wistfully.

" I'll tell you when I come back." Wasn't there some other subject she could start ? Her mind felt blank.

" Poor kid ; you did take a toss for him, didn't you ? "

" Sixteen's quite an age for ' tosses.' "

" Deb. I never asked you before. That first time you went to Paris—after the Armistice—it was to see him, wasn't it ? "

" Yes," she heard herself answer, after a pause. She wanted to scream out, And what about it ? What in sweet heaven have I done, to invite this insensate questioning ? Why, because you are my mother, does that give you the right to submit me to a cross-examination you'd never have thought of imposing on an acquaintance ?

" I hope to God the pair of you behaved yourselves ! " The belated fervour of the hope checked by its absurdity the bitter outburst that sprang to Aldebaran's lips.

" It's a bit late, now, to trouble the Almighty ! "

" Your Uncle Joe would be out of his mind. He was always

at me for letting you go off by yourself—though goodness knows, things were different after the war, and kids in their 'teens were doing as they pleased. And you'd got me at my wits' end, you and Harry, between you: always fighting and snapping—I knew there'd be no peace in the place till you got your own way," said Polly, her soft brows knitted over memories of the past.

"All right—I'm quite prepared to admit I was a menace to conjugal bliss."

"And there's no need to be sarcastic!" rapped Polly. "P'raps Harry wasn't up to the class of you and your friends, but he was a good husband and he wanted to like you for my sake. You may believe it or not, but you really hurt his feelings when you took yourself off to that ungodly place in Cornwall. He said it looked as if he'd driven you out of your home——"

"The flat was never 'home' to me, and where had I got to do my writing? I'd have gone to Uncle Joe's if his mother had not turned up, after all those years, and planted herself down in what was supposed to be my room——"

"And the next thing we hear is you've gone careering back to Paris, and nobody gets a line from you for weeks!" cried Polly.

"One has to grow up some time." Can we really, thought Aldebaran, be having all this to-do about something that happened ten—no, eleven—years ago? Something I thought had been blown to pieces in all Mother's angry letters—scattered, like dust, in the wind of her rages? It was like coming face to face with a new Polly; it was curiously disconcerting. From earliest childhood she had been accustomed to her mother's brief furies, whose violence was only matched by Polly's capacity for forgetting them when they were over. There was even something refreshing about them: like a downpour which leaves the earth smelling more sweetly when it is past. Could it really be Polly who had stored up these old resentments and grudges, to liberate them now, of all times? Out of her disconcertion, Aldebaran spoke more mildly than she was feeling. "You can't hold me to account, now, for the sins of my youth!"

" And you came back looking like a ghost ! " accused Polly.
" You've never got your weight up since ! " Incredible as it
seemed, there were tears in her eyes and in her voice : tears, not
of anger or petulance, but—Polly was hurt. Aldebaran hardened
herself in self-defence against that outburst of sentimentality,
as she had hardened herself in her childhood against her mother's
attempts to cover some wounding negligence or injustice with
a sudden, disconcerting gush of affection.

" Weight isn't a very good subject for discussion between
you and me." It sounded brutal, but Polly herself was usually
the first to make jokes about her increasing girth—or, according
to her mood, to swear when another inch of satin had to be let
into the cage of elastic and whalebone that controlled her obstrep-
erous flesh. The jest, on this occasion, missed fire—badly.
Leaning back in her chair, Polly lifted overflowing eyes to her
daughter.

" I sometimes feel you're not happy, and I wonder if it's my
fault."

" Why on earth should it be ? "

" Well "—Polly's gaze returned to her glass—" I sometimes
hear women talking about their daughters : talking about how
they've got no secrets from one another——"

" Then you can bet your sweet life they're lying. No girl
in her right mind tells her mother everything. Your generation's
quick enough to stand out for its privacy ; why shouldn't we
keep ours ? " She softened her voice to add, " Don't worry
about me, Mother. I've done pretty well, haven't I ?—a place
of my own, lots of fun, and—while it lasts !—money to burn.
What more can one ask for ? "

" You've said it : ' while it lasts.' Those things don't last,
Debby. You've got to have more in your life than that."

" Have you ? " asked Aldebaran, when she recovered from
her astonishment.

Polly nodded, almost apologetically.

" I've not got your brains, dear—I know that ; and I've
made a lot of mistakes. But when you get to my time of life
it's what you've got to remember that counts. Things you

hardly notice while they're happening—that add up to happiness."

Feeling like a schoolgirl, Aldebaran moved restlessly. At the same time, the realization—which rarely troubled her—that she was speaking to the " great " Polly Bowling held flippancy in check. Polly's public, although not so wide, was more personal than hers ; this big, simple and in many ways stupid woman was the idol of thousands who found in her the reflection of their instincts and their emotions. Many a time she had sat and watched, almost incredulously, her mother pouring sympathy and loving kindness across the footlights, until it was reflected back from the gross and unthinking faces in front of her. The words of her songs were often what Aldebaran, in the critical 'teens, had considered " tooth-jumping," yet Polly Bowling sent them like arrows into the hearts of her audiences and smiled the sting away.

" You've had a lot of fun out of your job, Mother—and so have I."

" Job ? " said Polly vaguely. " Oh yes ! " She gave her radiant smile. " It's funny, isn't it ? I wasn't thinking of that. If that little squit's right, my job's about over," she asserted stoutly. " I'm a back number—and who cares ? " *You* care, thought Aldebaran ; you'll care when it's time to go down to the stage door, and there's no stage door to go to ; when there's no gallery to shout " Good old Polly ! "—a pang of intolerable tenderness shot through her, and, at the same time, misgiving. What's going to make up for all that ? As though her daughter's thoughts had communicated themselves to her, Polly continued, " It won't be so good, but we'll live it down ! After all, there's other things to live for : folks you're fond of, and are fond of you. Folks that depend on you—there's always plenty of them about ! " She gave her rich chuckle, and sobered suddenly. "I never let anybody down—except Joe."

And your daughter. That strange trail of husbands : Johnny Flood, my Father. Then Bert, Harry, Tommy. Are those the memories that make up her happiness ? Bert, who though common, was kind and sweet, and died of a tired heart when

I was only six or seven; Harry who had rocketed his way down from the top of the bill, and was a confirmed alcoholic by the time he met Mother and persuaded her that she alone could save him from his inevitable end; Tommy, who drained her of every penny she earned . . .

She's happy because she's never been in love, came to Aldebaran, in a blinding flash of intuition. She's loved them, and mothered them, and sacrificed herself for them—but she's never been *in love* . . .

Something ripped across her brain like a surgeon's knife, laid it open and let in the light. Before I give Orlando his answer, I've got to find Lee! Surely it couldn't be—it was !— as simple as all that.

"What's making you smile?" asked Polly suspiciously.

She could feel the smile, tender and frail as a feather, brushing her lips into softness. She got up, and, no less to her own surprise than to Polly's, dropped a kiss on the glossy parting of her mother's hair.

III

It was Bob Winter's fault they were late in starting. He arrived in a taxi, full of apologies. An author had arrived—one of the elusive and difficult kind, who, materializing once a year, find it incredible that the entire organization is not instantly at their disposal.

"It's all right—but we may get caught in the midday crush."

And so it proved. It was Saturday. All of London was pouring out along the Great West Road. They found themselves in a queue that stretched through Chiswick out to the by-pass.

"I'd better fill up here." Orlando glanced at the petrol gauge and scowled; knowing he was going to Southampton the garage should not have turned him out short of gas.

When he got back into the car, Aldebaran had slid over into the driving seat.

D

" Darling, please let me ?   I shan't have another chance until I get back."

" If that girl of mine's going to drive, you can let me out ! " From her seat at the back, with Bob and Agnes, Polly registered a protest of which no one took any notice. They burned up the track, regardless of traffic lights, and were nearly three-quarters of an hour behind schedule at Basingstoke. Once or twice Bob touched her shoulder.

" Take it easy. A cop's got his eye on you."

" Maybe you'd rather drive ? I can't help having to hurry, can I ? " inquired Aldebaran sweetly, at which Bob, deflated, lay back and devoted his energies to calming Polly, in turns blasphemous or resigned.

At Winchester, Orlando murmured, " We're in plenty of time." He was not paying much attention to the driving ; his mind was centred on the coming parting. Would there be any hope of getting her alone ?—perhaps in the stateroom, with the others tactfully out of the way ? He knew Agnes was on his side, was not so sure of Polly. The difficult relationship between mother and daughter had prevented his deliberately attempting to enlist Polly's support. She had always shown herself friendly, but that was her way with everyone. He had tried to sound Aldebaran about her possible reactions to an engagement.

" I don't know—I wouldn't expect her to be enthusiastic," was the discouraging reply.

" But why not ? She hasn't got anything against me."

" Except the title, darling ! You forget—or maybe I've forgotten to mention—she went through enough for ' marrying above her ' not exactly to welcome the same sort of thing for her daughter," said Aldebaran dryly.

His optimism about the time proved to be misplaced ; as usual, in Winchester, half of the streets were " up "; they were side-tracked, forced into traffic diversions, held up again and again by " Stop "-" Go " signs that made Aldebaran grit her teeth with impatience, although, as luck had it, they had so far picked up on schedule that they could afford the delay.

It was at the Swarthling crossroads that the trouble happened.

Trying to shoot them ahead of an oncoming van, she ran it too close, tipped the wing of the van and swung the Bentley into a corner of the stone wall.

" Sorry, Landy." She sat still, feeling silly. There was no need for the hurry, but she had been driving ahead of her own thoughts ; driving ahead of Orlando's thoughts, as he sat there beside her, planning, trying to force her to conclusions. . . .

" What did I tell you ? She's not fit to be trusted with anything that'll do more than ten m.p.h. ! " Polly's shrill protest was damped down by Agnes. Bob Winter got out, with Orlando, to deal with the irate van-driver.

It ended in the three women being picked up by a passing car, while Orlando and Bob, having failed to start the Bentley, waited for the inevitable policeman.

When, at last, they got down to the dock, the stateroom was crowded with flowers ; Orlando's contribution, violets, was deliberately insignificant ; his parting gift, a gold lighter, he slipped, when she was not looking, into a half-emptied tin of cigarettes which Agnes had thrown on the table after filling Aldebaran's case.

Already the floor was littered with the gilt envelopes of " greeting " telegrams, the air full of laughter, of exaggeratedly affectionate farewells. To Orlando's dismay, the brilliant idea of " seeing her off " had communicated itself to her innumerable friends of the stage and screen. A vast Alfa-Romeo had swept a bunch of them down to the dock ; Aldebaran was surrounded, engulfed in waves of Chanel 5, her shoulders encircled by arms in pale, manly tweeds, her pale face smudged with lipstick. Bob Winter gave him a look, laughed and went out on the promenade deck ; if he had any sense, thought Orlando, he would do the same. But he felt stupidly obliged to remain there, with a glass of champagne in his hand—and not even Polly came to his rescue. Then the whole crowd—Aldebaran in their midst—rushed out, chattering like birds, and he was left alone. . . .

" We're well out of it ! " Agnes, slipping back, offered him the comfort of her grin. " The camera-boys are at it, and Polly, as usual, is stealing her daughter's thunder ! The whole engine room is clamouring for her autograph and it'll be a miracle if we're away by midnight."

I must be generous, Orlando reminded himself. This is the kind of thing that will happen after we're married. This is what she likes, what she's accustomed to.

They came swilling back into the stateroom; more champagne, more laughter, Aldebaran, in tense discussion with a young man he recognized as the writer of the script of *Bells*, occasionally lifted her eyebrows at him, giving a little shrug as though to say, "Well, you see how it is—and you wanted to come." He was monopolized by a blonde with incredible eyelashes who appeared to take it for granted he was acquainted with her every appearance on the stage (or was it the screen?) in the last six months. He became slowly furious, and had almost reached the decision to stride over and tear her out of the heart of the group in which she was imbedded, when the "Visitors off the ship" siren sounded: Polly rushed in, her face pink, her eyes brimming, and clutched Aldebaran to her bosom: he was thrust aside through an orgy of kissing and embracing —wondering whether, after all, he really wanted this so-much-kissed, so-much-embraced Aldebaran—and suddenly found himself alone with her, with her pale face stamped with women's lipstick, and her wild hair, and her excited eyes.

"Darling, I'm terribly sorry about the car."

"It doesn't matter in the least." It sounded impossibly stilted. "Promise me," he heard himself saying, "you won't drive until you come back."

Her laughter had a little edge of offence on it.

"Oh—so you think I'm in the habit of smashing cars?"

"I don't give a damn about the cars—I want you back, in one piece!"

"Silly! I'm a very good driver." She was smiling, but he felt antagonism in the smile. It was not possible they should say Goodbye like this. He tried to find words, and could only say the thing that was in his sore heart.

"I didn't expect to find all those people here."

"Didn't you?" She sounded almost casual. "I'm sorry,

darling ; it was a bore, wasn't it ? But you know what they are "—and he realized that she had known about the Alfa Romeo and the blonde and the young men in Hollywood tweeds and, purposely, had not warned him. She pushed her hands in her pockets and flung her head back, but betrayed herself by the flicker in her eyes. " Darling, if you don't go, you'll have to jump ship—literally ! "

" Is that all you've got to say to me ? "

" L-look after Uncle Joe for me—and Mother. Oh, Landy," she stammered, " I *do* love you ! "

Their mouths touched briefly. It's the first time I have ever kissed her without meaning it, thought Orlando. Even that had no power to shock him, because she had hurt him into numbness. The whole moment was meaningless as a dream. He told himself he would not see her for four—perhaps five— months, and the knowledge meant nothing. He said, " I hope you'll have a good trip "—and could not believe in the sound of his own voice.

" I'll cable you from New York." To her also the moment was unreal ; she wanted to break out of it, to have done with it, with Orlando's cold face, his baffled eyes. She felt, if he looked at her a moment longer, she would fling herself in his arms, say something mad and irrevocable. " Tell Uncle Joe to write to me : tell him I'll want to know *everything*. He'll understand." And you won't ; was that what she meant ?

They were half-way down the Channel when his cable was brought to her.

" Bon voyage don't forget send me your travel list "—to which she replied :

" Sending list air mail I love you." The last three words caused an acidulated young operator to expectorate before picking up his key.

Chapter Three

I

THROUGH AUTUMN mist, the towering cenotaphs, the obelisks and pylons of a giants' graveyard—strangely antique, even druidical, in the exhausted light—rose into a milky sky. Wistful, necromantic, profoundly melancholy, the Manhattan skyline wrote itself in the blurred terms of a Whistlerian nocturne across the bows of the ship ; drifted to starboard as she swung in towards Hoboken.

Aldebaran pressed her bosom against her crossed arms and caught her breath ; never, no, never had she foreseen this. There had never been such a moment in her life—a hushed, exquisite, inimitable moment : a moment of apprehension—in which all of that fair and miraculous vision, five wind-driven ocean days distant from familiar earth, might dissolve, to float away in sea-wrack beyond reach of mortal eye. Monument to esoteric cults, hung with its autumn haze as with elegiac veils. New York—the beautiful and damned.

An hour later, with the ordeal of the Customs behind her, the ordeal of reporters, the ordeal of her agent's welcome, she was in a car speeding towards the East Fifties. Stripped of its ashes by the setting sun, Manhattan rose, a delicate fire-colour, against the thin blue sky. Roseate, transparent almost as light itself—she watched its pyramids solidify at her approach. A million windows spurted flame. A faint, premature refulgence of sky-signs cast, here and there, a ghostly rainbow across the façades. She thrust her spine back against the upholstery, returning superficial answers to her companions' comments, while her brain raced away from them and wove its private fantasies.

Manhattan—Magnificat in stone ! My soul doth magnify

Mammon, and my spirit doth rejoice in my lord the Dollar : it comes at you off the fronts of the buildings : stunning and stimulating at the same time. It excites me ! Just the smell and taste of it—Orlando's right ; I'm vulgar. Success : money— well, I can't help it. I'm a Flood ! We've been in commerce two hundred years : I can't help thrilling to all this.

A terrible beauty, spiring up into the twilight ; a thousand blessed damosels, collected along their golden bars, looking down with envy on the profane splendour of Fifth Avenue, on Park and Madison, on Saks and Bendel and Tiffany, and the Waldorf and the Stork and the haunts of swing and jazz. I'm being shown New York. A faint strain of the blues crosses the sound of lutes. . . .

She sent cables to Orlando and Polly, and she and Agnes dined out of doors, under striped awnings and shaded lights, with the hot New York night pressing on their bare shoulders. Agnes was good company ; she knew when not to talk. A first night in New York, alone, would have been rather damping —although it was entirely her own fault, Aldebaran's, that they were by themselves. Her publishers had fixed a party ; her agent wanted to take them to some famous roof garden ; it had taken considerable ingenuity and lavish exercise of " the Flood charm " to get out of these, leaving no ill feeling behind—espe- cially the party, which, fortunately, was a more or less intimate affair at an apartment up on the East Seventies. In the end, she left Agnes to handle that, and bluntly, in propria persona, announced that she wanted to spend this first evening quietly, unpacking, " getting herself organized," and go early to bed. There were ten days before they started out on their travels, and she felt she needed this small space in which to " adjust." The first few hours of New York had been to her, as they are to most sensitive people, rather like a crack on the head ; she felt as yet too uncertain of herself to be confident of doing herself justice among strangers.

With her second Old-fashioned, however, she became con- versational.

" Do you see any of them ? "

"I thought I saw Lorelei Lee, just slipping out." That was the best of Agnes : she never missed a cue. It was a frightful extravagance, bringing Agnes, but it would, she assured herself, pay in the end. Agnes knew every inch of the States ; she would be efficient, and, if need arose—which heaven forbid— "home-sy": a word of Aldebaran's own coining which, in her youth, applied exclusively to Uncle Joe. Agnes continued, "It's a bit early for the Barrymores—but there's rather a good Peter Arno over there."

"I was always brought up to believe"—she cleared her throat and assumed what they called her "lecture" voice— "that the population of the United States of America falls into two categories : one, of witty, cultured sophisticates who can repeat from memory—but without giving themselves away— any two columns from the *Saturday Review*, and invent all the jokes in *The New Yorker*. Judging from the dialogue that's been rippling into my left ear ever since I started this vichysoisse, it strikes me we've tuned in on the wrong programme."

"What about the other category ? " encouraged Agnes.

"*They* "—she waved her spoon largely—"nourish themselves on grits and either live Across the Tracks or Overlooked by the El."

"Don't omit," Agnes reminded her, " the exaggerated subdivisions of the second category who spend their lives on porches in the Deep South till the floorboards give way and let them down on top of the family of skunks that took up residence there somewhere around the time when Sherman was playing mayhem with the Low Country."

"Actually," said Aldebaran, " I've left out the Babbits, the Old South'n Colonel and his daughter the South'n Belle ; Joe di Maggio, the Little Flower, Mehitabel the Cat and about ten million bobby-soxers who train for necking on the campus by watching Cary Grant make love to Jean Harlow." She cast a comprehensively reproachful glance round the surrounding tables. " It looks like they're all out of town. These people are really depressingly like the sort of thing you see any day of the week in the Savoy grill. It'll be a pity if all my generalizations fall down."

"Come again." Agnes grinned at Aldebaran's stare. "You'd better remember that one; it means ' go on '—in the polite sense, of course. Tell me more about your preconceptions; they remind me of my own, the first time I came over."

"All mothers," said Aldebaran, warming to her subject, "are white-haired, and answer to the collective surname, O'Mine: leading to the conclusion that the race is carried on exclusively through females of Irish derivation who give birth regularly to red-haired policemen named Doherty——"

"Geogehan," corrected Agnes, with a straight face.

"Can't spell it," said Aldebaran tersely. "There's quite a piece, incidentally, to be said about the American Woman. All old ladies are gracious, and were born in Boston or South Carolina."

"What about the mid-Western hellions who wield the bludgeon of enormous wealth inherited from share-pushing poppas over their reluctant families ? "

"All young women are exquisite and steel-smooth—Northern type—or exquisite and magnolia-like—Southern type."

"How about the young men ? "

"No girl over the age of ten is a virgin," said Aldebaran, sticking to her subject, "and the boys adolesce, with the co-operation of a Polack house-girl, about a fortnight after they go into rompers. Kindly note the neat correlation of the two subjects."

Heads turned as their laughter pealed across the tables. Aldebaran kicked Agnes and bent her own grin towards her plate.

"That's better; now I'm relaxed! Strictly between ourselves, I was feeling the least in life reduced. It does rather shake one, you know—no matter how hard-boiled one fancies oneself. If it was just sheer size, one could laugh it off; but why doesn't anyone tell one New York is *beautiful* ? ". She leaned back, to draw a deep breath and look up at the stars. "If I were to stop a long time, I almost believe I'd start writing poetry again. Look "—her voice quickened and sank—" talking of signs and portents : isn't that *me* up there ? " A corner of Taurus showed indeed above the roofs. " Aldebaran ; it's a hell of a name. I wonder what they'll make of it here ? I wonder, if you put the number of times I've had to tell people how to pronounce it end to end, whether it would reach round the British Isles."

" It's a good name for a poet," conceded Agnes. " Not so hot for a popular novelist."

" Shut up about the popular novelist. It's no worse than Sacheverell," scowled Aldebaran. " The accent's in the same place and it scans the same. Sachy hits a different public—but may be some day I'll write for people who know how Aldebaran's pronounced."

" *Oo*," observed Agnes abruptly. She had laid down her spoon and was leaning forward stiffly. Her face looked drawn.

" What's the matter ? "

" I don't know—a kind of a ' stitch '—I guess it's indigestion," muttered Agnes, ducking her head. " It's all right—it will be gone in a minute—but I guess I'll go easy on the next course. While I think of it, there's a letter——"

" Oh poops to letters. You aren't going to be sick, are you ? " scowled Aldebaran. The mauve-ish dress Agnes was wearing gave her a grey look. Agnes was not clever about clothes ; before quitting New York she would have to be taken in hand. Aldebaran, who had a weakness for having well-dressed people about her, frowned at the mauve frock which she had always disliked ; Agnes might have found something else to put on, their first night in New York. " Do you want to go to bed ? "

Agnes shook her head ; she knew it was not part of a secretary's duties to retire to bed when her employer was " rar'-ing " to be abroad.

" It was only a twinge—it's nearly gone. And if we're really going down to the Village you'd better knock back the rest of your dinner and get changed ; that creation of yours won't be exactly convenient for strolling around Bleecker Street. I'll go up and put your grey suit out. It's all right; you needn't glower! I expect I had one drink too many just now with Max and Phil Hardman."

She sat alone, absently eating, but mainly watching people— the novelist's favourite occupation; trying to overhear their conversations, trying to place them—difficult: because most of the women looked as though, at a push, they might be in the Social Register, while the men—— ! Her lips pursed themselves for a whistle. The American male did surely let his womenfolk down when it came to the social and sartorial graces. There was an exception at a distant table: the man who sat there alone was one of the few wearing a dinner jacket; an elderly middle age, his fine, fastidious profile and well-shaped head, together with his cold air of deliberate aloofness, distinguished him among the rest. There was something aloof and a little disdainful about him. From time to time, without speaking, he indicated his wants to the waiter who hovered behind him. Once or twice the captain went to his table, received some brief comment and nodded sharply to the waiter, who increased his assiduity.

"Mr. Tollemache," Aldebaran's waiter replied to her question. "Comes about once a month. Comes from the South— from Charleston."

The last name went into her like a pin-prick. She swallowed the last mouthful, balled up her napkin and rose abruptly. Half-way across the court she was caught by the waiter, to sign the check, and found, as usual, she had no money for the expected tip. Like most English people she had yet to get used to the American custom of cash down for service. . . .

Agnes was leaning over the desk in their sittingroom, Aldebaran smiled slowly as she opened the door and took in her face the overpowering scent of freesia, tuberose and clove carnation. The floor was scattered with florists' boxes and tissue paper.

"It's the first time I've known what it feels like to be a *poule de luxe*!—or," she amended, "a leading lady on a first night. I have a ghastly sort of suspicion we don't do this sort of thing, when American writers visit London!" She sank her nose into a bowl of freesia. " Whee-ee ; heaven—vases, I mean vayses, and all. Who's mine cordially, Berni Brunner ? "

" Give me the card ; I've got a collection of them here. We'll do them tomorrow, when Max comes round."

" Are you all right now ? "

Agnes nodded.

" Look, those dark red roses are from somebody called Ruth Rodríguez ; does that mean anything in your young life ? "

" Not a thing ; ought it to ? "

" Here's her letter. She says she, or her husband, I forget which, is related to you. She wants you to stay with her when you go down to the South."

" I never heard of her," scowled Aldebaran. " And I thought we agreed I shouldn't do any extra social stuff while I'm lecturing ? It was you who said——"

" Yes ; but this comes right at the end of the tour. Mrs. Rodríguez lives near Charleston——"

Again the pin-prick. Aldebaran muttered something and slouched towards the door communicating with their bedrooms.

" And that reminds me "—Agnes was fumbling in her handbag : much too big and clumsy a handbag for a smart young woman in New York—and pulled out a small, leather-covered book. " I've been making up the new addresses, so we don't have to tool that tome of yours about with us—and I'd just like to check up on something. Somebody called Anderson, and it might be *Cove* Street or *Cone* Street : I can't read your writing. I couldn't make out the number, either ; I suppose you can't remember, off-hand, if it's 75 or 78 ? "

" What do you want that for ? "

Agnes, surprised, lifted her head.

" Don't you remember ? You threw a whole heap of little old address books at me, and told me to copy out all the American addresses. I think the date of that one was 1917—but as ' Anderson ' had a tick against it I thought it might be someone important." She held the book out for Aldebaran's inspection. " Mrs. Rodríguez' letter reminded me of it, because that's Charleston as well."

Aldebaran snatched the book from her furiously, glared at the neat page of writing—and flung it across the room.

" You *fool*—— ! "

Agnes gaped ; went on gaping, while a smothered babble of incoherencies poured from Aldebaran's lips.

" 1917—no one but an idiot—— "

Agnes recovered her breath and her spirit and was about to point out that, among her qualifications, second sight did not happen to be included, when—" *Oo!* "—she was obliged to double up again. Drawn up tautly in the doorway, Aldebaran's eyes glittered resentment of the interruption.

" *Now* what's the matter ? Oh, really ! What do you want —an aspirin or some bicarbonate ? Where *are* the things ?— Agnes." She crept across the room to drop her hand on Agnes's bowed shoulders. " Agnes. I'm sorry I snarled. Do you feel awful ? Would you like to have a doctor ? "

Agnes shook her head ; she put her handkerchief up to her face and wiped away the sweat that had gathered in the roots of her hair.

" Heavens, no. I tell you, it's just plain over-eating and over-drinking ; I made a pig of myself at lunch—why do they have such marvellous chefs on board ship ? But would you think me an utter wet if we didn't go out tonight ? "

" Of course not, you half-wit ! " said Aldebaran tenderly. " Go on ; get your things off ; tell me where I can find the bi-carb., and I'll mix you a charge that will jolt your ridiculous stomach into order inside half an hour. Then you can take one of my sleeping pills. . . ."

II

Hands in pockets, heedless of North, South, East or West, she strode along the sidewalk until, out of the shining shuttle of the night traffic, she managed to snatch one of the yellow taxicabs, and told the driver, " The Village."

" Sure ; whe'bouts in de Village ? "

While her brain plunged about, trying from Agnes's half-remembered descriptions to seize on a place, on a name, she noticed he was coloured.

"Washington Square : isn't that the Village ? Listen," she was obliged to appeal to him. "I don't know New York. I want to go some place where there's music."

A smile of ivory split his face like a burst fruit.

"You wanna dance ? "

"Not particularly." (He thinks I'm a pick-up ! Who would I dance with, anyhow ?) "Just take me some place where they—where they play—*you* know : jazz, blues, whatever you call it."

"Sure."

The chains of lights streamed by, drops of moving gold strung on invisible threads, two endless skeins moving in opposite directions, crossing at intervals, to weave the rich texture of New York night. Slowly the skeins thinned out. A space with tall trees and strolling couples she guessed was Washington Square. Then the night became short tunnels, flashed with red or green or the vitreous blue of neon, and terminating in distant bonfires. They stopped in front of an archway with red and blue light-bubbles over the steps.

"What's this ? "

Taking his tip, the taxidriver told her a name that conveyed nothing. After a brief hesitation, she walked in. There were tables on the left, a long bar on the right. She appeared to be the only person alone ; all the women had men, the men were hung in clumps along the bar, or had their elbows propped on the tables. Noise came at her—solid : in rainbow-coloured blocks, in sharp angles and splinters, like a Picasso canvas ; she saw it proceeded from the far end where the room broke into a dance hall, and there was a brightly lit stage and a pyramid of bandsmen in white tuxedos, all flashed and mixed up with the glitter of their instruments. One man stood up for a solo with an immensely long thin horn—like a jazz-time archangel sounding the Last Trump for the couples seething darkly on the floor. She looked at her watch. Twenty to twelve.

. . . Twenty to one. There was a narrow staircase leading down, with red light-bulbs and a lantern-jawed youth in a plaid shirt, who held a curtain aside. She found herself in a kind of cellar, dark, except for some concealed lighting that brought up Village drawings in blue and pink chalk on cream walls. The low ceiling was arched and the space between the tables and the ceiling was packed solid with smoke, although the place was not particularly full. She found without difficulty a seat on the plush bench that ran along the back wall. A piano was being played by a light coloured youth with hair so far rubbed back from his forehead that from in front he looked as though he were bald. He was smiling, but his eyes and knitted brow held the anxious fear of the performer who knows he is not making good.

She pulled out her cigarette case and found it empty.

" Thanks—no ; that's all right. I can get some for myself." She had been about to accept one from the pack pushed towards her from her right-hand neighbour when she saw there were only two left. He insisted, shaking the pack impatiently.

" Sure ; me too. What are you—British ? "

She nodded.

" Been over here long ? "

She shook her head.

" Say "—came gravely, after a pause—" do you have an impediment ? "

" No ; why ? "

" Nothing. Just seems like you find it kind of hard to utter."

Aldebaran laughed. Apparently the offer of the cigarette was to be paid for in conversation. Across the flame of her lighter she looked at the speaker, who looked as though he might be in the late twenties : long, slack-limbed, out of place in a city, yet conforming to it in dress and the premature lining of a sallow, not unattractive face. Several men had tried to make her in the last place ; her experienced eye, summing up this stranger, found something different.

" Sorry. I just—wasn't thinking. What's his name ? " She nodded towards the pianist, now shambling his way into the darkness behind the musicians' empty stands. Only a few of the audience troubled to clap.

" Search me. This joint's dead, anyhow." He moved restlessly. " I guess he's just a fill-in till they close down."

The musicians had trickled back to their stands and proceeded to let rip a blare of noise. Suddenly her companion stood up.

" Let's go."

" Go where ? "

A slow smile broadened pleasantly on his face.

" Lady, will you do me the honour of dancing this one with me. Is that okay ? "

" A bit on the pedantic side "—her own mouth twitched— " but we'll leave it as meant. I'd rather not dance—it's too hot down here. What are they playing ? I don't know it."

" I bet you don't." He sat down again, as though relieved by her refusal. " That's an old number called 'Iceman's Rag.' Gee, we were dancing to that the year I graduated ; it's kind of nostalgic! It was all 'Iceman's Rag' those days: that and another thing called——"

She heard herself saying it ; it was like listening to herself talking in her sleep.

" ' Jehovah Blues.' "

" Say, what's this ? Are you a mind-reader ? "

" It doesn't take much reading. You must have graduated " —her slow glance bathed him briefly in liquid amber—" soon after the war. Everybody was playing it then. They're still playing it in England."

" Gee, I haven't heard that tune in ten years," he said slowly, and started to hum it.

" He never wrote anything else, did he ? "

" Who ? "

" Lee Marion ; the composer."

" Was that the guy who wrote it ? You're telling me something. I guess I don't pay much attention to composers—except the ones that play their own numbers, and you kind of tie up the tune with the guy's face."

" Then—he's not—well-known—over here."

Her companion wagged his head doubtfully.

" No-o, I guess he isn't. Anyway, I don't know him—though that doesn't mean much ! I've a wife and kids : we don't get around the way we used to before we got married ! There's a guy keeps a book store a few blocks from here : he'd know. He's got a collection of nearly a thousand records—right back to the old Pace and Handy numbers like ' The Cotton Fields of Dixie' and 'Jogo Blues,' that came out long before the war. I bet he's got that old blues—I must have him play it me some time." He leaned forward to stub out the cigarette in the saucer. " I'll go get another pack. You'll wait right here ? "

She nodded—wondering why ; but it was less effort to sit there, fanned by the hot rhythm of the band, than to get up and go. She sat there—and presently he came loping back, dropped a pack of cigarettes in front of her and opened his own.

" I was just thinking—what do you say they called that guy ? "

" Lee—Marion ? "

" Uh-huh. If he's anywhere around, I bet Karl knows him. Karl knows the whole of the café concert crowd as well as he knows his first editions." Then—inevitably it came, and she knew for what she had waited. " Say, would you like us to walk round there ? "

" What—to Karl's ? "

" Uh-huh. It's only a step from here."

She laughed, glancing at her watch.

" Have you any idea what the time is ? "

" What ? "

" It's after one o'clock ; nearly half-past."

" So what ? "

" Well—the shop will be shut, if course."

" Ses who ? "

" You don't really mean that one can buy *books* at half-past one in the morning ? "

" Why not ? "

E

" Oh my God," sighed Aldebaran. " Does one really have to cross the Atlantic to find civilization ? "

The book store was a little illuminated box in the darkened street. It appeared to be as much club as shop : youths and girls were sitting around, perching on the counter. Somewhere in the back a gramophone was playing *l'Après-midi d'un Faune.* Two coloured men leaned against one of the shelves, reading the same book ; one lifted his head to smile shyly at Aldebaran's companion.

" Hi, Dave."

" Hi, Saunders. Hi, Jex. Hi, Karl ! "—as a freckled youth in a thin blue shirt came from the back of the store. " Karl, meet—— ? "

" Barry "—as it appeared to be Christian names all round. Out of the corner of her eye she had seen several copies of *Bells on her Fingers* on one of the shelves ; luckily they were not new ; the jackets were gone and the spines rubbed. Karl was fixing her with bright blue eyes like pebbles.

" It's queer ; I kind of know your face."

" I dare say you do ; it's quite an—ordinary face," she floundered, raising a laugh.

" May be we don't use ' ordinary ' the way you do in England. Sorry ; customers," said Karl briefly.

A young woman in beech-green slacks and a turban of twisted silk wanted to buy a copy of *Bells.*

" I suppose you know that ? " He showed it to Aldebaran as he strolled towards the cash register. " We've sold twenty copies—second hand, of course—this week ; this makes the twenty-first. What do you know ? " He savagely rang up the sale.

" Have you read it ? " faltered Aldebaran.

" Jesus, no." Karl laughed, and handed the copy, with the change, to the customer, who gave Aldebaran a sweet, dental smile.

" Karl's just too intellectual ; he's always kidding me," she complained. " A girl can't be intellectual all the time, can she ? And this Aldy-bairan Flood—she's quite a famous author :

isn't she, Dave ? I don't see Karl should kid me for reading what everybody's reading. I mean, this *Bells on her Fingers*. I mean, a girl's at a disadvantage if she doesn't keep up on her reading——" She frowned like a baby. " Isn't she, Dave ? "

" Sure." Dave laughed easily. " What's wrong with it ? Martha left it for me to read while she was away——"

" For Chrissake," breathed Karl.

" Hell—it's just one of these ' women's books,' but I got a quarter the way through before I went to sleep. It's pretty slick—as a matter of fact, it's pretty good writing : in spots."

" Yeah ; good enough to be better," sneered Karl.

" I thought you hadn't read it ! " chorused Dave, the purchaser and two or three others who had drifted into the group.

" I read the first two chapters and then I vomited." He swung on Aldebaran. " Do you know Aldebaran Flood ? " At least he had the name rightly.

" Well—well—as a matter of fact, she's my worst enemy," she stammered—and drew another laugh.

" I guess you must know her pretty well ! She's over here lecturing, isn't she ? My, she must have made plenny dollars out of that book ! "

Dave was saying,

" Karl : do you know a guy called Lee Marion ? "

" ' Jehovah Blues ' ? "

Dave made an elaborate gesture, as to say, " What did I tell you ? " The two coloured men lifted their heads.

" Is he anywhere around ? "

Karl shrugged his shoulders.

" I wouldn't know. Do you know, Jex ?—Saunders ? "

The Negroes shook their heads ; their eyes of onyx seemed to dwell upon Aldebaran.

" Queer you should bring that up. I was playing the old Columbia disc a night or two ago."

" So it was recorded."

" How do you mean—' So it was——' ? There's seven or eight recordings of ' Jehovah Blues.' "

" *Band* recordings," put in Aldebaran.

" I know what you mean," said Karl. " Marion recorded it himself—once—in Europe. I've been trying for years to get that record. There was a French guy here, once, said he'd got it, and he'd mail me a copy——"

" But he didn't."

" Sure he did ; and it arrived in splinters. There's only one way to get records from Europe : have someone bring them over. But I guess it's obsolete ; it's not in any of the lists I've had. It's what they call a ' collectors' item,' and it's darned hard to get hold of those, unless you know somebody willing to part with them."

" But if it's all that good, why doesn't the guy make another recording ? "

Karl hitched his shoulders again under the thin blue stuff.

" ' Jehovah's ' an old number. The bands have cornered it. If the guy'd got himself in the lights, the gramophone companies would jump at a new recording. But I bet if you asked a hundred people, not more than one—I guess not even one—would know who wrote ' Jehovah Blues.' "

" Then—he's not around New York."

" I wouldn't know. There's scores of little joints where he might be working out—but I guess that guy's kind of dumb. He ought to be cashing in big with bands and the radio and recording companies, but, some way or other, he's never made the big time."

" Seems queer he only did the one thing."

" May be he didn't. May be he lifted ' Jehovah Blues ' from some other guy." The one they called Saunders spoke in a slow voice like a bassoon.

" He did write it ! " She checked herself just in time.

" May be the other guy's put him on the spot ! " Saunders was smiling, as though the idea gave him pleasure. " May be the other guy got kind of tired, listening to his tune being played and thinking about the dough trickling into this guy's pocket——"

" Say, Saunders, why don't you write books ? " His friend broke into a guffaw. " This Marion guy—he could be a dozen places : some of those bug-joints down the Bowery and West

River : or up in Harlem. Jeeze, he don't have to be in town, anyhow."

" Sure ; who cares ? " Saunders' smile broadened ; the two nodded ; Jex chucked the book they had been reading back in its place on the shelves ; beyond the radius of the store's lit frontage, darkness blotted them out.

A little man propped in the doorway threw a wary look after them, another round the shop—now empty, save for Aldebaran, Dave and Karl—and hitched himself a step or two towards the latter who, apparently recognizing a customer, nodded and picked up a handful of old pulps from the bench on which he was leaning.

" We've not gotten much in your line tonight, Gus."

It appeared, however, that the little man's present preoccupation was not with literature.

" Say, was de dame asking 'bout Red Marion ? "

" Is he a buddy of yours ? "

" Dat's de junkie was woiking Harry's spot on West 138th. Dat guy's sure got more hot licks dan all de piano boys put togedder ! " The speaker's face cracked open in a grin over septic gums.

" Could be. But he's not dragging down much at a joint like Harry's." Karl shrugged his shoulders.

" I told ya he's a junkie, din't I ? " said the little man aggressively. Karl laughed.

" It takes more than five dollars a week to make a junkie ! "

" What's this place—Harry's—anyhow ? " she broke in ; the unfamiliar vocabulary, the all but unintelligible accent set up a crackling in her brain ; was there no way of forcing them to speak English ? " Where is it ? Is it a club, or a dance place—— ? "

After a silence—" Kind of," said Dave, reluctantly.

" Well ? Let's go ! " Her voice sounded high-pitched, not like her own. Karl laughed again, Dave scowled, and the little man called Gus wiped his mouth on the back of his hand and looked furtively out of the corners of his eyes.

" Dey run him out."

" What for ? " Karl sounded bored.

" Got after Harry's ofay chick——"

" What does he *mean* ? " she appealed to Dave.

" Seems like he's quitted."

" Left the—the club ? But he must be working somewhere : mustn't he ? "

Although neither Dave nor Karl looked at her she could feel their curiosity and it was not difficult to imagine what they were thinking. She stiffened.

" I met Lee Marion during the war. I've got messages for him—from friends in England." (Surely a novelist should have been able to think up something more convincing than that. Knowing that they knew she was lying, she went on defiantly.) " You have agents, don't you—like we do over there ? People who handle the music-hall "—she remembered Agnes's coaching and changed it to " vaudeville," which she spoilt by pronouncing it in the English fashion—" people who handle the vaudeville turns, and the night clubs and floor shows ? "

Karl mumbled some names ; it was Dave who told her,

" You've got to be somebody, to have an agent. If he's working joints like Harry's, it doesn't sound as if . . . Hi, Karl ; you've gotten the contacts ; why don't you go into this, and I'll get in touch with Barry ? " His determination to reserve the rights of intermediary would have made her smile, if a smile had been in her.

They captured a taxi on Broadway—that imponderable thoroughfare which plays havoc with the neat geography of New York—and Dave produced a fountain pen and a notebook ; she could see his face, politely eager for the information she had so far withheld.

" Name—please ! "

She said, after a moment's desperation,

" Swear before God you won't tell."

" Sure I won't tell." But she felt his interest sharpen. " The name's not Garbo, is it ? "

She told him.

" You're kidding."

" Ask them at the desk—at the reception—whatever you call it," she said wearily, " if you don't believe me."

They had reached the quiet East Fifties when she asked him,

" What's a junkie ? "

" A junkie——? Well "—he laughed awkwardly—" junk's dope : cocaine, or heroin. Or morphia. There's quite a lot of it around, since Prohibition. But it costs plenty, and you've got to be in the big money, to be a junkie ! "

Her pride resisted the note of kindly reassurance in his voice.

" Who the hell cares, anyhow ? "

The hotel was bathed in its silent, interior glow of before dawn. She was in the elevator, with a yawning boy—who carried her books to the door of her apartment. Then in her bedroom—with the great golden night-blur of New York rising to her twelfth-floor window, before she switched on the lamps.

She opened the door into Agnes's room a crack ; darkness and silence. Thank God, Agnes was sleeping. She closed it again.

Before getting into bed, she went again to lean against the window. A veil lay over her mind. It was as though the whole thing were illusion : the speckle of lights which, climbing higher, confused itself with the stars ; russet veil of illuminated midnight drawn across the blue dark ; thunder of the subway ; howl of police cars, fire engines, ambulances—unfinished, interminable symphony . . . interminable blues . . .

When she awoke dawn had come. Again she crept to the window, to watch the gradual detachment of the city from its spell of darkness. Pale, forgotten buds of light waning before the rising sun. Waking pigeons sleeking their plumage within reach of her outstretched hand.

Way down on 48th, foreshortened to pinheads, moved a few figures. She felt young, tremulous, and very lonely.

Chapter Four

I

(ALDEBARAN TO ORLANDO)

... We've been here nearly a week, and it's only two more days before the circus opens ! I feel sicker in the stomach than an amateur slack-wire walker making her first appearance at Olympia. They've all, so far, assured me that I'll be a terrific success, and, it needs no saying, cracked themselves to give Agnes and me a good time. Cocktails, lunches, dinner parties and theatres—all organized to a degree that makes one rather shudder to think how *we* blunder along. I've come to the conclusion that what the Americans excel in is detail ; in fact, realizing its importance, they specialize in it—and the result is a kind of exquisite ease that floats one along as it were in a bubble of rarified air. In spite, however, of all this " spoiling," this place has done more than any other to disturb my egoism : to make me aware of a vast and important world in which I'm merely a grain—but a grain passionately anxious to preserve its integrity.

... Already my intonation isn't quite English ! I shall have to take care of this, because, apart from there being a section of society that makes a *culte* of the English accent, nothing makes the average American see red like the foreigner trying to ape their accent. You know how offensive we find it when Americans come over and proceed to acquire what they think is Oxford English ! The problem is, to strike the happy medium : to shorten, somewhat, my long As, and remember to say " Pardon me " instead of " I beg your pardon " when I jolt somebody getting into the lift

—hell; elevator. You'd be surprised how much antagonism it arouses, if people get the idea you're high-hatting them.

Two things are going on that make me realize I'm in a " foreign " country : one's the Depression—and if you believe all you read you'll get the idea the air is black with bodies pitching themselves off the top of the Woolworth building. The other is Prohibition, which, since I've gotten me a tame bootlegger, doesn't mean a thing except toting round with me a pint-sized flask which fits very neatly into the specially-constructed bottom of a handbag (called, for some godforsaken reason, a " pocketbook ") given me by a fan with more dollars than horse sense.

If I continue any longer in this vein, you'll say this is not a letter, but a Press column. You're so right ; down under all my braggarty and assurance I'm just a coward. I've been funking this part of the letter, because—oh well, I suppose because I can't bear not being sincere, and, at the moment, sincerity just terrifies me. I can't bear admitting the many times, in a crowd, I've looked for your nice face, and felt chilled and somehow disappointed to remember how far away you are ! I feel I have no right to say, or feel, such things, considering the way in which I've treated you ; no right, during the last twelve months, to come so utterly to depend on your presence—and at the same time to resent my dependence. Even here, all these hundreds of miles away, when I wake—perhaps for a few minutes in the night, in the most awful sweat about this misbegotten tour and all the deathly lunches and conferences I've got to live through before I come back again !—the thought of you makes the world seem a safer and more bearable place.

Oh dear ; isn't all this just saying " I love you "—in perhaps a little more convincing way than cabling the bare words ? I had to write just that, because there was no time to think of something rather less *brut* ! But at least you can never accuse me of letting concealment like a worm, etc., prey on my cheek, which, far from being " damask " at this moment, is—since I am in the seclusion of my chamber—

rather greyer than usual : the result of never seeing my bed until three and four in the morning. I think I've rather startled my New York friends by the determination with which I sweep them into the night life of this most nocturnal city. And *not* the elegant resorts to which they are acclimatized. My taste for low life comes out, I fear, in my shameless choice of the downtown and off-Broadway joints in preference to the Stork Club, etc. I explain it as local colour !

My dear, dear Landy. I've tried so hard to think of some phrase that would give you the same confidence in me I have in you ! Oh darling ; I wish, for your sake, that it wasn't me you care for ; and yet I can't even begin to imagine what I'd do without the assurance of your love, to steady me up. And I can't imagine myself marrying anyone else. . . .

Agnes has been rather under the weather since we came out, and has done a good deal of snoozing and resting ! She calls it indigestion, but I have more than a suspicion that I about ran her to a standstill in those last few weeks before we sailed, and that this is what they call " reaction." Anyhow, she's getting it over under the best possible conditions, and will be all right—D.V.—by the time we set out on our travels : list enclosed. . . .

As she signed this letter, the telephone rang, and the easy voice of Dave overlaid with its calm the ragged edges of her nerves.

" Gee, I was scared you'd not be ' at home.' That's English isn't it ? "

" It depends." She felt herself smiling. " I rather think the telephone formula is ' engaged.' "

" What a hell of a language. I've located, I ought to say Karl's located, your—friend."

He's being discreet, not fresh, she told herself, and made herself say coolly,

" That's good work. Where is he ? "

" In Detroit. I'll give you the *ad*-dress, if you've got a pencil and a bit of paper."

" Carry on. . . . Thank you," said Aldebaran, when, at last, she hung up the receiver.

II

First they flung her to Chicago, and Chicago flung her to a dozen cities that registered themselves on her confused brain only as faces : as the great multiple, American Face, obstinately female, strenuously earnest. As hotel bedrooms—by the end of a fortnight she had a formula worked out for those, and could have walked blindfold into any one (lobby ; tub and shower on left ; sittingroom and bedroom straight ahead—the latter with twin beds, near-silk spreads and curtains—she learned to call them drapes—which, first, are not draped, and second are never intended to be drawn. Tug on the " drapes "—as she embar-rassingly discovered her first night in Detroit—and they descend complete with pelmet, on one's strengthless head) straight to the corkscrew and bottle-opener behind the bathroom door. What do Americans do in England ? How do they cope, in the bedroom of an English hotel, with their Coca-Cola, their Old Grandad and their smuggled bottles of French wine ? How many are found dead, their dry mouths gaping in the last agonies of thirst, before the floor waiter gets to them with the corkscrew —to part with which is like asking a British waiter to give up his life ? Often and seriously she and Agnes discussed this : and likewise—how large a percentage of American energy goes into drawing corks and yanking off tin caps ? In the earlier and gayer moments there was considerable diversion to be had out of compiling a list of statistics on this and other peculiarities of travel ; but gaiety was soon spent, or gave way to the grim mono-tony of the lecturer's schedule.

She began to feel like a ball, a tossed ball, flung, caught, flung again, without personal volition. Each town was orchids—once her favourite flower—tied with satin bows and stuck with pearl-headed pins : pins and ribbons the only tangible harvest, so far, of her pilgrimage. Was the great American Hand held out for the quarter or the dime—usually when one was in bed, or scrambling for the shower.

"It seems at first "—she wrote in one of her letters to Joe—
"as though there's a religious objection to performing the smallest service for nothing, in this country : but gradually, as you get used to it, the reason seeps through. High as wages are, they aren't high enough to give every man the things he covets : the super-car, the radiogram, the fur coat for his wife. These are the ambitions that lie behind the hints, the reminders, the ever-open hands. Nobody here feels he is lowering his dignity by a system of begging which is part of the economic scheme, and no American resents a form of highwaymanry which he fully understands, and with which he is in sympathy. The man who drops a buck in the bell captain's hand is in a position to do so because he held out his own hand in the past. It's all part of the ideal which is persistently held before every American from the hour he's old enough to accept an ideal : which is preached verbally, in homes, in schools and colleges and even from the pulpit. The ideal of wealth.

"Well, hell, Uncle Joe, what's wrong with money ? And when they've got it—what then ? I'll tell you : superb libraries, galleries, concert halls and museums ! It breaks my heart, the towns we pass through, when I don't have a minute to look at the glory this country has made its own.

"If you ask me, this eternal what we would call 'begging' is less undignified than the manœuvres with which a London waiter conjures the extra half-crown out of one's pocket. It may be less graceful, but it has at least the merit of honesty! "

To which, in due course, she got Joe's reply :

"My dear Debby,
"Your letter was a treat. One of these days I shall have to take a trip and a look for myself at these wonderful places you are exploring. It's always been an ambition of mine to visit the States but it seemed as though there was

never time and now it looks as if there will be less time than ever till we've got things straightened out over here. As you'll guess from the papers I've sent you and hope you got them we're handling ' a load of mischief ' and wasting a lot of time in the courts that would be better spent on Company affairs which by heck are in a mess and don't you make any mistake about it. Officially they are no business of mine but Goring's on the line from Liverpool two and three times a day and this new Malayan combine has properly put the wind up the Company. It seems they've not yet appointed another director in my place and its my private view that Goring has been told off to sweeten me! There's a lot of cuts going on and I feel like advising them to economize on the telephone account. Between ourselves, things are *bad*, and though I don't give a continental for Purcell I mind a lot about Flood and shall do all in my power to prevent us being discredited. I won't say it's got me down but the outlook's pretty gloomy.

"I've been seeing plenty of your friend Lord Orlando. As you know, your Uncle Harcourt had it properly in for Saxes but perhaps time alters families the way it alters people and I always found Lord Mildenhall a very affable old gentle-man though not over-gifted in matters of business. Orlando's got all his buttons on, as they say, and at the same time he isn't one of those young chaps that think they've got all the answers and act sorry for my generation! I was a bit taken aback the other day when he invited me to dinner at Paragon but he wouldn't take No for an answer so over I went and I don't need tell you what dinner at Paragon is like. His lordship went early to bed and Orlando and I sat in the study and talked. He made me tell him something about our early venturing and how Floods got to be the great firm it was under your ancestors and then again under your Uncle Har-court. It's a pleasure talking to somebody who really cares. Young folk today talk a lot about the future but don't seem to realize that the future is built up out of the past and you can't arrive at greatness by sacrificing continuity. That's

Orlando's way of putting it. It's a pity you weren't there, you would have appreciated some of the things he said. Something about a phoenix rising, and if there'd been no fires there'd be no phoenix. You can work that out I expect better than me all the same I know what he meant.

"Anyhow it's good to have somebody to talk to and ginger you up when you feel a bit low. As you can imagine, we talk a lot about you . . ."

At this point she had to drop the neatly written pages and fling herself flat on the bed. That made matters worse, so she had to sit up and stiffen her neck and shut her eyes and press her hands hard against the soft spot under her ribs : wondering if this was hooch—against which she had been warned in every town they reached—and if she would now go blind, or mad, and die. Her brain was rocking, and the bed and the room with it. How furious Agnes would be if she knew . . .

This was Detroit, and she had known, even while driving to the address given to her by Dave, that Lee would not be there. Three of the four people she had cautiously asked had never heard of the place ; the fourth—the youth at the news stand of the hotel in which they were staying—looked at her out of the corners of his eyes and mumbled there was no such joint in town, in a way that told her he was lying. The truth, it appeared, was valued at two bucks ; yeah, he knew Rocky's, but "it wasn't a place for dames." She asked casually what time he came off duty.

The bed keeled over like a boat, and she clutched at the night table and felt her clothes, her skin, her lips, her teeth impregnated with smoke and the smell of human bodies and the peculiar, insidious-sickly smell of the cellar to which, his unwillingness finally conquered, he took her : where for the first few minutes the heat, the low ceiling and the squalor afflicted her with so powerful a claustrophobia that she had to clench her teeth, not to scream out to them to let her out. People sitting around, and crammed against the walls, and a jockey-type yellow boy doing a buck-and-wing in the five-foot floor space in the middle of the chairs. She did not need to look at the man at the piano to know it was not Lee. She made herself smile at the news stand boy, whose name was Mannie.

" I'm thirsty ; what about a drink ? "

He gave her a dubious, almost a sullen look and slouched away to the bar. The drink came, she took a gulp, felt her jaws contract in a spasm and set it down hurriedly beside the chair a girl had just vacated when she stood up to dance with her partner. Conversation was out of the question ; walls and flooring throbbed with the din of voices, the jangle of the piano. She lit a cigarette and, through its smoke, watched the company : floozies, men and youths of unimaginable occupation. No one looked at her, but she could feel their furtive awareness as though they stroked her with dirty fingers. Presently, absently, she lifted the glass again and took another sip ; this time, probably because the heat and smoke had made her thirst unbearable, it did not taste so bad. She finished it, and signed to Mannie for another, slipping him the notes to pay for it, and for his evidently distasteful occupation.

When he came back the dancing had stopped again and he had found a friend. She sought for the particular brand of charm (the Flood charm—false as hell !) that would suit with her present company.

Yeah, she was British. She was just crazy about jazz. She liked the piano sort best. That guy that had just played " Shake That Thing "—out of *Africana*, wasn't it ?—was pretty good. No, she'd not seen *Africana* ; it was her first trip. But she'd heard some of the numbers in New York. She'd bought a record of " Shake That Thing " to take home.

"You wanna get some of the Blackbirds' numbers ; *Africana's* kinda B.C. stuff."

(B.C. stuff ? She got it, and grinned.)

" Tunes—I mean numbers—don't go out of date as fast in London as they do over here. We're still playing ' Jehovah Blues.' "

The others exchanged blank glances ; Mannie guffawed.

" I guess that was before we was born."

" 'The composer—the guy that wrote it—he's been performing here, hasn't he ? "

Their eyes were blank.

" L-Lee Marion. Perhaps you call him ' Red.' "

" Where's Rocky ? Hi, Rocky ; you know a guy calls himself Red—Red Marion ? "

She felt the air stiff with suspicion, and herself as its focus. A barrel-shaped man avoided looking at her and spat truculently.

" Who's asking for him ? "

" I'm an English writer. Lee—Red, you call him—wrote a blues that made a big hit back home. They told me in New York I'd find him in this place and—and I thought perhaps he'd let me give him a write-up . . ."

The silence, the taut attention of those immediately around her, warned her that patrons of Rocky's did not invite the notice of the Press.

" What I write is strictly for the British public and it's only concerned with Lee—with Red."

" Red ain't here."

" No ; I see he isn't. How long has he been gone ? "

" A coupla weeks."

" I suppose he's working—somewhere else ? "

" He ain't in town."

" Has he gone back to New York ? " Her heart sank.

" Nope. He's gone South."

" Where—where to ? " she stammered.

She forced herself not to flinch as she met a pair of eyes pitiless, devoid of humanity. She heard Mannie say, in a high-pitched, nervous voice,

" This dame's okay, Rocky. You don' have to go tough on this dame. That line about being a writer—that's okay. I got the dope on her—she's staying our place——"

The other cut him short with a downward movement of a thick hand that in some way swept Mannie and his protestations out of existence. The room had gone quiet. Everyone was listening.

"Red Marion ain't here. Dat guy trimmed me for five bucks and I guess he knows better dan come around till he's chiselled it off some udder guy to pay me back."

"He'll need do some chiselling in Charleston!"

She caught the almost inaudible snigger behind her shoulder and made herself turn slowly to look the one she took to be the speaker in the face.

"Has he gone to Charleston?"

"I din't say so, did I? Dere's plenny places between here and Charleston, Red can do his chiselling—if he feels dat way!"

"But you said Charleston." She ignored the warning drive of Mannie's elbow into her side.

There was some cautious mumbling.

"Red's a sweet piano boy—he's got the riffs to beat all the coloured guys——"

"They just haven't given him his break——"

"What made you say Charleston?" She heard her own voice swim up, like a slim, silver fish, from eddies of chatter.

The answer came in a whisper into her left ear, and, quickly as she turned, she had no idea who had spoken.

"Dat's where his folks live—dat's where Red goes back each time he hits bottom. Sooner or later, dat's where you'll find him—but dere's plenny places he could be, 'tween here and Charleston . . ."

"Let's scram," came Mannie's urgent mutter into her other ear.

"Gee . . ." They were in the taxi; she was feeling terrible, and hoped she was not going to be sick. "I'm kinda glad to be out of there!"

"I thought you'd been there before."

"Sure. But not with a dame!" said Mannie fervently. "I guess The Boss would give me the run-out if he knew I'd taken a dame down there!"

"Relax; I won't give you away," said Aldebaran absently, wondering how many notes were left in her bag, and deciding to settle the matter in the morning. Mannie was looking at her sidelong.

F

" Din't you smell it ? "

" I certainly smelt something funny—and rather nasty——"

" Rocky'll do time one of these days ; it's a hop joint."

" Hop joint—— ? "

" Joy-bangers—the opium guys . . ."

. . . The walls, the furniture, tilted themselves at odd angles about her ; she saw, down a long tunnel, the squalid track she had to follow, to find Lee.

Each town was talking, was synthetic sparkle and increasing difficulty in infusing threadbare material with an illusion of spontaneity. Was a losing struggle to keep one's end up against the endless resources of American vitality. This one paid for writing a book which, for some imponderable reason, had gone into innumerable editions, been rushed through the studios, and now occupied some seventy per cent of the screens between the East and West coasts. Already she hated its title ; shrank from the posters ; from the lights that blazoned the names of the stars into the darkness of every town, so far, she had visited. Already she was impatient to write something better : something slow, and painful, and probably unpopular, which would help her to regain the self-respect she had sold for a sum sufficient to keep her for the rest of her life in modest affluence. (Only modesty was not in the Flood tradition. Already she had over-spent by half as much again the proceeds of the tour.)

There came the day—or, rather, the night—when Agnes attacked her. At four in the morning, bedraggled, weary, not quite sober, she dragged herself into their apartment. Agnes, in her dressing-gown, glowered from the sofa.

" What in hades do you imagine you're doing ? How, at this rate, do you think you're going to make out ? "

Muttering something, Aldebaran made across the room for the whisky. In a flash, Agnes was beside her, had snatched it from her hands. Brushing Aldebaran aside with atrocious ease, she carried the bottle into the bathroom, and poured its contents into the lavatory pan. When she went back to the sittingroom, Aldebaran was crying.

" What *is* the game, A. F. ? That's the third night this

week you've gone on the racket with people you wouldn't be
seen dead with at home. Have you lost your senses? Apart
from the fact you'll never stay the course at this rate, it
won't do you any good if the report of this goes back to New
York."

"New York be damned," said Aldebaran indistinctly.

"Just think of the day you've had. We got in at half-past
one and it was after three by the time you were in bed. At
twelve you were on the air, and then there was the lunch club.
Then there was that cocktail, and you gave two interviews before
the lecture. You had dinner with the editor of—I can't remember——"

"All right, all *right*! I did the job I'm paid for! At the
end of that, don't you think I've earned a bit of fun?"

"Depends what you call fun. You and your pal the editor
were all set to go on to the Van Burens'; you'd have had a lovely
time and met writers and painters and the worth-while end of
local society. Then those types turn up, and you just give
who's-it—Walcott Dean—the brush-off and depart on a high
wind for some gut-bucket joint——"

"'Bartender, give me a bracer,'" hummed Aldebaran, her
eyes glinting with malice, "'double beer chaser, 'cause I got
the low-down, mean, rent-man blues'! Ya-a-ah!" She yawned
expansively. "It just happened. I was feeling more like 'gut-
bucket,' as you call it—and I must say," said Aldebaran, with the
sudden assumption of dignity of the un-sober, "I think it's
a most unpleasant term; *most* unpleasant. Rather vulgar in
fact—what was I saying?"

"Nothing of the least importance," said Agnes loftily.
"And I think we'd better say good night."

The dressing-gown folded around her, she swept to her
room; but she was angry, disturbed and a little scared. This
kind of thing had been going on too long. Every place they
came to—sooner or later—it happened; some short while after
dinner, Aldebaran would get restless; would make an excuse to
leave whatever company they were in. Agnes, in search of her,
would find her dragging on a wrap; "I'm going out a while

—no, I'd sooner go by myself." Or there might be a note—
" Don't wait up." Once or twice Agnes had waited ; had started
from sleep on a sofa to find Aldebaran in the room, dispensing
drinks to a cluster of strangers—youngish, flashy men, and
perhaps a girl or two . . . Agnes held her tongue, not knowing
but that this might be " material "; who is to know what is at
the back of the novelist's mind ? Sooner or later it would
transpire that Aldebaran had picked them up at some club or
dance-joint. It usually fell to Agnes to get them out before the
hotel management complained of the noise.

It was odd, and rather amusing, to begin with. There had
been nothing like this in London. Plenty of company, plenty
of parties ; dancing, sometimes, in the drawingroom, with the
rugs rolled up and the furniture pushed back, until dawn. A
few expensive nights in the clubs of the West End—but *work* ;
always work, before everything. A few days, or nights, of
extravagance, then the shutter came down between Park Village
West and the outer world. Never since she had worked with
her had Agnes seen Aldebaran surrender herself to this verti-
ginous mixture, this night-and-day expenditure of forces—that
could only come to one end.

The end was reached, and Agnes, secretly, was frightened.
Apart from the scandal which Aldebaran was inviting, particularly in the small towns they visited, whose grape-vine carried
every ripple in the social pool, there was the growing danger of
a breakdown.

Leaving her wrap on the floor of the sittingroom, Aldebaran
blundered into the bathroom. She felt sick. She felt like hell.
She looked in the glass at her ghastly face. The dress she had
on was a lime-green taffeta : a last-moment extravagance in New
York, too hurriedly chosen, never very becoming, and tonight,
a disaster. A disaster. Absently she turned on the shower and
returned to the contemplation of her own image against the
background of falling water. Is that really *me* ? The atmosphere
she had been in during the last few hours seemed as though it
had left streaks on her ; the smoke and the heat had dissolved
the sharp lines of her face, slackened it, lent it a dissolute look,

at which, with a shiver of disgust, her pride revolted. That—just—can't—be *me* !

She turned and stepped, just as she was, under the shower. The water spattered like fine gravel on the taffeta. Leaning back with her eyes closed, against the tiled wall, she felt the stiff silk flattening against her thighs ; felt her court shoes filling with water and her underclothes plastering her with a cold, silken paste. Presently she turned round and, bracing herself with her hands against the tiles, let the hail of water break on the base of her neck. Her drenched hair hung like seaweed over her breast. She was quite, quite sober. Her hand was icy when she turned off the shower and stepped back on the swimming floor ; she shivered as she stripped off the clothes—the taffeta cracked and tore as she pulled at it—snatched a bath-towel from the rail and wrapped it round herself. She bound another round her dripping hair, and, after a moment's hesitation, opened the door into Agnes's dark room.

" Hi. I'm all right now," she said, in a small sheepish voice.

" I heard you having a shower."

" Yes." Aldebaran giggled. " It was quite a shower. I wonder what's under the bathroom ? "

" Another bathroom, I expect." Agnes switched on the bed lamp, and smiled uncertainly at her employer. " I didn't mean to bawl you out."

" I bought it," admitted Aldebaran, helping herself to a cigarette from Agnes's pack. She let herself drop in an armchair and smoked for a couple of minutes silently. " You know what it is," she burst out ; her head against the back of the chair, her eyes, avoiding Agnes's, were fixed on a corner of the ceiling. " It's—I've not taken to the bottle. But you sit there—or you dance—and you buy somebody a drink—or somebody buys you a drink."

After another silence, each caught the other's eye ; Agnes began to laugh, and Aldebaran, after a moment's uncertainty, joined her.

" Let's skip it," smiled Agnes presently. " It's only that —well, you do rather put the wind up me, when I remember we've got to hang out nearly three more months. At this rate you'll finish the tour in an ambulance. It's a pity we don't do a bit more travelling; the only place I'm sure of you is when we're on the train." She paused, before asking, "Where, actually, did you get to, tonight?"

"Just where you said: a gut-bucket joint."

"What do you find in them?"

"Oh—I suppose I'm a push-over for that sort of thing."

"But *what* sort of thing?" persisted Agnes, a crease between her worried eyes. "What is it?—the noise, the atmosphere, the people?" As Aldebaran did not immediately answer, she continued, "I know it's not my affair, and the last thing I want's to make myself a bore and a nuisance. It's just—well, it's so unlike you, mixing yourself up with the sort of gin-mill crowd you've managed to pick up, almost everywhere we've been. Setting aside the gipsy's warning and all that—I've got a fairly good nose for the human species, and unless I'm much mistaken, some of these new buddies of yours aren't more than a couple of jumps ahead of the lock-up. I suppose what you're really after is a book."

"Could be," admitted Aldebaran, noncommittally.

"Yes; but would it do any harm if you got somebody decent—somebody out of your own stable—to take you around? I bet Walcott Dean knows all that's worth knowing about night life in this town. He looks like a good dancer. And he could be depended on to deliver you home, in one piece, this side up with care!" Agnes gave an apologetic little laugh. "I know I'm being a crashing bore; but I've got to admit these night jaunts of yours give me the crawls in the roots of my hair. A neat paragraph in the Press about the author of *Bells* getting herself into some kind of a liquor-fest in an off-colour bar would put the jitters into every woman's club between here and New Orleans—and even you can't afford that sort of publicity!"

Aldebaran leaned over to pat her hand.

"Relax, sweetheart. I don't get myself into any liquor-fests. I only go to dance and listen to the band."

Agnes's jaw dropped.

" For sweet heaven's sake ! In almost every town so far there's been a dinner-and-dance place——"

" Listen : when I've spent most of my day between breakfast and dinner being shot at by my devoted public, do you think I want to go out somewhere where they'll nudge one another and say ' That's Bells-on-her-Fingers-Flood ' ? And after I've been running a ' line ' with an editor or a publisher or a woman's page-writer, do you think there's much relaxation in the prospect of keeping it up to the tune of Panther Jag ? What I want is to get out by myself——"

" By *yourself* ? But——"

" I can pick and choose, can't I. If I want to brush someone off, I can do it, if he's a stranger ; I can ride along for a bit, if he's prepared to accept my pace. There's something you probably don't realize about jazz : it sounds different, in those down-to-earth joints, than it sounds in a smart restaurant with tuxedos and naked spines and powder rooms stinking of Chanel Number 5. I'd sooner hear it from a jukebox than watch the élite doing the Charleston to a tune that started somewhere down on a Mississippi levee——"

" You've got it badly," said Agnes dryly. " What happens when you go into these jukebox joints ? How do people look at you ? "

" Hell, I don't know. I buy myself a hot dog, or a Coca Cola——"

" Yeah ? "

" It was Bourbon tonight, because I happened to pick up with a drinking crowd. I danced with somebody—and the others tailed along," said Aldebaran vaguely. " They rode me home. It was kind of awkward."

" It wasn't the first time," murmured Agnes.

" These things happen. I don't want them to happen."

" Well," sighed Agnes, " I suppose you'll square it with Walcott Dean in the morning."

" The morning ? Do I have to see him again ? " faltered Aldebaran.

" He's taking you out to that library for the twelve o'clock

' talk,' isn't he ?—and you're on the air again at a quarter to one. Come along." Agnes swung her long, pyjama-ed legs out of bed. " I'll tuck you up, and, please heaven, you'll sleep until they bring up your orange-juice at half past ten. But your hair's wringing wet ! " she cried, as she touched the towel round Aldebaran's head.

" Yes. You'll have to get me a date with the hairdresser in the morning. Agnes. I do give you hell, don't I ? "

Agnes's lips twisted into a smile.

" Yes, you do, rather ! "

" You—you don't have those pains any longer, do you ? " It was like a little girl, trying to make amends for bad behaviour. Agnes's brows drew down over her level eyes : there were moments when she—eighteen months younger—felt much older than Aldebaran. What was the good of saying that the " pains " had been growing sharper, and her resource to the sedative tablets she had bought in New York more frequent during the past weeks ? She, herself privately, was in a panic about it. What would happen, if she were taken ill, and Aldebaran obliged to continue on her travels alone ?

" Good lord, no. Now, go to sleep, and for goodness' sake, don't start a cold in the head with that wet hair of yours."

III

(ALDEBARAN TO ORLANDO)

I've just left Agnes in hospital, having had an appendec-tomy—as they call it here, where nobody ever uses a three-syllabled word when a six-syllabled one is available. I got a doctor to her as soon as we arrived, and she was rushed into hospital and operated on just before noon ! Angelic doctor, who, with his wife, is going to look after her when they let her out ; it's perfectly hopeless, of course, to think of her racketing round with me. Darling, *don't* get into a flap. It was perfectly idiotic, bringing Agnes at all : just one of those extravagances I can't—now I'm "in the money!"—resist. Nobody, so far as I know, brings a secretary on a lecture tour; of course, it was terrific for prestige, and sheer bliss for me, because I never had to think about anything. But every place I go there's the most super organisation, and Agnes was just a tribute to my self-indulgence. It was like having a highly educated personal maid, because, having very little to do, beyond a few letters, she looked after my clothes, etc.—and now I'm down to sweet earth, and *not* before I ought to be! From one point of view, it's positively an advantage: because Agnes spared me the personal impact with all sorts of people I ought, as a novelist, to contact: bell boys and waiters and valets and chambermaids, with all of whom, by now, I'm "on terms," and this realistic kind of living, although less luxurious, is certainly better for me as a writer.

They seem to be pleased with my lectures, but I sometimes wonder how long I can keep it up. It's not the lecturing, but all the social nonsense that goes with it, that wears one down, and in some queer way unnerves one.

Did I tell you in my last how *glad I* am of your letters? *Truly.* And more than ever now. It is rather odd being by oneself and leaves one a good deal of time for thinking. Sometimes I try to delude myself I can just lift the telephone and hear your voice, in the midst of all these American voices —for which, let's admit it, I'm getting a great prejudice! They vary enormously, of course, just as ours do, but there's something heart-warming about them. I've lost, to a great extent, my sense of being a foreigner, but, oh, it would be good to hear your long As and your clipped consonants again: like a forgotten music! That's a wonderful idea of yours, darling, to ring me up: as soon as I can be quite sure of where I'll be, at a certain time, I'll let you know; I haven't yet quite digested this itinerary of mine, that Agnes used to look after: and at every place there'll probably be additions and alterations—but 2 a.m., New York time, ought to be fairly safe. Anyhow, I'll let you know.

. . . Whenever I get up to " say my piece," I try to imagine
that you are there . . .

IV

The farther she went South, the more her throat tightened
and her nerves tensed themselves, and the more she missed
Agnes. Waiting for the sleeping pills to take effect, she held on
to her jangled nerves and tried to discipline her mind towards
the next day's effort—of which the lecture itself was a minor
event. A scribbled list of her engagements lay beside the
telephone, and she felt it jagging at her through the dark : the
editress of a women's page coming to breakfast ; interview with
the local Press at ten ; broadcast at eleven, followed by a
luncheon that would probably go on until four. Rush back to
the hotel ; change ; another interview. Cocktails arranged by
a local leader of society, and then—the lecture. After that,
dinner, and on to the train. Or, perhaps, another night in the
hotel . . .

She had given her word, under pressure, that " until Agnes
rejoined her," she would give up her solitary jaunts. Agnes
had in fact made it a condition of her departure into hospital ;
knotted up, her face leaden with pain, her feverish hands clutched
Aldebaran's ; she held off the irritated doctor and the orderlies
waiting to carry her down to the ambulance ; she knocked
the needle out of the doctor's hand and clutched Aldebaran's
with her own, which were burning. In some odd way, the
fact that the thermometer check had shown 104.8, and that
she probably did not know what she was saying, made it more
impressive.

" I won't be moved—I won't be operated unless you
promise—— ! "

The doctor's hand was squeezing her arm above the elbow ;
she knew what the pressure meant : Go on—for chrissake can't
you promise—whatever it is ? And she knew she could neither
dishonour Agnes nor herself like that.

" Don't be an idiot," she muttered. " I'm coming with you in the ambulance—look, everybody's waiting——"

" Let them wait," said Agnes with remarkable distinctness. " Let the dam' thing get on with it—it can burst—I'm not going to be operated until you promise——"

She could feel the impatience of the watchers, all antagonistic to her. What was the good of arguing—of pointing out that Agnes, dead of a burst appendix, was of even less use than Agnes in hospital ? Of course, everyone would say that a promise given under such conditions was not a promise. Fool ! Sentimentalist ! Traditionalist ! she apostrophized herself, as she mumbled the words that would bring peace to Agnes's troubled mind. In the ambulance, with Agnes " out " after the injection to which, suddenly, like a lamb, she had submitted, it came to her with a sense of shock how much she must care about Agnes. Their relationship—cool, casual, for neither was addicted to the turgid attachments that obtain between women—had, in the last seven years, grown deep roots. And she had allowed it to betray her into a surrender of her personal freedom . . . The fact that Agnes, normal and in her right mind, would never have exacted such a surrender, made no difference to actuality. She had promised, and, being herself, could not go back on her word. It did not stop, of course, her ridiculous, her useless search. There would always be someone gratified to pander to Aldebaran Flood's craze for " café society "; her taste for the unexploited, the unconventional . . .

There was the night when Orlando's call came through.

" Are you all right ? "

" Yes, of course I am."

" Because—I'm pretty sure I could fix things up so as to come over for a few days."

" Good God, no—darling ! " she gasped. Orlando—in this circus to which she was committed : the mere thought of it jolted the breath out of one. They exchanged brief questions and answers about Agnes. The danger-point was over, and Agnes was making a steady, although slow, recovery. But it was good sharing past panic, present misgivings with one who, in some strange, calm way, seemed to take possession of one's life! It was—it was like talking to someone to whom one was peacefully married: the thought ticked suddenly in her brain, and echoed in her heart.

" How near you sound," observed Orlando.

" And you. But I can't help wondering what the hell this is costing you!" said the daughter of the house of Flood. She heard him chuckle.

" I backed an outsider today at Newbury! I made up my mind to put the proceeds into this call!"

" Oh, darling; back some more!" she breathed.

. . . The moment when they were cut off was a moment like death. The air in the room felt dead, yet restless. Her brain ached again with the pressure of her uncompleted task. She had an acute sense of aloneness in a land more foreign than any European country she had visited.

Landy; oh, dear, dear Landy. Am I really in love with you? enough in love to make you the kind of wife you want, and deserve? Or, when the first bliss is over, should we both realize it was a mistake—that the bridge between your circumstances and mine is too frail to bear the *va-et-vient* between your world and mine? Have I the strength, the assurance of my own rightness, to stand up with dignity to the antagonism of your family—all of whom, with the exception of Cat, are scandalized by the mere possibility of seeing Polly Bowling's daughter in Vanessa's place—the future Marchioness of Mildenhall? Would this be, as you so confidently claim, the end of the long and rather ridiculous feud between our two families, or would it start a deeper and bitterer quarrel, for which others will suffer, after we're gone?

. . . Theoretically, Orlando supported her contention that a woman has as good a right to pre-nuptial freedom as a man. Or was he only pretending, to humour her?—was he just trying, on her account, to conform to the post-war view, that it was as fashionable for a woman as for a man, to be " a bit of a rake "?

She had said, pretending to be airy, " I take it you don't want references?" And he, forcing his good, his honest smile:

"I don't think we—either of us—belong to the kiss-and-tell school!" That was the moment when all the confused liking, and passion, and even tenderness of the past months fused positively into love : when her impulse was to fling her arms round him, to trail her pride in the dust and declare herself unworthy of his trust and fidelity. Instead, she lived up to her unhappy generation. She laughed a little, and lifted her glass :

"To our purple past!"

"I'm afraid mine's only a washy sort of mauve." He said it with a wry air of apology. "You know about mine—of course."

"What? Lydia?" burst from her, before, flushing and stammering, she realized this was not playing the game. She had no business to bring in Lydia's name and to withhold Lee's. "I suppose you know about me and Lee?" It ought to have been easy to toss it off, just like that, but her mouth went dry, the unspoken words tasted evil on her tongue. She scorned herself, afterwards. All this adolescent preoccupation with virginity! She and Orlando, two responsible and sophisticated people being solemn about a thing which no adult, in this hard-bitten third decade of the century, took seriously! But— it's not that; not that, Orlando. After all, you knew Lee, and you never guessed, did you? You would never have believed ...

She switched off the light, wondering if Agnes, by now, was sleeping—mildly doped, probably, in a Philadelphia apartment. How fantastically generous Americans are! How many English doctors would take an unknown patient to convalesce into their own homes, or doctors' wives accept the imposition of a helpless guest, for an indefinite period, on their households? The generosity was to her, of course, as much as to Agnes ; it would have been the last straw—wandering on by oneself, worrying about Agnes's comfort, her needs, her infernal propensity for economizing where her own luxury was concerned.

She lay there, wondering why she had ever undertaken this futile pilgrimage. Life—the life of a novelist—is so short, and so much to be crammed into it! Four precious months, frittered away in gratifying the idle curiosity of a public that never stops to think how, for the sake of an hour's indulgence, it forfeits

weeks of the pleasure it professes to derive from reading an
author's works! How many words she could have written in
these four squandered months. The idea for a play was nagging
her, and there was still the coming season's novel to be revised.

For the next hour Aldebaran went through all the sick apprehension of failure which is the penalty of enormous success.
Suppose Bob Winter turned down her next book? Suppose the
critics turned sour—as they were said to do, over the successor
to a spectacular-best seller?

Down to Atlanta and New Orleans, with a plague of little
towns on the way, then back to Charleston, and—finish. After
that, no more drawingroom cars, sleeping cars, endless drum of
railroad track under one's sleepless pillow; no more dispensing
charm (the Flood charm false as hell) together with signed
copies; no more interviews, appearances in book stores (the
ultimate indignity), dates on the local network; no more
luncheons, teas, cocktails in the houses of strangers. . . .

Ruth Rodríguez. What would this Ruth Rodríguez, who
through her husband's family, claimed cousinship, be like?

" You have got relatives in Cuba, called Rodríguez ": where
did that come from? Lines scrawled on thin ruled paper with
indelible pencil, scrawled in the heart of African jungle, before
she was born. On her fifteenth birthday—she never knew what
determined the act—Polly had pushed the crumpled envelope
into her hand, and hurried out of the room, her handkerchief to
her nose. She remembered how she had sat looking at it, with
all the angry antagonism, the faint disgust and sense of superiority
her mother's bursts of emotionalism roused in her; how, to
begin with, she tossed it aside, resolved out of perversity not
to open it, and how, eventually, curiosity, not wholly unmixed
with fear, made her pick it up again, and read—Johnny Flood's
last message to his unborn son.

Father. What was Father like? How would we have got
on together? It was rather—grim: like touching hands with
the dead. She swallowed two or three times. Presently she put
it away. Neither of them referred to it again; she was resolved
not to show that she was touched, but once or twice an impulse

of cruelty to Polly—the froth of the increasing tension between them as Aldebaran passed from girl into young womanhood—was checked by the recollection of Johnny's exhortation to his son to "look after his mother." I've done as you asked me, Father—in my fashion.

And how came Rodríguez in South Carolina? It might be worth while to solve that mystery, in the short interval between the final lecture and departure for Southampton.

And Charleston. There was something—beside the lecture—to be done in Charleston . . .

V

The desk clerk threw a contemptuous glance at the direction on the envelope, tossed it aside and resumed his conversation with the man in grey lounging on the end of the counter. The slim girl in a tussore suit waited, her white hat shading her face, her white gloves and shoes lending her an air of delicate immaculacy. The grey man's eyes crawled over her; he winked at the clerk, stared at the girl again with a half-smile of insolence, and blew the smoke of his cigar in her direction. She gave no sign of awareness, but continued lightly to balance against her own shadow, her eyes on the narrow gloved hands clasped about her pocketbook.

A messenger clamped down two long florist's boxes on the counter; the girl's eyes rose for a second, hopefully, and fell again. Two men, arguing vociferously, possessed themselves of the house telephone, gave a room number, and entered into blasphemous colloquy with its occupant; at a particularly gross word, one nudged the other, jerking his head towards the girl; the speaker looked round, sneered, and finished his sentence.

The lobby filled with newcomers and baggage. The girl's slim body was caught in the swirl, spun out of the way. She found the grey man looking down at her, his cigar plugged between blatant dentures, his lips twisted in a disagreeable smile.

"You waiting for your beau, Nancy Lee?"

Her face became dead clay.

"I've got—business." Her lips moved stiffly over beautiful teeth.

"Is that so?" His smile grew more lickerish. "May be you and me might find some business?"

She moved quickly back to the counter, where the clerk scowled at her.

"You still around?"

"That letter I gave you. There's an answer."

"They're out," he told her glibly, and turned away.

"Pardon me." She caught her breath. "I saw the lady come in, a little while ago."

"You calling me a liar?" He tried to browbeat her.

"Could be you didn't notice. She came in and went up in the elevator. In *that* one"—she pointed, to convince him. "The room number," she added helpfully, "is seven twenty-two."

"As you're so smart, baby"—he snatched up the letter and pushed it at her—"you can tote it up yourself. And the elevator for you-all is round the corner!"

She kept her hands folded.

"I sooner it go up by a boy."

"Anything more you'd 'sooner'?" But her steady eyes and modest manner—added, perhaps, to her beauty—conquered his insolence to the extent of beckoning to one of the bell boys. "Hey, you! Your sister wants you do an errand for her!"

The boy's eyes flicked Janet's briefly; his expression did not alter as he vanished into the lift. She told herself, I must not be angry, because I've invited this. I must keep very calm, because this is important.

When the tap came on the door, Aldebaran had just stretched herself on the bed. In less than an hour she would be eating one of those interminable platform meals, watched by the avidly smiling eyes of the eight hundred members of the Skeeterville Ladies' Luncheon Club. She would scatter shredded lettuce and cold tongue about her plate, do her best to sparkle to the Chairman on her right and the secretary on her left, and eventually rise to deliver the " talk " from which four months of repetition had drained the last vestiges of spontaneity. She knew her platform manner had gone off, that an artificial animation had taken the place of former sincerity, and that the shallowness of her own performance was reflected in the shallowness of her audiences' appreciation. No one, she reminded herself indignantly, could remain at concert pitch over sixteen weeks of sheer talking !— weeks in which solitude had become a thing to be craved for, hardly to be imagined, and when briefly won, to be defended with all the passion of one's weary soul. Closing her eyes, she resolved to ignore the summons, yet, when it was repeated more imperatively, habit made her crawl off the bed and peevishly open the door.

" Sorry, I've got no change." She took the note from the bell boy, glanced at it, and tried to determine from the writing whether it stood for an autograph, a " little party " (only a couple of hundred people, animated by the curious desire to drink cocktails and eat canapés in the same room with someone who had written a successful novel !), or whether it contained some last-moment instructions from the agent, and could therefore not safely be dropped in the wastepaper bin.

She found her spectacles, tore open the envelope and ran her eye without interest down the neatly written page.

" Dear Madam,
" I hope you will excuse the great liberty I take in writing to you. I am sure you have many claims on your time, but I could not resist writing these few words to ask if you would be so kind as to grant me a short personal interview. I know it is asking a great deal of one so fully occupied and famous, but I hope you will forgive me as I have taken the liberty of waiting in the lobby and will promise not to detain you for more than a few minutes. Permit me to add that I am one of your most sincere admirers, since reading *The Sad Dove* . . ."

" I don't believe it," said Aldebaran aloud. She turned the page quickly to look at the signature : " Mrs " Janet Jackson.

The only blot on the fair face of the composition. A fake, of course. How in the name of fortune could someone living in Skeeterville, South Carolina, have got hold of a book of youthful verse, meagrely received in England, and never published in the United States?

College girl, diagnosed Aldebaran; young, newly married. Got the title, of course, from the fly-leaf of *Bells*—a bad shot! Yet, with her hand on the receiver to tell the receptionist she was engaged, she hesitated.

It was odd that, out of a list of titles, the girl should have picked on that, published—how many years ago? It all came back: the thrill of seeing one's words in print; the pride, excitement and mystification of Polly—"I can't make head or tail of it, but I'm sure it's clever, dear. Now, why can't you sit down and run me off a good number or two?"; Uncle Joe's solemn, persevering efforts to read it, and his honest admission of defeat; Cat's awe, her candid—"I don't know much about poetry, but I'll show it to Orlando"; and, best of all, the secret triumph in having captured—if only in a line here or there—the elusive music of one's heart. Nothing else had brought that sweet, that holy sense of achievement.

I suppose, she thought, it's possible—just possible—the girl's been to Europe; she might, in London, if she's interested in poetry, have picked up a copy in one of the boxes down Charing Cross Road.

"A Mrs. Janet Jackson is asking for me. Will you send her up in about ten minutes?"

"Surely." The warm voice reminded her she was in the Deep South, and she smiled as though face to face with the speaker.

She took a quick shower, brushed out her hair and slid into the thin black gown she had chosen for the luncheon; it was limp from continual pressing, but the triple string of pearls and inevitable corsage of orchids—waiting in its cellophane box on the bureau—would revive it. And a soft velvet cloche, chosen for its packing qualities. It would be good to get rid of these —the stale uniform of her pilgrimage.

When she again looked at her watch, nearly twenty-five minutes had passed. With an exclamation of annoyance, she again picked up the receiver.

" Did you give my message to the reception ? "

" Sure, ma'am. Just a minute—I'll put you through."

Another voice came on the line.

" Bell captain."

" A Mrs. Janet Jackson's been asking for me. I asked them to send her up ten minutes ago."

" A Mrs. who d'ya say ? "

" Jackson—Mrs. Janet Jackson. Please find her as fast as you can ; I have to go out in a few minutes."

" Theah's no Mis' Jackson heah, ma'am," came, after a long pause, the glutinous voice.

Surely the girl might have waited a little longer ? An irrational wave of disappointment swept over her, as she turned back to the glass. Fixing the pearls into her small, fine ears, she tried to recall some of the lines of *The Sad Dove*.

She had taken the title, she remembered, from a *folia* of the Canary Islands, which she and Uncle Joe had visited on one of the Flood cargo boats, after her return for the second time from Paris. The boat was going to the Gold Coast, and she had bitterly resented his refusal to take her on with him. She remembered how her resentment had faded, under the silver shadow of Teide, and how the nights striped with moonlight and threaded with the sound of guitars had revived the brief poetic impulse of her school days ; and how she began by translating the local songs—

> *Yo soy la paloma triste*
> *la triste la desconsolada*
> *que bebía en agua turbia*
> *y no puede beber clara—*

—I the sad dove, the sad, disconsolate . . . Aldebaran dismissed such memories with an impatient shake of the shoulders, and, hearing the door click, turned sharply.

" Oh ; is it Mrs. Jackson ? "

Chapter Five

I

THE GIRL was standing shrinkingly in the lobby between the inner and outer doors. The breath caught in Aldebaran's throat. After a pause she prayed the other had not noticed, she held out her hand.

"I'm so glad you didn't go." Her voice fluttered, and she paused for a moment to steady it. "It was nice of you to come and see me." The girl's hand burned through the thin glove of cotton; Aldebaran drew hers quickly away and picked up at random a pack of Virginias lying on the bureau. "Do you smoke?"

Janet Jackson shook her head shyly.

"No, thanks."

"I'm afraid everything's wildly untidy—I've had to manage without anyone to look after me the last few weeks, and I'm not a very orderly person. Have a drink!" said Aldebaran desperately.

"Thank you, I just don't take liquor."

"I think there's some White Rock somewhere——"

"Thank you, ma'am—thank you, Miss Flood. I don't want a thing—and I surely am bothering you!" The voice was like rough honey, rich with apology.

"Do sit down, Mrs. Jackson." She began to screw stoppers in bottles, to replace lids, to put in some kind of order the litter of the dresser. It was necessary to do something! not just to sit and stare at the girl, in all her meek, dark beauty, whose self-possession put her confusion to shame. "Have you really read *The Sad Dove*?" burst out Aldebaran.

"I surely have. I read it over and over. I know some of it by heart. I like it most of all the poetry I know."

" But how did you come by it ? It's never been done in the States, and it's been out of print for years "—to be accurate, since the year after its publication, when the unsold two-thirds of its single edition were forlornly remaindered, and most of the copies bought up and addressed as gifts from the author to dubiously appreciative friends. " Have you ever been to England ? "

The question seemed to amuse Janet.

" Oh no, ma'am ! Somebody left it here, in the hotel, and a friend of mine found it and brought it to me. I guess they all know I'm crazy about poetry."

" I'll—I'll write in it, if you like."

" That's just too kind of you. I wish I'd brought it with me."

Wrong again. Aldebaran forced a laugh.

" I'm sorry ; most people do ! If you'd like to bring it to the luncheon." Her voice dried in her throat. After an almost imperceptible silence, Janet replied, with exquisite, mechanical formality,

" I guess you're really too kind "—and Aldebaran wondered what punishment applies to a gaffe so brutal that there can be no forgiveness for it under heaven. " And thank you for letting me tell you I like your poetry—and now—I guess—I'd better go."

" Janet ! I beg your pardon : Mrs. Jackson ! " She sprang to her feet. " Please don't go. That wasn't what you came to see me for, was it ?—just to tell me that ? "

A veil seemed to draw itself across the girl's face.

" Yes, Miss Flood—it was just—that."

" Nonsense. Sit down." She sought for another opening, stubbed out her cigarette and lit another before it burst from her. " You remind me of something—of someone I knew a little—years ago, in Paris." Janet waited politely. " His name was Naimbanna. I'm afraid I've forgotten his other name."

" There were some French girls at college——" She left the remainder of the thought in the air.

" Let's not waste our little time," said Aldebaran. " Perhaps we'll never meet again. You aren't the foolish kind of person who comes just to see what an author looks like ! " How crude it sounded, how distant from what she meant to say. " Something made you trust me enough to come here. If I've said or done anything to disturb that trust—please believe I didn't mean it."

Seated in the chair, the girl's slender spine reared into dignity ; it reminded Aldebaran in some way of the innocent beauty of a young cobra, unaware of her lethal potentialities.

" Yes, ma'am, I did come for something else—but I guess I was wrong. I guess, when you read and think a lot about something in particular, you kind of imagine things. You kind of mix up what *is* with what *could be*——"

" You mean, you're disillusioned." Aldebaran spoke in a very small voice for a successful author.

" My folk don't have many illusions." Janet brushed this gently aside. " Dreaming and illusion are different, aren't they ? There's no harm dreaming, so long you don't let it lead you across the tracks where you lose hold of it. But illusion "—she had a way of leaving her sentences unfinished, of leaning her pretty head a little to one side, as though listening for their echoes, as though following them to their mysterious conclusion in some secret recess of her soul.

" I'm not sure I understand you." Because she was moved, Aldebaran spoke brusquely ; her eyes went involuntarily to the travelling clock on the writing table, and, quick to take the hint, Janet rose. They faced each other—the white girl in black, the black girl in white—each aware of a straining to make things as easy as possible for the other.

" If I explain," said Janet, " you must please take no notice ! —because now I've met you, I realize it's just one of those pipe dreams : like a child asking Santa Claus to bring it a whole railway, and when it comes to Christmas morning, being quite content with one little truck."

" That's not like any child I've met ! Go on, Mrs. Jackson."

" A while ago you called me Janet."

" I did. It was very impertinent of me, but I didn't mean it that way. I called you Janet because I felt—I felt," blundered

Aldebaran, " that we were—or might become—friends. And— people over here use Christian names a good deal, don't they ? "

A fine smile sketched itself about the other's lips.

" Yes, in a casual way. Only—well, it's wrong ; it's ridi- culous, and touchy of us, of course. Most of us—the educated ones—resent being called by our Christian names by your people." She went on quickly as Aldebaran was about to speak, " I like it, when you call me Janet."

" That's a big honour—Janet." It was like crossing a stream into a foreign land. " And now you can tell me the rest, can't you ? "

" There's quite a few of us," she began, " here in Skeeterville, who have been through college. I was mighty lucky ; my mother taught school—under the Rosenwald foundation. Excuse me—you won't know about our educational system down here ; but you can pretty well take it for granted, if a coloured boy or girl talks properly and takes an intelligent interest in the com- munity, they can thank the Rosenwald Fund. After that I went through college. I graduated four years ago "—there was a trace of pride in the modest voice—" and came back here."

" And got a job ? "

" We've got a paper here of our own. Sometimes they take what I write——"

" Oh, but you're not a newspaper woman ? " No one so gentle and diffident could make good in the thrust and drive of the newspaper world. She had probably given it up when she married. " You don't want to run an interview, do you ? " she asked, half-joking.

" Oh no, Miss Flood ! " As though, thought Aldebaran, castigating herself, they would give space to a white author in the coloured Press ! " My idea was much wilder than that. You see, when we come down from college, there's quite a lot of things we miss. Sometimes we get together and try to act like we're still on the campus, listening to the professors. Some- body reads a thesis and the others criticize it. Or we have a discussion on something we've read in the Press. Sometimes one of us gets up and talks about a book——"

"A kind of club," nodded Aldebaran, and wondered what the Skeeterville Ladies would make of this rival to their intellectual pretensions.

"Last week I read them out of *The Sad Dove*."

"Did anyone like it, beside you?"

"One or two did," said Janet honestly. "A few are prejudiced; we had a discussion about that afterwards. 'White poetry means nothing to black people.' 'The whites don't make poetry, only rhymes.' That kind of thing. It sounds childish," she apologized, "but most of us haven't had much chance to read since we left college. Some are so stubborn, they'll only read the works of Negro authors. I tried to argue that there's no 'black' or 'white' in poetry, but the boys shouted me down. Then one of them—a boy who's visiting; he's reading law, he's got much more culture than the rest of us —he did object that our poetry's always sad, and that we're clogging ourselves with race consciousness, and till we've worn that out there'll never be a *great* Negro poet"

"But surely——"

"Of course; everybody started yelling about Countee Cullen and Langston Hughes. But essentially he was right. No Negro can take colour in his stride, and with the poets it's an obsession. It narrows us down as artists, just as it narrows us down socially. Poetry *is* universal, isn't it, Miss Flood? —anyhow, that's the way I read *The Sad Dove*. When it comes down to deep moments, colour makes no difference."

Why isn't she talking to someone who can give her what she wants? Aldebaran veiled her face with the smoke of her cigarette. I write one little trivial book of verse, and she comes to *me* . . .

"Well—I guess I was crazy." Janet's face melted into a smile so defenceless that it was like talking to a child. "But I just wondered—after the luncheon—if you'd got time—there's only about a dozen of us—would you read one of your poems." As Aldebaran flung out her hand, Janet hurried on, "Of course I see now it was foolish, and quite impossible——"

"Why should you say that?" She tried to think how *un-*

mpossible it might be, and knew, unhappily, that Janet was
ight; but not for her own reasons. " Of course I'd have
done it; but I've got interviewers after the luncheon, and a long
ourney by car after that—I'm speaking in Charleston tonight——"

" I told you; I'm crazy," said Janet calmly. " I do crazy
things; I dream about something till I believe I've only got to
walk across the road and get it—whatever it is."

" Blind faith. They say that's the basis of the miracle," said
Aldebaran absently. " I'd give all I've got, Janet, to ' pass your
miracle ' for you, but——"

" I'm just as grateful as though you had."

" If you'd written to me earlier——"

For the first time, the smile, while losing none of its polite-
ness, was faintly derisive.

" That's mighty kind of you. When I do mad things, they
kind of have to happen, on the spur of the minute."

" But this really could have worked out, if——" The snarl
of the telephone tore into her words. She snatched up the
receiver. " Yes ? "

A female voice blared into the room.

" Is that Miss Flood ? This is Mrs. Howard Clark, Miss
Flood! And I've got a great admirer of yours, Mrs. George
Delaney Paterson. She just can't wait to meet you. Shall we
come right up ? "

A sudden dilation in Janet's eyes checked her assent.

" I'm terribly sorry—I'm late; you'll have to excuse me,
just for a few minutes. I'll come right down." She hung up
on a chilly " Okay—if you'd rather," and turned back to Janet.
" I hate stopping our talk, but you see I'm in a spot."

Janet's lips curled with unexpected mischief.

" Nothing like the spot you'd have been in, if you'd come to
read poetry to us ! I ought to apologize. Miss Flood "—she
hesitated—" is this your first visit to the States ? "

Aldebaran nodded, as she turned to the glass.

" Would you think me rude, if I gave you some advice ?
For your own sake, Miss Flood, don't let anybody get you

mixed up in the 'colour question'!" Her intonation se
the two words into italics as clearly as though she had writter
them.

"Well, but you——"

"That's what I was apologizing for," said Janet quickly.

"I've got your address and I'll give you mine. Let's write
—oh God, I'd forgotten these." She snatched up the orchids
fumbling at the cellophane ; Janet took the box quietly out of
her hands, broke open the lid and took out the fabulous bloom
with its knot of cyclamen ribbon.

"Let me fix it for you."

"You should be wearing it ; it's more your colour than
mine."

"I've never owned an orchid," said Janet simply. Her
delicate fingers occupied themselves with the iridescent pins ;
the frail magenta petals, spread across Aldebaran's breast and
shoulder, lent luxury to the much-worn gown. "Thank you,"
she said, as she finished, "for being sweet to me."

"Look, Janet : I'll be back here some time before five.
Couldn't you come in—just for a few minutes ? I've got my
packing to do—and it will be a frightful rush—but I'd love to
see you, to say Goodbye !"

"May be I could help you ?" The girl's face brightened,
then fell again. "I'll—try to be here. You've been too terribly
sweet to me ! I won't ever forget it. So, in case I can't come
back—Goodbye, Miss Flood."

"Wait—I'm coming down with you." She snatched her
bag and gloves and hastened through the door held open by
Janet.

The illuminated pointer over the lift at the end of the corridor
was swinging towards 7.

"It's going down. Come on—we'll catch it if we run."

She caught Janet's hand and raced towards the doors, which
slid open to disgorge two heavily upholstered matrons in summer
crêpes with jewelled clips, and hairs and skins of the pampered
perfection to which, by this time, Aldebaran's eye was so accustomed that she neither looked nor envied. She felt Janet's hand

jerk itself out of hers, stepped in quickly, heard the doors click behind her, and observed, as she drew on her glove,

"That was lucky!"—then, turning, saw Janet was not beside her.

"My friend! You've left my friend behind!"

The gum-chewing girl on the brake rotated her jaws and stared at the lift ceiling. The lift continued to descend. Aldebaran became aware of her companions: a blonde prostitute and a gross individual in grey whose hat hung on the back of his head and the corners of whose mouth slobbered the juice of the cigar he had not troubled to remove at her entrance. She averted her eyes from the distasteful spectacle and smoothed the fingers of her gloves. The air of the lift tightened.

"You—English?"

She admitted it, not troubling to look at the speaker, whose eyes, like blobs of dull jelly, projected through a starfish-like arrangement of stiffened lashes. Through the stench of the woman's scent and the man's cigar she smelt enmity, and wondered what it was about.

When the lift checked at street level and the prostitute tottered out on her lofty heels, Aldebaran, about to follow her, found her way blocked by the man, and looking up, met his leer, only a few inches from her face.

"You British broads better remember you're in Jim Crow country down here!"

It took her a few disgusted seconds to grasp the implication: that Janet Jackson, the girl who could talk about the universality of poetry, was forbidden by the state to travel in the same elevator with a half-drunk sales executive and his whore.

II

Shaking a few hands, signing a few copies of her book, Aldebaran held back a grimace. There was one thing about American audiences: they left you in no doubt as to whether or not you had registered!

It was the worst "talk" she had ever given; she was pre-occupied, lost the thread of her argument several times, and found herself more than once at a loss for the word she needed —than which nothing so panics the impromptu speaker. At the beginning of the tour she had used notes, but soon abandoned them. She would have given much for them, when her memory plunged and stumbled, and she felt the attention of her audience flagging.

She spoke much too long; several people rose and left their tables; their creaking, tiptoe exit increased her confusion. Far down the room, facing the platform, a woman was wearing a superb diamond; the light streaming from its facets created a hypnotic focus to which her eyes were constantly drawn. The woman sat as though mummified. Apart from her, there was a good deal of shifting and whispering. She dragged her final paragraph to its desperate finish and sat down; listened to the usual phrases about the "great privilege" of meeting "this celebrated lady"—during which most of the audience was shrugging its way into its coats and hunting for gloves and handbags—and noticed a large number of copies of *Bells* under people's arms and lying beside their plates. Not more than a dozen came up for autographs. She had run over her time and not inspired her listeners with any particular urge further to delay their departure.

"And now, Miss Flood," said the secretary, with an intrepid brightness that did not conceal her disappointment in the lecturer, "I'm going to take you back in my own car and hand you over to our brilliant young reporter Tom Turpin! Tom's just devastated he couldn't make your lunch, but his editor sent him out on an assignment before we got started."

"I'm sorry, but I have an appointment." No interview under heaven was going to make her let Janet down. For sixteen weeks she had put duty to her agent and her publishers first, but this was almost the end, and it could not possibly matter.

"He'll keep you ten minutes, not a second more; I've made him swear it! I've told him Mrs. Rodríguez's car will be here at

half-past five. My, it would never do—if we kept Mrs. Rodríguez
waiting ! "

She found herself being shepherded, swiftly and skilfully, to
a waiting Cadillac.

" And you're visiting with Mrs. Rodríguez after the lecture ?
My, isn't that fine ! Hammock Hall : it's just a dream place !—
one of the real old plantation houses, kept up in the old style.
Wait till you hear the darkies singing their spirituals on the porch
after dinner. You'll just fall for everything." Mrs. Howard
Clark pulled dashingly out into the traffic stream. " Hammock's
between here, you know, and Charleston ; you'll pass it on your
way into town. No, you can't see it from the road ; it's set
way back, the other side of the swamp, inside a kind of formal
garden they copied from their place in Havana——"

" Is Mr. Rodríguez alive ? " asked Aldebaran, to stem the
tide of Baedeker.

" Oh, didn't you know ? She divorced him a year or more
ago. He's married a Spanish girl and gone back to Cuba.
Ruth's just back from Europe with her little girl—my, that
child's elegant ! She'll come into a quarter of a million dollars
under her grandfather's will when she's of age. Ruth's in for
quite a time," chattered Mrs. Howard Clark, crowding a Negro
jalopy out of her way and slithering to a standstill against the
curb outside the hotel. " Now see here, Jeff." She addressed
the Negro hall porter who came down to open the door of the
car with the confidence of old acquaintance. " I'm going to park
here ten minutes. Just ten minutes—so you don't go pulling
a face ! Find Mr. Turpin and say we're here—I expect he's in
the bar ! " with a roguish look at Alderbaran. " You know these
reporters."

" I must go to the desk. I'm expecting someone and I've
got to leave word to show her to my room when she comes."
A glance round the lobby had not discovered Janet, and the
incident of the lift had made her uneasy about leaving the girl
to wait in a public place.

The expression on the clerk's face when he said No to her
question, had anyone asked for her, convinced her he was lying.

She tapped her fingers on the polished wood, wondering what to do next. Finally she lifted her head and looked the man in the face. His half-smile faded, as smiles were wont to fade before that black-browed stare. She said, hardly moving her lips.

"I am inquiring for Mrs. Janet Jackson." She paused. "Mrs. Jackson is—a coloured lady."

"Say—you mean Jenny Jackson?"—with a start of affected recollection. "Now you mention it, it seems like she was hanging around." He trailed an indifferent glance round the lobby. "I didn't know you was asking for *her*! We don't call niggers 'Missis' and 'Mister' in Skeeterville."

She found Mrs. Howard Clark at her elbow with a good-looking, lanky youth whose eyes crossed Mrs. Clark's millinery to settle with interest on the famous author, Aldebaran Flood. They shook hands briefly.

"What do you think Jeff's been telling us?" tittered Mrs. Clark. "There's been a nigger girl here, asking for you! Did you ever hear such impudence?—though I suppose the blacks go to our movies and some of them read. Jeff got rid of her, of course." She turned a glance of bland approval on the porter, vanishing through the revolving door. "Jeff's got no more use than we have for uppity nigs!"

An assertion of friendship trembled on Aldebaran's lips, but instinct warned her to withhold it. She was on dangerous unknown ground; open partisanship might do harm to Janet.

"I guess you could use a drink, Miss Flood."

Mrs. Clark was waving a coquettish farewell from the door. Aldebaran nodded, stuck her hands in her pockets and stalked ahead of her companion towards the neon-lit bar at the end of the lobby; stared around and let herself drop on the padded bench along the wall.

"What'll you have—Martini?—Manhattan?—Bob, here, shakes a cute Manhattan."

"Was that true, what she said—about the hall porter?"

"What did she say?—I don't remember." Turpin was obviously taken aback by her abrupt demand.

" That he—how did she put it ?—that he'd ' got no use for uppity nigs ' ? "

" I don't know.   Could be."   The point plainly did not interest him, but she persisted.

" But he's a Negro himself."

He shrugged his shoulders.

" Nigs aren't supposed to come in the lobby, except they're hotel servants, or from the stores,   Jeff's a whale of a good guy on the door.   I guess it pays him to do a bit of Uncle-Tomming."

" Uncle-Tomming ? " she scowled.

" They call a nig an Uncle Tom if he goes out of his way to please white folk.   ' Lawd bless you, Mars Charles—dis am sho nuff sweet weather fo' de vimes ! '—Brer Rabbit stuff.   Jeff can talk as good English as you or me ; he takes the Baltimore Afro-American, he's a member of the NAACP, and I've heard him addressing a meeting on the Fourteenth Amendment in an oratorical style that licks most of our senators !   But there's a good many folks don't care for that sort of thing.   Taking things on the whole, the educated nigger isn't popular this side the Mason-Dixon line, and if Jeff was to air his information he'd pretty soon be out on the sidewalk, looking for a bootblack's job, or may be stoking somebody's furnace."

" That's a pretty goddam state of affairs, for a country that boasts of its freedom ! "

Turpin raised his light, furry eyebrows and laughed.

" For Jesus' sake, don't start on colour !   We like to look on it as our own little private skeleton—though," he admitted, " it's not little and a lot of folks have made it their business to see it's no longer private.   Sooner or later something's going up with a big bang.   Still, there's no need you should spoil a nice trip to the South by getting yourself a headache over the nigger ! "

" I'm interested in Janet Jackson."

He gave her a cautious look.

" Well—may be she's an interesting sample.   The guy she married's a janitor in our building ; he's kind of ornery darkie and Janet's supposed, in coloured society, to have married beneath her. Her mother's a big shot in the NACW and administers some sort of fund to help with the legal defence of niggers had up on false charges."

"Do you mind," said Aldebaran carefully, " not calling them ' niggers ' ? It's rather unnecessarily offensive, isn't it ? "

" Say, you're kind of interested in colour ? "

Under the curiosity she sensed a faint antagonism. His sullenness was not, she reminded herself, unreasonable ; this was not much of an interview to take back to an impatient editor ! She gave him her most gracious smile and, for the next half hour, all he wanted for his paper, and was rewarded by his gratitude as he pushed the notebook in his pocket.

" Thanks a lot. It's mighty good of you, Miss Flood, to spare us your time ; you must get pretty tired of this sort of thing ! " To her surprise, the hard-bitten, pressman look had peeled off his face ; she realized he was much younger than, in their first moments of meeting, she had imagined. His eyes were bright and shy as he patted the pocket with the notebook in it, and his smile was very young, and, in some way, apologetic. " You've been so nice, I guess I ought to tell you—before somebody else does—I sure hope you won't get mad——" He gulped. " I'm not Tom Turpin."

" You wouldn't know how little that shakes me," said Aldebaran, after a pause, " as I never heard of the gentleman in my life."

He laughed nervously.

" He's the big guy. He's the one who does the profiles in the Saturday edition. He gets all the visiting big shots——" He gulped. " But there's been a kind of tangle ; there's a conference here this week—political ; I guess you've noticed this hotel's crawling with senators."

" I hadn't," said Aldebaran, as he paused. He smiled wanly.

" Sure ; you wouldn't know. Well, Tom rang through about an hour ago to say he couldn't make it. So I—well, it's my first real break since I was on the paper ! I might as well come clean : it's the first time I've ever interviewed a—a celebrity. I guess I was pretty raw ! "

"On the contrary; particularly hard-boiled," Aldebaran assured him gravely. "There were moments when you practically had me rattled——"

"Nuts; it would take more than I've got to rattle you!" He grinned, then sobered. "But—thanks a lot for giving me my first big break. And—and for being swell about it. Lots of folk would be mad—Tom's quite a guy, you know——"

"I told you: I've never heard of him. And I hope you'll 'make out' on this—if that's the expression."

"You bet I will! I guess you get all your stuff from a clipping bureau, but I'd like to mail you the Saturday edition, if you'll let me. And I'd like to show my appreciation—if you'll let me—say, Miss Flood: you're a jazz fan, aren't you?"

"Where did you get that?"

"Jeeze, the old office grape-vine!" He chuckled; confidence flowed back in him. "The press gets hold of plenty of stuff we don't let out in our columns. Yeah; I know we got a name for opening our mouths too darn wide. May be that goes for the North. But you're in the deep South now, and the layout's different. If you'd care to let me escort you tonight, Miss Flood——"

"I can't. I'm talking at Charleston tonight."

His face fell.

"That's too bad."

"I'm sorry."

"Me too. I'd like to have taken you to a joint I know——" He seemed to hesitate. "It's not a place a woman—a lady—can go alone; but—I guess that doesn't go for a writer! They got a guy this week—gee; he'd send you crazy. Most all the guys got what he's got get sucked into New York. He can make the old piano sound like it's a five-piece band. He's got a few numbers of his own, but mostly he plays the old Pace and Handy numbers: 'Memphis Blues,' 'Brown Skin,' 'Joe Turner'——"

"What's he called?" she heard her own voice saying from far away.

He laughed.

H

"You know how these guys get called! The fans give them a name and it sticks, or may be it doesn't. I got talking to one of his buddies the other night; every time I said ' Honey Joe ' the other guy says ' Lee.' "

The lights of the bar whirled before Aldebaran's eyes.

"Seems like his mother called him Leroy ! "—it seemed to amuse him. " ' Lee ' mostly stands for that ! "

"Lee—Lee—Lee—Marion." She heard herself say it.

"You know the guy ? "

"Red hair—very white skin—eyes—like a—cat——"

"Gee ! " He let out a roar of laughter. "My, my, you got it all wrong ! Most all these guys are niggers—I mean, Negroes. You've seen that, surely ? This Honey Joe—Lee—whatever he calls himself—he's kind of high yellow ; pale sort of café-au-lait colour, but hair—well, you know the way a nig—Negro's hair grows—and eyes——"

When the cold tide of relief settled in her veins, she found herself wondering : If it had been Lee, what should I have done ? What would have become of Charleston, and the lecture, and Ruth Rodríguez ? How far would discipline—the discipline of a paid job, of a waiting audience, have gone to control the impulse which had risen to bursting-point while he was talking ?

"Well, I guess it's just too bad," he was saying. "Is it your first trip ? They'll give you a swell time, in Charleston."

"Yes. I've been looking forward to it."

"Got friends there ? "

"Not exactly. Just somebody I might look up—if I can find the house. Cone Street ; is there such a place ? "

"There is." His expression was surprised, then doubtful. "But I guess you'd better look up your friends in the directory before you go visiting in Cone Street. Cone Street—well, it kind of doesn't grade, socially ! "

She laughed as she held out her hand.

"Thanks for the compliment. I may have made a mistake —but I should think quite a few of my friends wouldn't grade, socially ! A writer can't afford to be a snob, you know ! "

While she was flinging her belongings at random into a suitcase—thinking how neatly and carefully Janet would pack : there were no grounds for the assumption, but it went with her fastidious personality—the telephone chirred. She picked it up, hoping it might be Janet.

" There's Mis' Rodríguez' car here."

" Thanks. Send up for the baggage, will you ? "

She reddened her lips and brushed the powder from her eyebrows and the bosom of the black gown. Her grey-white face stared at her from the glass, slashed with black and vermilion : a good platform face ; a face that photographed well, in spite of—or because of ?—its irregularities. After seeing it reproduced on some thousands of book-jackets, on publishers' show-cards and in the social pages of the glossies, it had ceased, as a face, to interest her. But it occurred to her to wonder how it would strike the unknown Ruth Rodríguez, who, from some far reach of the genealogical river, claimed relationship.

A jaded spectacle she was, to meet Ruth Rodríguez, and to face her Charleston audience. But when she went out on the sidewalk, a coloured chauffeur held the door open into an empty car.

" Good evening, ma'am. Mis' Rodríguez will meet you at the hall wheah yo' giving yo' talk."

Was this indifference, or kindly imagination ? Hardly the former ; she had already experienced the vast resources of Southern hospitality. Predisposed to like her unknown cousin, she sank gratefully into the deep upholstery, had her knees covered with a thin sheet of monogrammed linen, was shown where the cigarettes were, and the electric lighter, and a thermos flask that clinked with the ice within. She closed her eyes. Silence, solitude, coolness ; out of these she could recharge herself for the last—the very last—ordeal. I must be good to-night, on account of Ruth. I'll relax ; I'll make myself go to sleep . . .

Only it did not work out that way. The humming of the car was the humming of a dynamo inside her. Lee. Supposing it *had* been Lee. It was like the reaction, after being rescued from falling down a precipice.　It left one tremulous and sweating. And there was another precipice ahead.　Cone Street . . .

That boy had known something about Cone Street.　Why had she not questioned him further ?　The answer came back from some distant gulf in the subconscious : *Because you did not dare.　Because you know the answer* . . .

I may have made a mistake.　I—must—have—made—a—mistake.　Jesus—it's *got* to be a mistake !　Orlando, my only love, it *has* to be a mistake.

Chapter Six

I

WHEN SHE opened the screens on morning, on the liveoaks in their tapestry of grey lace stirred by scarlet tanagers, it was like stepping into a new world. An over-powering fragrance of tea-olive rose from under her window, as the sun sucked up the dews of night : it went like a strain of light music through the heavy obbligato of spicy air, held down by the canopy of trees. She stifled an exclamation at the sight of innumerable magnolias, clustered like pale bulbs of light on the trusses of waxen foliage.

At right angles to the wing in which her rooms were situated was the towering Ionic façade, whose pillars, interrupted by the gallery that ran along the second storey, soared to the pediment behind which rose the steep mansard penetrated by a row of dormer windows. Lit by the headlights of the car, it had seemed, at midnight, like a Pompeian temple, set in between the two lower and recently added wings, whose design scrupulously observed the proportions of the original house. Screened by its perpetual curtains of Spanish moss, the place was as silent as the palace of the Belle au Bois Dormant, save for the hissing of the unseen swamp.

Across a sweep of grass greener than emeralds, a ring-fence with hitching posts held off the highway, along which, as though to complete the fabulous picture, came riding a young man on a glossy chestnut. Lost from time to time behind the cascades of moss, they came at last into full view in the sun-filled clearing, and the rider, swinging himself to the ground, lifted a thin, pale face to yell " Sam ! " A Negro appeared round a corner of the outbuildings at a loping trot, looped the reins over his arm, and shambled back into shadow.

The young man, his hands thrust into the pockets of a pair of well-cut breeches, sauntered towards a block of buildings partly concealed by a tall clipped hedge. Handsome, young and discontented. Aldebaran, enjoying her point of vantage, wondered what life in this somnambulistic region held for those in whom the ardent blood of youth was bubbling. Even in this early hour of morning the air was oppressive, as though all its freshness had been sucked up by the exuberant vegetation. The lovely, languid, deep, deep South !—for all its beauty, a little sinister. She allowed her eye to be caught by a flicker of white away to her left.

A girl had appeared on the upper porch ; flickering like a butterfly from pillar to pillar, she reached the angle at the extremity from Aldebaran's window. Graceful and furtive, she looked back towards the doors from which she had emerged, hung over the balcony rail and whistled once, sharply. The man's head came up ; he faltered, stared at her across the top of the hedge, and, without sign or smile, walked on.

" Diamond ! " called Ruth's voice. The girl raced back closing the screens behind her.

M'm, a romance. And not approved by Mamma. What, she entertained herself by wondering, while brushing her hair, were the objections to a good-looking young man, possessed at least of a beautiful chestnut horse (now tranquilly cropping the grass), and himself—at a glance—not destitute of breeding ? Possibly youth—Diamond's. The girl looked seventeen, but girls grow up more quickly in the Deep South than in Northern climates. Ruth herself seemed hardly old enough to have a daughter of seventeen.

Someone was speaking, so close that Aldebaran looked round with a start, almost expecting to see the speaker in the room : then remembered the angle of the wing.

" You'd better put on your candy-stripe, honey."

" What for ? "

" We're going into Charleston."

" Oh Mother, what *for* ? "

" I want to shop, and you can show your cousin the town."

" Oh—*blight*. What is there to show ? It's such punk, after Paris. Can't I stay home and go swimming ? "

" We'll all swim, after tea. Don't make comparisons between Charleston and Paris, honey ; it only makes you sound a very silly little girl. There's some camellias ; take them in and tell your cousin Aldebaran good morning."

" I thought I was supposed to change."

" Go tell your cousin good morning," said Ruth's calm voice, " and don't forget to ask if she had a good night."

" Come in," called Aldebaran to a tap on her door.

A sullenly beautiful child stood there, her hands full of camellias. So this was Ruth's problem. Thank God it's not mine, thought Aldebaran. Slim as a reed, with a golden tea-rose complexion and full crimson bud of a mouth, Diamond, in a short white seersucker dress, buttoned and widely belted with scarlet, was lovely enough to send any mother's heart into her boots. Her youthfully critical eyes went over Aldebaran's mandarin-yellow dressing-gown and over her articles of toilet, and flicked away, admitting nothing.

" Hallo," said Aldebaran, and wondered if she passed muster.

" Good morning. I'm Diamond Rodríguez. Mother says, did you sleep well ? "

" Like a top." Ungracious because she's unhappy about something ; probably about the Adonis in riding breeches. " I got in rather late, last night."

" One o'clock ? " The child's lifted brows, her pouting lips, held a faint insolence of patronage. " We were never in until one or two, in Paris."

" You don't notice time "—Aldebaran repressed a smile— " when you're amusing yourself. Did you get the candy-stripe in Paris ? "

" Oh ! You were listening ! " Diamond's face flushed from pointed chin to the deliciously clean line of her blue-black hair.

" It would be rather difficult not to," shrugged Aldebaran, " in this house "—and rose as Ruth appeared in the doorway, flinging her arm round her daughter's narrow waist, drawing her to her, as she smiled in welcome at the visitor. They certainly made an entrancing pair : Ruth, although dark, almost fair in comparison with her raven-haired daughter, with eyes like dark velvet in a small, animated, heart-shaped face, alight with wisdom and tenderness.

" Look, honey ! " She squeezed Diamond's waist and laughed. " She's got your eyebrows ! "

It was true ; the silky bands across the girl's eyes were shaped and coloured like Aldebaran's. Diamond's brows, although thinner, described the same swift, impatient line from temple to temple.

" They suit Diamond better than they do me. It's ridiculous to have black eyebrows and ginger hair ! "

" It's a lot more distinguished. Listen : do you feel like coming in to Charleston ? I've got to shop and see the lawyer. Diamond will show you the old houses and the Slave Mart, if you like, but if you want any reliable information, you'd better buy a guide-book. Considering my child's practically grown up in Charleston, she couldn't know less about local history."

" Oh Mother—as if she cares about that parochial stuff."

Ruth nodded tranquilly at Aldebaran.

" Since we got back from Paris everything's parochial. The car'll be round in half an hour, but don't hurry. We don't need to be back before dinner."

" You said we could go swimming after tea ! " An edge of anxiety on Diamond's voice did not escape Aldebaran's attention, or, apparently, her mother's. Ruth turned to look quietly into her daughter's eyes.

" And we can go swimming tomorrow, and the day after that. You can have a dip when we get home—if it's not too dark."

" It's sure to be dark. Joe drives like he was driving a hearse ! "

" Joe drives my car the way I like it."

There's no want of command in her, thought Aldebaran, as she professed readiness to be shown the sights of Charleston. Presently she discovered in her cupboard the freshly pressed rows of her dresses, and chose with relief a light silk suit she had

kept for this visit. As she added lizard shoes and a lizard bag
to the scheme, and slid a pair of powder-coloured gloves from
their folder of satin, she reflected that, next to a man—a special
man—nothing stimulates one's vanity like the unspoken criticism
of a schoolgirl.

Talking to the chauffeur, when the three of them came out
on the porch, was the youth she had seen from her window.
At close quarters, not so good. There was something decadent
in the long and admittedly graceful structure of his body ; the
skin of his face was papery, his eyes, of a curiously flat grey, had
bruises, that looked like dissipation, under them. When Ruth
wished him a pleasant " Good morning, Alger," he returned
the greeting without a smile ; he studiously kept his eyes from
Diamond, who had taken advantage of the pause to thrust a
camellia under the knot of her hair-ribbon. She lounged on the
stone terminal of the stair rail, apparently indifferent, but every
line of her young body expressing awareness of the observant
male.

" Anything in particular, Alger ? " asked Ruth crisply.

He answered in the marked drawl of the Southerner, his
lids half-covering eyes which avoided Ruth, equally with her
daughter.

" Sam's house is down again."

" You mean, they've pulled the bricks out ? " She laughed,
but let him see her exasperation. " What's it this time—a
barbecue ? You can tell them I'm not rebuilding. When they
get the swamp in, and may be a moccasin or two, they can shift
in with Betsy's mother. That cabin's big enough for two families
and it will do Betsy no harm to be under her mother's eye for a
while. Any more trouble with Jake ? "

He made a negative sideways motion with his head.

" Seems like Betsy's made up her mind to behave."

" Or her husband's made it up for her. Has Sam been
beating her up again ? "

A glimmer of humour lightened the reply.

" Could be he's too busy building barbecues."

" And barbecues mean poaching and poaching means the

can. Tell Sam I'm putting up no more bail for him if he can't lay off the Colonel's turkeys." She motioned towards the car and the coloured chauffeur swung the door open with a flourish. "Keep your eyes on those people, Alger; I don't want trouble in the cabins. Have the new shingles for the school come yet?"

"They'll be alawng today, or may be the day after," said Alger, in his oddly reluctant voice.

"They'll be along today, or I'll know why. You'd better ride straight down to the mill and say I'll have that roof on by Sunday or I'll take the job to Skeeterville. Alger's acting over-seer—don't you call it bailiff?—while our head man, Phil Curtis, is away," explained Ruth, as the car slid across the rollers at the gap in the ring fence.

"Then you still run the plantation? I mean, as a planta-tion?"

Ruth shook her head, pointing to a brick stack rising appar-ently from the heart of the swamp.

"That's one of the old rice mills. The Confederate war put paid to the rice industry. They say Hammock had seven hundred field hands, in those days: now we've got about forty workers, counting field and house servants and the boys that look after the livestock. Most of the stuff you'll eat here is raised on the premises; it's a nuisance, but it's a way of giving the people work. When you take over a plantation," explained Ruth, " you take over the darkies with it. Most of the boys trek off, sooner or later, but some of them come wandering back, when they find it's not exactly a Land of Promise across the Mason-Dixon line! Our numbers don't vary much between forty and fifty—apart from the piccanins. I've given up counting them; they're like little black pigs, all over the place."

"' Pigs ' is right! "

Ruth gave a sharp glance at the back of Diamond's slender neck, leaned forward and slid the glass panel between themselves and the driver's seat.

"All this bad temper is because we aren't going to school in Paris. You aren't married, are you? " she asked abruptly.

"Goodness, no. I thought you knew."

"I read you up in *Who's Who*," said Ruth candidly, "but it was an old copy I happened to pick up in the Crillon. Two or three years back, I should say. Things could have happened since."

"Things have." She smiled at the frank but inoffensive curiosity in her companion's eyes. "But not that particular one."

"I wish we'd met when Diamond and I were in Europe," said Ruth presently. "I was dumb enough to mention to my child the possibility of sending her to boarding school in Paris——"

"You changed your mind."

Ruth shrugged her shoulders.

"It just happened when I'd looked at two or three of the schools they gave me, I came to the conclusion Paris and Diamond Rodríguez don't mix. You'll have to tell me something about your English schools, as I don't mind admitting, the way things are, it's a race between my daughter and me for the bin—and, so far, Mother's winning!"

"How old is she?"

"What do you think? Fifteen. Isn't it appalling? All our friends in Europe took her for seventeen at least, and she got dreadfully spoiled. And of course "—Ruth's soft brows knitted—"we had young man trouble. I have to face the fact my child's a beauty: all the same, I didn't expect to have to take that fence for another couple of years, and when she sneaked up and crowded me on the rails, I felt we'd be better off at Hammock till I got my second wind. Now, what with one thing and another, the sooner I get her somewhere else, the better it suits me."

"I suppose one of the 'things' is called Alger."

"You're pretty sharp, aren't you?"

Aldebaran laughed.

"Oh—there's been an Alger or two in my past."

"And you brushed them off. As you've seen, Diamond's as likely to brush them off as a frolicsome young kitten meeting its first toms. The kitten usually gets damaged. I don't seem to like the idea of Diamond getting damaged—yet." She interrupted herself to lean forward and look at a clump of shacks at the fork of the rutted road, and rapped sharply on the panel. Diamond turned a bored head. "Tell Joe to stop. Joe," she said, when the chauffeur came to the door for orders, "go down and find out if the doctor's been to see Marie. If he hasn't, we must stop on the way and give him a dig."

They had passed from the lovely melancholy of the Spanish moss into a region of young pine; the rosy trunks rose like the masts of an innumerable fleet, and in their gilded tops roosted the buzzards. In the air was a sweetness of resin. A beneficent heat brooded on the clearing. From somewhere in the depth of the trees came the buzz of a sawmill and two piccanins, stark as nature made them, were playing gravely with a snake.

Ruth said absently,

"There's a girl here had a baby last week. Born dead, of course. The doctor couldn't—or wouldn't—get here in time. Usual thing—they didn't send for me until it was over: one of her relations did the job—with a pair of rusty scissors. The Lord knows why she isn't dead. I've been trying to get her to a hospital, but there's only one hospital for blacks in this part of the county, and they don't have a bed."

"But—Ruth—you don't mean that you—you yourself—go down and deliver children for the black women?" Ruth, in her frail muslin dress through whose folds glimmered the lacy petticoat; with her small gloved hands and fine, fastidious flesh—— ?

"I happened to take a hospital course, back in '17—you know, when we came into the war," Ruth told her casually. "It's almost hopeless to get any skilled attention here when our people are ill. Unless it's an occupational accident—somebody chopped an arm off in the sawmill or broken a leg tree-felling—the doctor won't come out. They tell me I'm a fool to fuss over pregnancies: the blacks litter like rabbits! Well, mostly they do; but just now and then—— What about it, Joe?"

" Looks like it's curtains, Mis' Rodríguez.   She don't know nuffin' and her breath's coming queer."

" Oh *Mother*!   You'll get fleas and your clothes will smell ! "

" Sorry to keep you waiting, Cousin Aldebaran.   Give me my case, Joe."

The chauffeur slid back a panel in front of the passengers' seats and took out an attaché-case, apparently kept there for emergencies.   Ruth plucked off her hat and swiftly folded her soft hair into a snowy square of linen, slid her arms into the white hospital coat the man held for her and rolled on a pair of rubber gloves.

" One of my housegirls I trained was supposed to be looking after her, but they're all born slipshod and she probably used a dirty pan."

" Can I come too ? "

Ruth, holding her gloved hands away from contact with her coat, looked at her doubtfully.

" I wouldn't, if I were you.   This isn't one of our ' show ' cabins and it takes a pretty strong stomach, at any time, to go into quarters.   When you've got sickness, on top of dirt——! "

" If you can take it, I guess I can."

Their eyes met ;   after a moment, Ruth shrugged her shoulders.

" You can carry my First-Aid box for me if you like.   I guess it's copy.   Keep your eye skinned for snakes."

II

A carved wooden pillar supported the wreckage of a shingle roof.   As they stepped up from the long grass on a broken porch a plank gave under Aldebaran's high heels and she saved herself with a lurch.

" And remember," frowned Ruth, " don't touch anything. And that means *anything*."

The air was like a filthy rag pressed over their mouths. Aldebaran drew in her breath and held it until her heart pounded; she had a shrinking that amounted—she scorned herself for the admission—to fear.

Barely distinguishable in the green gloom reflected from the trees through a paneless window were walls that let in streaks of light between thin planks of pine ; was a pine floor, rotted and partly sodden with swamp water. When her eyes accustomed themselves to darkness, she saw that the shack consisted of a single room, and that there was no furniture—in the sense furniture holds for civilized people—whatever. Some rags hung from nails on the wall which, at the end where Ruth was standing, was plastered with old wallpapers, as though someone had tried to secure at least one corner against the wind and the rain. A wooden crate pushed against the wall-boarding carried more newspapers, a pile of rusty and broken tin utensils and a pan of beans curdled in fat whose surface was spotted with mould. Over everything were flies, whose metallic bodies zinged against the newspapers.

On a thin layer of rags lay a girl with her knees dragged up towards the cave of her ribs. One arm was stretched out, its knuckles resting on the floor, and the other flung across her breasts. Her closed eyes showed a glint of white between the lids and her nostrils were inflated with each noisy breath. A feeble moaning that escaped her gritted teeth had drawn the children from their snake, to stand, like frightened fawns, in the opening of the door. Aldebaran whispered,

" What can I do ? "

Ruth thrust a metal tray at her, lit a flame, and gave her the needle to hold while she snipped the nipple off an ampoule and filled the syringe. Aldebaran watched her sink the needle into the girl's arm and swab the invisible wound with alcohol.

" She'll be dead before night." Ruth spoke, after a long silence, in the car.

" Does she have to die alone ? Hasn't she any people ? "

" Plenty ; you didn't see them dodging back in the wood as we came along. They may well ! Yesterday we'd got that place cleaned up—nearly; we used enough disinfectant to float the *Mauretania*. And I'd got Marie into a bedgown, of sorts, and a pair of sheets. Well—you saw how it was."

" They'd stolen the sheets ? "

" Oh hell," said Ruth, " I'm sorry you've had this. Give me a cigarette. We're late. I'd meant to show you Magnolia Gardens on the way in, but there isn't time. It's a pity you've missed the azalea festival." She turned her head sharply. " I know; you're wanting to ask a thousand questions: how come our darkies are the way they are, and why don't we give them proper medical service—and all that. That can wait for another day." She drew deeply on the cigarette.

" As a matter of fact, I was thinking of what you said about " copy." I don't see how anyone called Flood can look on Negroes as ' copy '."

" Flood, or Rodríguez either. Funny, to think of your ancestors and Jim's, partnering one another in the old trade. As for me—I've had it—or its results—under my nose as long as I can remember, here and in Cuba. It makes it rather difficult to be objective ! " Ruth laughed shortly, glancing at her watch. " We're nearly there. Is there anything you specially want to do, or see, while we're in town ? "

" No—except——" She bit her lip, but the words seemed to force themselves out. " Cone Street: do you happen to know it—Cone Street ? "

They were driving along South Battery, between the balconied mansions of Charleston's elect and the palmettos of White Point Gardens; the harbour danced gently in points of sunlight behind the Fort Moultrie monument.

" Seems like I disremember *Cone* Street, ma'am," came at last in Joe's slow voice.

" You're sure of the name? Joe knows Charleston like he knows the palms of his hands."

" Leastways," pursued Joe, in vindication of his character, " the only Cone Street I heard of's out on President, by Harmon Field."

" It's certainly not there ! " Ruth laughed at some private

joke. "What are your friends called? Joe can look them up in the telephone book while we're having lunch."

Again the struggle between her will and some irresistible compulsion took place within her; as she spoke the word "Anderson" she was thinking, What a fool you are to betray yourself. But it was safe; Ruth would certainly not know.

"That's a pretty common name; there are probably a dozen in the directory. Joe"—before Aldebaran could interpose—"take a pencil, Joe, and copy all the Andersons out of the telephone book; Miss Flood's looking for some friends and she's forgotten the address. Hallo, Henry!" A tall man in a pale suit had come to the door of the car; Ruth gave him her hand and allowed herself to be drawn out. "We're late, aren't we?"

"I have never been able to decide," said the person addressed as Henry, "whether the correct answer to that—from a gentleman to a lady—is 'Not at all' or 'Indeed you are!'—the latter connoting the impatience of the speaker——"

"All right, Henry! We take that for granted." She turned to Aldebaran. "This is an old friend of ours, Henry Tollemache. This is my cousin—or rather, Jim's cousin, Henry—Miss Aldebaran Flood, the celebrated author!"

Aldebaran found herself looking at the man she had seen dining on Chatham Walk, on her first night in New York.

Seen close at hand, he appeared a little younger than from a distance, the pale tan covering an extraordinary smoothness of skin, abnormally free of lines for a man in his forties. He was good-looking and well-bred—yet the impression he made was not agreeable. A pair of icy eyes cancelled the smile courtesy drew about his thin lips. She was relieved when he allowed her to withdraw her hand. The light reference she was about to have made, on its not being their first meeting, faded, unspoken. He gave her, for some reason, a sense of insecurity, a warning of caution; all this in spite of his graceful acceptance of Ruth's introduction.

"Henry looks after us at Hammock," Ruth was saying, rather vaguely; in what, wondered Aldebaran, did the looking-after consist ? He was certainly not to be fitted into the picture of the divorce, of which Ruth, characteristically, had given her an outline on the night of her arrival. " You're coming back with us tonight, aren't you ? That's fine," as he admitted the invitation with a bend of the head. " Now "—again she glanced at her watch—" I've got to do some shopping, no, it's too late for that ; that will do after lunch—but I've got to catch Del Morgan before he goes out——"

" Why not telephone him from the club ? He can join us for a cocktail—or lunch, if you prefer."

She shook her head smilingly.

" No, Henry ; although I know you like to believe you're in all my secrets, this is estate palaver, and you don't always approve of my methods of doing business. Take Diamond and give her a lemonade or something, and if I'm late, don't wait lunch for me ; I'll be back as quickly as possible. What would you rather do ? " she asked Aldebaran. " Go to the club and have one of Henry's ravishing mint juleps, or tote around with me ? " She laughed as Aldebaran hesitated. " That's putting you in a spot, isn't it ? Well, I'd like my cousin's company, Henry—so don't let Diamond bore you about Paris."

" *A bientôt*—I hope." His smile, although agreeable, was wanting in sincerity. " I hope you are making a long visit, Miss Flood. We Charlestonians are proud of our city, and it gives us great pleasure to show our guests its charms."

" Uncle Henry ought to be appointed as town guide ! " chanted Diamond, flickering her eyelashes at him ; the presence of a male—even an old stiff like Uncle Henry !—was sufficient to banish her ill-humour. " He knows every brick and every date and all the ghost stories and where you usedn't to be allowed to smoke a cigar—he's frightfully ante bellum : aren't you, darling ? "

" In brief, a museum piece. Still, if it would not bore you—— ? "

" I was brought up on antiquity," said Aldebaran coolly. " My home town is Bristol—although it wasn't my birthplace. We should have something in common." She had involuntarily

I

stressed the word "something," and wondered if he noticed. Ruth had, and looked at her curiously when they were settled again in the car.

" You don't care for Henry ? He's a bit of a bore, but not a bad sort ; I could hardly manage without him, since Jim walked out on me. We fight like cat and dog, he's always at me about extravagance and spoiling the people, and he disapproves of Alger—but he's not going to get his way over *that*." Not for the first time, Aldebaran noticed the firmness of the small, pointed chin. " We'll get him to fix you a dinner party—his house on Tradd Street is a dream. What a fool I am ! " she burst out. " Of course, Henry's the person to know all about your friends the Andersons ; why on earth didn't you remind me ? "

" They aren't friends." She was surprised by the smoothness of her voice. " Actually, they're relatives of someone I used to know—and it doesn't matter in the least. I don't know why I bothered. They'd probably be mystified if I turned up ! "

" Then that's all right. Here's my lawyer's. Look, this is going to be an awful bore for you . . . Would you care to take a stroll while I'm talking to Del ? It shouldn't take more than a few minutes—perhaps you'd better come in and we'll see how long he's likely to be."

The Boss, they were informed, was in conference, but was expecting Mrs. Rodríguez and hoped she would do him the favour of waiting a few minutes.

" Blight." Ruth borrowed an expletive from her daughter. " I know Del's few minutes !—they may be thirty seconds or half an hour. I ought to have left you at the club. I'll tell you what : I'll tell Joe to take you a short ride round the town and be back here at a quarter past one. It won't be as dull as sitting in Del's lobby or listening to my daughter's raptures on the Pré-Catalan ! "

" I think I'd sooner walk a little. It's rather warm in the car." *I was meant to say this. This is how it was meant to be.* Again she listened, wonderingly, to her own voice.

" Well—don't get lost, will you ? " Ruth sounded doubtful.

hey stood for the moment on the steps, looking down the reet laid with a lilac carpet of shadow and a creamy carpet of un. "Look, down there, that's Meeting Street: lots of rather ice old houses and gardens. If you stroll along to your right will bring you back to the Gardens, and we'll pick you up hen I'm through with Del; it will save your coming back ere," said Ruth.

Yes, it was meant to be like this. Walking alone between wns and trees, shadowy vines and clustered azaleas and delicate rills of iron. Walking with the ghosts of crinolined ladies ollowed by their Negro pages. Walking with the sure knowledge f finding what one was looking for—at last. Walking with hivers in one's knees and a light, empty feeling, a sick feeling, feeling of dread, of knowing, yet not knowing—this was how was meant to be. At last all the pieces were falling into place: he visit to Charleston, Ruth's invitation, Ruth's appointment vith the lawyer, the easy disentanglement from Ruth and Diamond and Henry Tollemache. With the sense of one very lose to the end of a long journey, she lifted her hand to a ruising taxi.

"Seventy-eight, Cone Street."

She did not notice the driver's look. She pressed her hands hard down on the padded seat to stop the tremors in her wrists, nd her knees, and her ankles.

III

Dust and rubble and tin cans. More cans than could con-ceivably be imagined—rolling across the broadwalk, piled in the gutters, cluttering the corners of doorsteps. Boys kicking a ball between the wheels of traffic and the legs of pedestrians. Tub-shaped women, in Mother Hubbards, rolling along with bundles on their heads, or propped against walls, or resting immense breasts on their forearms, planted on broken windowsills.

Din. Shapeless, indescribable, sub-human din, knitted together by the film of dust hanging in the air. But most of it

the jangling din of cans—the all-purpose unit of the neighbourhood.   Children beating cans for drums, a chocolate-coloured
youth in faded cotton breeches and torn sweater eating some
yellow mess out of a can, two little boys, crouched in the gutter
trying with immense application to force an enormous dead rat
into a can.   Barefooted girl in a red and white spotted dress
carefully carrying a brimming can of liquid up a flight of steps
and, a moment later, pitching the empty can out of a window:
Cone Street's easy disposal of its garbage problem.   Two boys
starting a scrimmage in imitation of the footballers, with a
corn-beef can toed at random out of the pile at the foot of a
lamp-post.   A young woman teetering past on high heels, with
more cans—presently to swell Cone Street's debris—in a string
bag.

The taxi halted half-way down Cone Street.   She sat still
with her hands clenched in her lap.   The driver twisted his head
round.

" Yo' gonna stop heah all day ? "   She noticed for the first
time that he was coloured.

She doubled herself to get out on the pavement—and felt
the whole street petrify to attention.   She heard her own voice,
unnecessarily loud, say to the driver,

" Wait.   You'll have to take me back."

He gave her a look of bitter distrust and looked ahead, over
his wheel.

As she crossed the broken sidewalk, her slim pale skirt
clinging to the heat of her thighs, her face chalk-white and
drained of expression, the suspicion of coloured people of a
white woman, dressed like rich white folk and arriving in a
taxi-cab, pushed through the silent light and broke against her
like a wave ; she could feel it physically.   She remembered, as
she reached the doorstep, that she had not stopped to verify
the number ; this might be seventy-eight, or it might not—the
driver had given her no indication.   The only thing clear was
that she must not turn back or falter.   She lifted her face steadily
towards the dark ones looking down.

" Does anybody called Anderson live here ? "

All of her vision seemed to be invaded by a pattern of dark
eyes motionless on balls of yellowed ivory. No one spoke. She
asked again,

" Does this house belong to a Mrs. Anderson?" and someone
uttered. " Belong to !" She felt the skin of her face tighten
and her lips shrivel, but was resolved not to flinch. She stood
there, waiting for the answer.

" Seems like yo' got the wrawng ad-dress, ma'am." It was
a man in a paper-thin chalk-stripe suit ; he ran his eyes down
to her waist and up again to her mouth, insolently. She forced
herself to look back at him.

" Well, do you know of any Andersons, in this street, or the
next ? "

A mumble of argument rose among the women ; the men
clumped together, silent, eyeing her with enmity. To them she
stood for danger : for false accusations, for jail, and lynchings,
and all the perils that beset black folk in the Deep South. Without
having a finger laid on her, this white woman could go back and
tell a tale that would bring the police cars wailing down Cone
Street. They stood and hated her, while their women argued.
Out of the argument broke, finally, a mutter that sounded to
Aldebaran like " Ball Street."

" Did you say Ball Street ? "

Quickly as she spoke, the betrayer was shuffled by her companions to the back of the group now wedged in the opening
—there was no door—to the derelict house.

As a last resource, Aldebaran pulled a dollar bill out of her
handbag and said to the company at large,

" I'll give this to anyone who'll show me where the Andersons
—any Andersons—live."

She fancied she saw a gleam in the eyes of a thin boy of
fourteen or fifteen, who had crushed himself in at the side of the
steps, but as she looked at him he dropped his head and his face
went blank.

Twelve years ago : and Negro populations were, without
doubt, as transient as poor whites. Twelve years ago, Cone
Street might probably have been a respectable if impecunious

neighbourhood : why had she never thought of that? Th houses were well built, the small, old-fashioned bricks hand made ; there were even traces of porticoes over one or two o the doorways, and the glassless transoms with their broke spokes were of the old, elegant fan pattern. In twelve years street can come down in the world. Telling herself all this, sh stumbled back to the taxi.

"Why don yuh say yuh lookin foh Andersons?" Th driver accused her bitterly. "Deys plenny Andersons arou heah. My sistuh—she done marry a Anderson."

"Go on—please go on!" She was seized with horror o the dark faces that now were pressing against the window "Drive till I tell you to stop—and tell me about your sister——

"Den," said the driver, yawning to let her see that, at th end of ten minutes, he was bored with the saga of Andersons they had crawled out of the coloured quarter into a region o small, squalid shops, "dere was a Mis' Anderson—I disre membered her. Lived on Cone Street a mighty long time Yassuh! I reckon she lived on Cone Street fi'-six year. It mu be fi'-six year she gone nawth—dey say she gone to Harlem. He yawned again. "Useta teach school—fi'-six year ago."

"Fi'-six year," apparently, was his only unit of time. Hov long had Cone Street been a coloured quarter? Fi'-six year, h guessed. She gave up at last. She bade him put her dow where he had picked her up on Meeting Street, and added th promised dollar to the fare.

"Where *have* you been?" cried Ruth. Their anxious face —Henry Tollemache's and Ruth's, and Diamond's sharpl curious little mask—peered at her from the car at White Poin Gardens. "We've been looking for you for nearly an hour When you didn't turn up, I rushed to the club, and Henry insiste on coming back with me——"

"I'm *famished*!" wailed Diamond. "Do you know it' nearly two o'clock? We've been crawling all over the tow for you——"

"I'm so terribly sorry—I'd no idea of the time ; I left m watch at home." This happened to be the truth. "Yes, I go lost—and I couldn't remember what to tell the taxi-driver——"

" Well, all our troubles are over now." Tollemache's cold
eyes smiled into hers as he helped her into the car, and she
knew he had not believed a word she said. " The immediate
consideration, I imagine, is to get some food——! "

" And a stiff drink for Aldebaran, by the look of things ! "
Ruth's warm hand closed over hers ; Ruth's anger had melted
at the sight of Aldebaran's face. " My, honey, you're done in !
I didn't know Charleston was *that* large——! "

" I should think you've walked over every inch of it," was
Diamond's contribution, " and, oh Uncle Henry, I'm *dying* for
crabmeat in avocado pears——! "

IV

The young man called Alger rose out of the dusk as the car
swung in to the steps of the porch ; he was greeted curtly by
Tollemache and eagerly by Ruth, who followed him as he turned
aside. Aldebaran noticed that Tollemache took Diamond's
arm and steered her promptly into the house, murmuring about
a cocktail. Ruth turned her head to call,

" Marie's still alive ! Alger went in to see on his way from
the sawmill. You'd better tell them to get out the station
wagon," she told him. " I'm going to move her up to quarters
—and they can grumble all they like ": a parenthesis that
mystified Aldebaran, listening from the top of the steps. " You're
late tonight, aren't you, Alger ? Nothing wrong, is there ? "

" There's this." She saw him hold out what looked from the
distance like a crumpled sheet of paper ; saw Ruth stare at it,
then start, and push it in her pocket. Her laugh did not sound
quite convincing.

" Cheer up, Alger ! We've done nothing to invite the
attentions of that outfit."

Alger was silent. Aldebaran, glancing up at the wing
opposite her own, caught a flicker of white at a window, and
guessed it was Diamond, listening in to the conversation.

"Well—Mr. Tollemache is here. You'd better have a word with him before dinner."

"I'm sticking around. I've had some food."

"Really, Alger! You're not taking this seriously?" Ruth patted her pocket; there was a little note of bravado in her voice that made Aldebaran curious.

"Yeah, it's not that. Diamond's pony's running a temperature; I telephoned the vet, but they can't get out before morning. They told me what to do, but I don't feel like leaving it to Jake. That pony wants watching, and Jake's interested in something else for the present."

"What's the matter with Peppermint?" Diamond was hanging out of the window.

"Alger says she's got a temperature," answered Ruth shortly. "All right, Alger; stay around, will you—and I'll let you know when Mr. Tollemache is ready."

"Okay, ma'am." He collapsed into his former position on the steps.

Diamond whirled down the stairs to meet them as they walked into the hall.

"I'm going to see Peppermint."

Ruth caught her by the arm.

"No, you're not. Listen, honey: I'm sending Barbara down with some things for Marie and you've got to help me dress. It's that grey thing—I can't do it up by myself."

"Then why do you have to wear it? It won't take me a minute, to see Peppermint—and I'm going to have a swim before I change." An exiguous garment of pink wool swung from her wrist.

"It's too late for swimming."

"No, it's not; the moon will be up any minute."

"You know I don't let you go swimming alone after sundown, so stop arguing. Go ask your uncle if Alger can speak to him—and then, if you like, run down and see Peppermint. But, for the sweet love of heaven, be back to do up my dress."

Diamond's interest, however, in Peppermint had suddenly evaporated. She came back rather sullenly to say that Uncle

Henry was waiting for Alger in the gunroom, and ran up the stairs ahead of her mother and Aldebaran.

"It's a good thing Marie didn't die," said Ruth, as they mounted the stairs arm in arm, "because the servants are going to sing after dinner, and the concert would have turned into a wake with a corpse on the premises! Are you sure you're all right? You look awfully tired. You scared Henry and me stiff, you know, this afternoon."

"I'm dreadfully sorry. But surely nothing very serious could happen to one in a place like Charleston!"

"You wouldn't rather have your dinner in bed?"

"Goodness, no—thank you all the same!"

They had paused on the gallery; the light of the great chandelier that dripped its crystals into the well struck upward on Ruth's face—and, she supposed, on her own—sharpening its planes, stripping it of youth.

"Something's worrying you, Ruth."

"Me? Oh no. Nothing much. Perhaps I might tell you —later." With a wave of the hand, she slipped into her room.

The big, pale chamber with its softly faded chintzes sent, for some reason, a shudder through her. She could not stay up there alone; she must dress quickly, go downstairs, get herself a drink . . .

Although no one appeared as she descended the stairs, she was aware of a quiet attentiveness. Whatever one did in Hammock was observed. By the living, or the dead. "Plantation houses have their ghosts, little, wrinkled, old ladies, with sad, questioning faces, beautiful young women in their wedding finery, waiting for loves tragically cut off": she had read that somewhere—ah, in a book that Ruth had put in her room last night. Loves tragically cut off. Were they gathering round her, feeling her one of themselves, since—oh God. Oh Landy. Oh, you deserted brides, don't you know how much easier it is to lose your love by death?

Through the empty hall and into a long room curving into a bay, beyond which, following its sweep, extended the screened porch on which the glass doors stood open. The room, like the rest of the house, was filled with the hissing of the swamp. Two broad fans of candles flung gold into the mirrors behind them. As she paused to look at her illuminated face, and the whiteness of her neck and shoulders, one of the men-servants entered noiselessly and lit more candles. The room stirred and awoke, as a landscape wakes, at the coming of dawn. Another servant came with soundless tread and offered her a deep frosted glass on a salver. To what a peak of perfection had Ruth trained her servants. How was it done? A cool draught slid down her spine; she hunched her shoulders and pulled a floating strip of chiffon across her naked spine.

" I hope you have not caught a chill ? "

Tollemache was standing behind her ; she was annoyed with herself for letting him see her start—an admission of nervousness which, from his smile, appeared to give him satisfaction. She was obliged to concede him his handsomeness, in the dinner jacket—he would call it a tuxedo : or would he ? He was inclined to stress, though faintly, the fact of his Europeanization —which he wore with an ease not common, so far as she had had opportunity of observing, to many Americans. His greying hair broke in a steely wave from its parting and he was faintly redolent of bath essence. His smile, as usual, was a little forced and formal, as though he had other things on his mind : perhaps the interview with Alger ? She laughed, reverting to the " chill."

" Don't you know the saying, ' Someone walking over my grave ' ? "

" You did not find your friends, the Andersons ? "

All the blood from her heart pumped suddenly into her spinning head. She managed to say coolly,

" No ; they have probably left Charleston by now."

" Ruth mentioned it to me. The *Heyward* Andersons are very old friends of my family, and would be charmed to meet you ! " She told herself it was absurd to suspect malice in his insistence. " I could ring them tonight and arrange for you to visit them. The house, at least, would interest you : one of our finest examples of ante bellum——"

"It is kind of you," she interrupted him, "but I am only here for a few days, and Hammock fascinates me! I feel it will take me all my time to discover its many charms." She had recovered her sangfroid; her smile defied him across the rim of her glass. His reaction, this time, was gratifying.

"Sheer folly!" snapped Henry Tollemache.

So you have emotions, like normal human beings! Aldebaran raised her brows, to observe,

"What? I don't follow you."

"All this. Her insistence on keeping it up. I wish"—he caught his lower lip in his teeth. "I suppose you have gathered by now that Hammock Hall, and its population, are Ruth's obsession?"

"A pleasant one, surely." It was her turn to be tiresome; Aldebaran's eyes glinted in the candlelight.

"Jaime Rodríguez—we called him Jim—bought it for her, as a man buys his wife a jewel when she is expecting his first child. A good diamond would have been more suitable, and much less troublesome."

"I think, like Ruth, I would have preferred Hammock."

"He owed her much. But for Rodríguez," said Tollemache solemnly, "Ruth would have been the Princess Modigliani."

She bit her lips to restrain her laughter; he sounded more like a match-making mamma, deploring her daughter's wasted opportunities, than a bachelor of forty-five, discussing the woman with whom, presumably, he was in love. Yes, she had noticed enough to be reasonably sure that Henry Tollemache thought he was in love with Ruth Rodríguez. That tetchy possessiveness, those rather overdone attentions, which she suspected Ruth rather endured than appreciated, were signs of that which he interpreted to himself as love.

"I wish to heaven you would add your persuasions to mine! We might, between us, induce her to dispose of it!"

She waived, with a smile, the proposed alliance.

"You forget I only met Ruth last night. She would have the right to consider me very pretentious, if I presumed to advise her on her private affairs!"

"But, now Jim is gone, there is no reasonable excuse for remaining here!" He seemed astonished at her lack of partisanship.

"I expect Ruth has her 'excuse'—if she needs one? She seems to devote her life to the people."

"She may do more than devote her life——!" She was startled by the shadow behind his words. "I am not exaggerating, Miss Flood; Ruth is in the gravest danger—as is any woman who meddles with the social structure in this part of the world. If she is obsessed by the colour problem—as indeed she is—why should she not put her theories into action back there in Cuba, where she is under adequate protection from her ex-husband's relations?"

"Thanks for the suggestion. I've given you the answer to that before, Henry."

Ruth was standing in the arch of the doorway, in the spread of her bell-like gown. With her small, proud head and vivid face, she looked like a fine miniature of an earlier period.

"Have you got nothing better to do, the pair of you, than gossip about me?" She gained control of her anger, laughed lightly, and moved towards the bell. "Don't pay any attention to Henry; where I'm concerned he's just a fussy old woman. You know you are, darling!" She allowed her hand to brush, as if in apology, his arm.

Suddenly and without warning, he splintered into rage that took Aldebaran by surprise.

"You have been told, times without number, that this is no place for a woman living by herself!"

"Oh, poops, Henry; don't shout."

"I will shout!" Incredibly he stamped his foot. "You may be indifferent to the risks you run, every time you go into those stinking cabins, every time you handle a diseased woman! But you have no right to disregard Diamond!"

"I have looked after my daughter for fifteen years." She lowered her voice deliberately. "I'm capable of looking after her for another fifteen, if necessary—which isn't likely. As for myself—will you get it into your thick head that I know what

I'm doing ? I take no risks that aren't taken ten times a day by the nurses in our own hospitals. The conditions I sometimes have to work under are, I'll allow you, worse than theirs ; I take so much the more precaution. I know you're squeamish about these matters, Henry, and I'm sorry to fling them in your teeth, and Aldebaran's ; but you drove me to it—and now, perhaps, you'll let the subject drop. It's hardly an agreeable prelude to a dinner party ! And I'll give you leave to start on me again, if you like, when the number of hospitals for coloured people equals the number of our own in this county ; when I can send my sick people straight off to the clinic with the assurance they'll get as quick and good attention as any white ; when the State appoints medical officers whose sole job is to look after the workers on the plantations. Then, may be, Henry, I'll listen to you. Then may be I'll consider passing Hammock over to somebody who knows more about running it than I do——"

" I have not said you can't run Hammock," he muttered. " What I repeat is—this is no place for a woman, young, attractive, and known to hold views that run at odds with local prejudice. How do you know how many of the people you entertain in this house are secretly your enemies ? One day, perhaps, you'll find out ! " He ran his hands grotesquely through his hair. "If you must play the fool at Hammock, get a man—get a man ! "

" Really, Henry ! " Her smile broadened, but her eyes were still bright with anger. " If I didn't realize this is one of your strange examples of a proposal, I'd be seriously offended. It's a most immoral suggestion."

" To hell with your flippancy ! " astonishingly cried Henry Tollemache.

" And to hell with your fussing." Ruth was suddenly cool. She turned to a glass to touch her hair.

" You call it fussing—in the face of this ? " He dragged from his pocket the crumpled sheet of paper which Aldebaran realized was the one she had previously seen in Alger's hands.

" Henry Tollemache." There was an authority in Ruth's

look and attitude that sobered him. " Once and for all, I won't have my friends dragged into our private disagreements and made uneasy by your bogey tales. You're worse than Little Orphant Annie ! Listen : that's the Lenwoods arriving. For heaven's sake go brush your hair and take that mean look off your face."

She grimaced at his retreating figure, then flung her arms round Aldebaran.

" Forgive that, honey ! It's only one of our spats."

" He must be crazy about you," Aldebaran was drawn to observe. " I can't, offhand, think of a man among my acquaintance who would take a pasting like that from a woman, and trot off on the next breath to do her bidding, as though she'd been patting his head."

" I guess Americans are different." Ruth spoke absently. " See, honey : don't let Henry give you the jitters. He's a little bit right, but mainly wrong. Now you've got a glimmer of why I want to get Diamond away as soon as I can find a suitable place for her : somewhere where she'll be disciplined without getting her dander up—and where they'll give her a hint now and again that there are things worth living for besides dates and dress shows ! You know," she added with her candid smile, " that was partly my reason for asking you here. They say English boarding schools are marvellous——"

" I hold no brief for the ' great ' boarding schools : they're too hot-house, too specialized—and they stink of snobbery," scowled Aldebaran, not at all beguiled by the prospect of being responsible for Diamond Rodríguez in England. " I'd have thought you had as good over here——"

" Oh, we've got plenty of our own brand of snobbery ! " smiled Ruth, as she turned to greet her guests.

It isn't real, thought Aldebaran, as, a little later, she looked round the candle-lit room at the women's dresses spread like flowers across the couches, at the tall, good-looking men with long, frosted glasses in their hands. Ruth's butler, followed by her maid with a big satin pin-cushion stabbed with jewelled pins, was offering a flat wicker tray of camellias to the women, who chose, with a ripple of discussion, corsages to match their gowns. No, it's not real ; it's just some lush novel of the Deep South.

The air dripped sweetly with compliments, grew anæsthetic with soft voices. Even Diamond, shedding the bored attitudes of a young woman just back from Europe (" Oh honey, I could just die of envy ! " " Sugar, I can't wait to see the heavenly clothes you've brought back ") slid under the gentle rain of flattery into her impersonation of the Southern belle. Was it a little too sweet, too candy-cloying ? Had Henry Tollemache —now recovered, at least to appearances, from his snubbing, and supporting his evidently accustomed role as the genial host—had he slipped some drop of henbane into the sugared draught, that left acid on the palate ?

" It's just too marvellous, to meet the authoress of *Bells on her Fingers* ! That's my dream book."

" Isn't it just Ruth, to give us a treat like this ? "

" My, how do you ever think of your stories, Miss Flood ? All—my—life "—the speaker sighed—" I've just ached to write a book : but there never seemed a thing to write about."

With their waxen skins, their somnambulistic gestures and the wistful echoes of their voices they seemed to be under the spell of the swamp, of the cypresses, of the Spanish moss. Under their delicate sparkle lay melancholy, deep-rooted as a chronic disease. They laughed, and it was in their laughter ; its shadow stirred in their smiles. And they were no more aware of it than one is of a creeping disease, until the day comes when the doctor is called in, to seal one's fate . . .

The beautiful, accursed South.

At the farther end of the room, the group of men round Henry Tollemache seemed by contrast curiously solid, curiously sober.

Chapter Seven

I

THE MOON rose and flooded the formal garden with creamy light. The senseless reiteration of a katydid competed with the chorus of frogs from the pool whose onyx shield was mosaicked with the broad leaves of lilies, each bearing its starry cup of pearl. The servants had started their singing.

She cast a quick look round her : at the men, the red tips of their cigars briefly lighting their satisfied faces ; at the swinging rockers, at Henry Tollemache fixing a cushion behind Ruth's head. How did they manage to look, all of them, as though there were nothing in the world but swinging on a moonlit porch ? Even Diamond had settled, for the time being, into stillness ; she and the two college boys who had been invited for her benefit, and whom she had consistently ignored throughout the evening, occupied the long slung couch opposite their elders. The three young, uplifted faces were pale, and the moonlight gathered in Diamond's eyes gave them a look of blindness. It was beautiful, Diamond's listening face.

" Oh Eve, weh is Adam ? " whispered the sweet voices.

> " *Adam in duh gyarden*
> *Pickin up leave.*"

" Oh Eve, weh is Adam ? " came the wistful query.

> " *Adam don answer*
> *Pickin up leave.*"

Then a pause ; then a banjo, jonking into a rhythm that went deep down and beat like a pulse in the blood. The moonlight ran a strip of silver down the toe of a satin slipper, absently tapping out the rhythm.

" *En uh wonduh wey Mosey*
    En e mus be dead
    En uh wonduh wey Mosey
    En e mus be dead
    En uh wonduh wey Mosey
    En e mus be dead
    Oh duh chillun ob duh wilduhness
    Moan foh bread."

" Oh Ruth, your darkies are cute. They sing much better than ours," whined one of the women.

" Like it ? " Ruth turned to Aldebaran. " Is it the first time you've heard plantation singing ? "

(Paris. A hot red room. " Nineveh, Tyre, Babylon "— Memphis Blues. Then a red-haired boy hitting the notes as if he hated them—" Upon the mountain Jehovah spoke.")

" It's lovely—but so terribly sad."

One of the men laughed.

" That's how they like it ! The less they've got to be sad about, the more they lay it on." The speaker's tone struck a discordant note in the midst of the sweet voices. " I guess none of Ruth's niggers has got anything to be sad about ! " He seemed determined to rub it in. She saw Henry Tollemache's hand close over the sharp angle of his knee. Ruth got up and went to call through the screen.

" Oh Pete. Let's have ' We'll walk around the fountain.' You can't call that sad ? " she referred back to her guest.

The boy they called Don supported her.

" And what about ' Ef yer wanter see dat preacher tickle ' ? "

Tollemache laughed, and leaned forward to encourage him.

" I don't know that one ; how does it go ? "

Don leapt from the hammock and went into a coon imitation —wagging knees, flapping feet, rolling eyes : cruel and clever. Everyone except Aldebaran laughed at this impersonation by a white boy of a coloured boy letting out the lightness of his heart on a sun-baked levee.

K

" Ef yer wanter see dat preacher tickle
Change a dime an gib him a nickel
Ef yer wanter see dat preacher laugh
Change a dollar an gib him half
Ef yer wanter see dat preacher holler
Change a fire an——"

"Oh, stop him, somebody—he's slaying me!" Laura Lenwood lifted her handkerchief to her streaming eyes.

"Oh religion, oh religion so sweet"—through the laughter and the levity and the patter of Don's agile feet came the grave strophes from under the window.

Aldebaran thrust out her foot, ostensibly by accident, and tripped the capering boy back into the hammock. Among an outcry of dismay and apologies, Diamond rose, rather grandly disassociating herself from the horse-play, and, followed by the other boy, Morton, still apologizing profusely for the clumsiness of his friend, went to lean against the pillar behind her mother's chair, looking out at the moonlight; her profile, cut against the shadow, was as aloof as an angel's. The rest of the group settled down again to listen to a solitary voice, rich and noble, that dominated the humming of the chorus.

" One moment in glory
To satisfy my min'
A-settin down wid Jesus
Eatin honey an drinkin wine
Marchin roun de throne
Wid Peter James an John
But yo body
got to lie
in de groun."

Two of the servants came back, to pass coffee and liqueurs again round the circle; their white suits and white gloves were immaculate, their movements soft and humble. They kept their eyes down, never raising them to those of their white masters. Lenwood was a little drunk, all were laughing and talking loudly, the laughter of Harriet Cort had grown shrill. Through all these went the servants, their human dignity as private and intact as their human bodies inside the sheaths of white that preserved, as completely as possible, the sensibilities of the white folk from the sight of, or contact with, dark flesh.

"Where's Diamond?" said Ruth suddenly.

Morton Lenwood volunteered she had gone for a wrap.

"She wouldn't have me fetch it for her," he justified himself to his mother's raised eyebrows. Both boys had returned to the hammock. It occurred to Aldebaran that they had been there quite a while, and that it must be at least a quarter of an hour since she missed the flicker of Diamond's gown from behind Ruth's chair.

"I'll go and look for her." Henry Tollemache intercepted Ruth's movement towards the door. She hesitated, lifted her shoulders, and, recalling her hostess's duty, returned to the rocker. As her small hand clutched the arm of the chair, a sudden diamond-flash betrayed her uneasiness to Aldebaran. To the latter's surprise, Tollemache was standing in the doorway, looking directly at her; he made an almost imperceptible motion of the head as he withdrew into the room. Aldebaran could see his shadow thrown by the candlelight, and realized he was expecting her to follow him. She murmured casually about fetching a wrap as well, and drifted through the door.

"I thought," he said with his unreal smile, "you might care to look at the magnolias; they are magnificent in this light."

She waived this with the flat inquiry,

"Do you think Diamond has gone out?"

"You had better put this round you"—he picked up a woman's gauze shawl from the hall bench. "The mosquitoes are savage—and you will have to change your shoes when you come in."

They walked for a little while in silence, before he observed, more to himself, apparently, than to his companions,

"If Diamond is in the house, as she may be, she will turn up when she pleases—I thought those boys rather bored her tonight ! " He turned his head towards her. " Did you gain that impression ? "

" I think, at Diamond's age, elder men are often more attractive than boys." She shrugged her shoulders.

" I am afraid most of her swains will find themselves at a disadvantage, since her return from Paris. Well, if a yearning for romance in the abstract has lured her out upon the greensward "—he narrowed his eyes across the long, pale lawns—" the spectacle of you and me, taking a moonlight stroll, may absolve me of the charge of spying on her movements. It is important that Diamond and I should continue, for the present, on friendly terms——"

If it struck Aldebaran that the pace at which they were walking was hardly to be classified as a stroll, she allowed the description to stand, remarking without much originality,

" It's a difficult age."

" It's difficult blood," said Henry Tollemache. " There, by the way, are the magnolias."

There they were, a pile of silvered snow, their perfume spiring into the humid air. Round the end of them, they came within sight of the swimming pool, a long rectangle cut in a sweep of turf fringed with cypresses. The surrounding hammocks, with their striped awnings, had been covered with their tarpaulin slips for the night, and the cane chairs were stacked in the summerhouse. On the moony surface of the water floated a rubber raft and a diving ring ; there was no other sign of occupation, except——

" What's that ? " said Aldebaran, pointing. They bent over a pink swimming suit, which she recognized as the one she had previously seen in Diamond's hand, and a wrap of towelling. " That means she's somewhere about, doesn't it ? " Her senses informed her that he was disturbed, rather than relieved, by the discovery.

The tiles of the pool, which she guessed to be blue, turned it into an immense moonstone at their feet. Delicious, too flat in moonlight on that sheet of crystal.

" Would you care for a dip ? " he astonished her by asking.

" Of course !—but——"

He led the way quickly to a pagoda-like building at the head of the pool, opened the door and switched on the lights, and found herself looking into a spacious dressingroom fitted with shower and toilet accessories. A selection of swimming suits hung on a rack over a dryer.

" Ruth and Jim used to be very fond of swimming by moonlight ; we don't use this much now, but, as you see, it is kept in order."

" Yes ; but I thought you wanted me to be with you——? "

" Diamond will come here," he stated positively. " I may possibly miss her—in fact, I shall certainly miss her." Again his lips curved into their cold smile. " She will have a pleasant surprise, when she finds you in the pool ! "

After some hesitation, she stripped, and forced her slim body into one of the suits which fortunately, although Ruth was much smaller, adapted itself to its present wearer's long limbs. In the door of the cabin she paused, to switch off the lights and sense for a moment the delicious solitude. What a place, to live and to write in !—but for the ever-present danger of surrendering to its languid beauty.

She pulled on the cap, fastened the strap under her chin and let herself into the water with a little gasp ; she was too tired and limp to dive. She swam a few strokes and, presently, turned over and floated. In the distance she could hear Tollemache, whistling up a dog. So that was what he meant, by " missing " Diamond. Amateur Machiavelli ! He was giving her full warning. " Tanner ! Tanner ! " His voice grew faint in the distance. She gave so sudden a start that she sank and had to strike out again.

What a fool I am : I ought to have remembered. It's her pony—what was it ? Peppermint. Of course ; that's where she is. How far away were the stables ? At any rate, on the evidence of the pink suit and the wrap, Diamond meant to come back and swim.

She was a long time in coming, and the water, tepid as it was, began to feel chill. Treading water at the deep end, Aldebaran listened. The din of the frogs made it hard to identify any but positive sounds, yet she imagined she heard a footstep brush the grass. Once again she swam the length of the pool.

She had just touched the bar at the end, and was about to draw herself upright, when it came—directly, it seemed, over her head.

"For Christ's sake—do you want to get me killed?"

The voice was male: so smothered in fear, or anger, that she could not recognize it. A moment later, she heard the lower branches of the cypresses crackle, as though someone were thrusting his way through.

She looked round, and Diamond, in her white dress, her hair swinging over her face, was crouched on the curb of the pool, wetting her swim suit.

If she called out suddenly, the girl might fall in—and serve her right! thought Aldebaran. Her elbows braced on the bar, her legs floating, she waited for Diamond to turn round. She did so, saw the figure in the pool, and her mouth made a black hole in her face.

"Oh-h-h!"

Aldebaran dropped her feet and climbed casually on to the curb. She saw that Diamond was both frightened and angry.

"I thought I'd like a moonlight dip." She picked up the wrap she had left on the grass—forgetting it would be sodden in dew—and, walking back to the pagoda, heard Diamond whirl after her.

"You were spying on me!"

"That's the second time you've accused me of spying: do you remember? I shouldn't call a swimming pool much of a place for spying myself." She switched the lights on her own smile and Diamond's small, dishevelled face, distorted with hate. I believe she would like to kill me, thought Aldebaran, interested, rather than dismayed, by the discovery. "Come in. I rather think your Uncle Henry's round somewhere."

"Who cares about Uncle Henry?" For all that, she slammed the pagoda door and leaned against it, her hands behind her back, glaring defiance. "For that matter—who cares about you ? You can tell if you want to ; it makes no odds to me ! "

Aldebaran turned round in the robe on which she was towelling herself. "Shut up." The dispassionate tone was no less disconcerting to Diamond than the brevity of the remark. "You won't get anywhere by being rude to me, so save it for somebody you can impress with it."

"I don't care about impressing people ! "

Aldebaran grinned broadly.

"Don't be foolish ; you live for it. Pass me my slippers."

The breath whistled audibly through Diamond's teeth.

"Why should I ? I'm not your servant ! "

"Pass me my slippers." The grin had vanished. Their eyes met. Diamond writhed, bent, and tossed the slippers to Aldebaran's feet. Patently, she was baffled. No one had ever spoken to her like that in her life. No grown-up person had ever treated her with that curious, adult contempt, the sort one only bestows on a contemporary. It was galling, yet, in a way flattering. It added to the flattery that the contemptuous person was tall, had a lovely figure and wonderful lingerie : through her rage these impressions penetrated, against her will, Diamond's consciousness.

Aldebaran stooped, snapped the clips of her garters casually to the tops of her stockings, and began to set her wave. So far as she was concerned, Diamond was not there.

"Well : are you going to tell ? "

She let the thin chiffon circle of her gown fall over her shoulders, and made sure of the line of the pleats before replying.

"You can hang my suit to dry with yours."

With a smothered exclamation, Diamond flung the bundle of wet pink wool that was still in her hand on the slab under the shower. That, said her gesture, is as far as hanging goes with me—and you can do the same with your own ! Aldebaran meditated on whether to press the point, and decided to let it go.

"All right." She shrugged her shoulders. "So long as you don't repeat tonight's antics, I don't mind standing by the evidence."

Diamond drew in her breath, but pride would not allow her to accept the concession outright.

" After all, it's no business of yours, is it ? "

Aldebaran allowed her eyelids to droop ; it lent her eyes an expression that made Diamond cringe.

" I'm not my cousin's keeper, if that's what you mean. It was Alger you were with, wasn't it ? "

" So what ? " Defiance flamed up again.

" So nothing," said Aldebaran, as if the subject bored her. " Only—another time—I mightn't stand by the swimming pool story."

Diamond laughed suddenly, shrilly.

" What a fuss ! " she said scornfully. " Anyhow, you won't be here."

" Nor shall I," said Aldebaran calmly. She turned with her hand on the light switch. " ' Do you want to get me killed ? ' That was a funny sort of thing to overhear, wasn't it ? " Diamond started ; her face grew crimson. " It doesn't sound like the kind of thing a boy says to a girl, in the way of an innocent friendship. That, anyhow, would be your Uncle Henry's view, I fancy."

" You're going to tell Uncle Henry ? " Her voice rustled with terror.

" I'm going to write it down on a sheet of paper "—she watched the girl's face—" complete with its context : you know —time, place, characters. And seal it. I'll give it to Mr. Tollemache before I go, and ask him to open it if—well, if you perform any more of these nocturnal antics."

" What a positively *filthy* thing to do," whispered Diamond. " Why, it's a sort of—blackmail."

" Don't use words you don't understand," said Aldebaran coolly.

Suddenly the child panicked.

" Why—he might open it any time—just for curiosity ! Oh no, cousin Aldebaran : you can't—— ! "

She melted at the pitiful appeal ; when she spoke again, her voice had lost its aloofness.

"Look, Diamond. I'm a grown-up person. I'm bound to take a grown-up's point of view. I've promised to tell, or act, a lie for your benefit tonight, but I'm not doing it for your sake. I'm giving you a chance to get yourself out of this mess—whatever it may be about—you're in, because I think you're old enough and intelligent enough to do it without other people butting in. You're old enough to have dignity, and behave like an important person, instead of acting like a little, cheap tramp, chasing someone who doesn't want to have anything to do with you——"

"Oh, but he does!" she quivered; but a tremor of her eyelids told Aldebaran that she had found the right note. "You didn't understand—I'll tell you all about it, if you like——"

"For God's sake——!" Aldebaran's lips twitched into a smile, as she passed her cigarette case to Diamond. "Keep your own secrets! It's one of the first principles of being grown-up."

II

Ruth had suggested Mah Jong; she had to make up to the boys for Diamond's disappearance. She had also, somehow, to wipe the look off the faces of Laura Lenwood and Harriet Cort. Their girls would not quit on their mothers' dinner parties; above all the Lenwoods, who lived on the outskirts of Charleston, would not allow any daughter of theirs to go wandering alone in the moonlight. Don's parents, too, the Frasers, who were frankly eager—more eager than Ruth herself—that the two children of adjoining plantations should make a match of it. Mrs. Fraser had pleaded neuralgia, and her husband had driven her home. No doubt the pair of them were talking, saying things about Diamond that no mother cares to have said about her daughter—matchmaking aside.

"Diamond's fretting about her pony," she said casually, as she sat down with the boys and Laura; Harriet said she was tired of Mah Jong, she would prefer to look over the photographs Ruth had brought back from Europe. The two men, withdrawn from the group, continued to rock and mumble on the porch. "I expect she's teased Mammy into going down to the stables with her." A polite murmur covered their unbelief. At this rate, Harriet's eyes distinctly said to Laura's, Diamond Rodríguez will be getting herself talked about.

"Is Phil back yet, Ruth?"

"No. Didn't I tell you his wife's had an operation? It seems like it's not quite gone off on schedule. Phil sounded a bit high when he rang last night." She set up her pieces and waited for Laura to play.

"You must miss him. How do you manage?"

Harriet's eyes were narrow, like a sleepy cat's, as she fanned herself with an enlargement of the Papal palace at Avignon.

"Alger's all right; he's only got to follow Phil's routine." Smoothly she caught Harriet's dart and held it, proving it harmless.

"Still, you can't depend on him, like—— ?"

"I don't depend on anyone, excepting myself!" she laughed.

Chandler Cort turned his head from the porch and looked at her. His face was dull, but there was a keen look in his eyes.

"Don't depend on yourself too far, Ruth. Henry showed us the letter."

"Did he? Trust Henry to play the skeleton at the feast." She slid the West Wind on to her ebony rack and smiled at Cort.

"When's Phil back?"

"How should I know? I guess it depends on Lucy."

"Can't you get someone to tide you over?" put in Lenwood. He got up from the rocker and came into the room to stand behind Laura.

Ruth laid her hands on the table, leaned back, and looked with raised eyebrows at the attentive faces of her guests.

"Hey, what's this? Have I lost my grip, or something?"

"There's quite a few things been happening, while you were in Europe." Lenwood's brows were knitted, as though he were angry with her, but she smiled back at him.

"I know, I know. Phil turned in his report. I've heard all about the trouble at the saw-mill and about Milo Adkins' funeral." Her mouth hardened. "So what? The law had its way with Milo, and I guess that's got nothing to do with his wife and children. Listen, Len: when first we settled here they told us we could do pretty much as we pleased on our own property, but not to start meddling with outside affairs. I've gone on that understanding—more or less——"

Chandler Cort, following Lenwood, broke in on the conversation.

"More or less! You've got away with murder, because you're a woman, and because Jim was popular: and neither of those arguments goes, as you dam' well know, with the Ku Klux."

Laura Lenwood gave a little scream and her husband glared at her.

"You took the Adkins in against everyone's advice," went on Cort, "and put them in that cabin by the old mill. And now, Henry tells me, you're fetching them up to quarters——!"

"I took Marie Adkins and her children in because her husband was on the run and she was seven months pregnant. They hadn't a crumb of food in the house, and she lost her baby partly through starvation. I've shifted her up here tonight because she's dying. Upon my soul!" cried Ruth, "I don't see why I've got to justify my actions to you and Len! You'd both take a pretty poor view of it if I were to butt in on your business!"

"That's true enough." Harriet came unexpectedly to her support, and Ruth was silent, mistrusting Harriet's partisanship. "Ruth's got plenty of people to advise her: she's got Henry, and she's got Phil—and, of course, Alger!" she concluded, with a brilliant smile at her husband.

Cort, who, during Ruth's speech, was pacing the long carpet between the Mah Jong table and the window, stopped short.

"Then here's another bit of advice for you, ma'am! As soon as Phil gets back, get rid of Alger Dunnock. If you don't, as there's a heaven above us, you're going to regret it."

"Get rid of *Alger*!" She let out her indignation full at him. "Honestly, Chandler, you must let me choose my own staff! I understand, of course : you've been talking to Henry, and he's got a gripe against Alger. Well, both Phil and I happen to disagree with him. Ever since he came to Hammock, Alger's been honest, hardworking and dependable. He understands the people——"

"I'll say he does ! "—with a sneer, from Cort.

"——and time and again we've found his advice invaluable in dealing with the problems that come up now and again in the cabins. Alger's worked himself up from a kind of jack of all trades about the place till he's Phil's right hand. If you think that because of an abominable prejudice I'm going to turn Alger adrift, you can think again—all of you. And now, for goodness' sake, let's change the subject."

The door swung suddenly open and Aldebaran—her head flung back, her eyes shining, her hands extended in apology—swept into the room. She knew the value of a dramatic entrance. The men's eyes lit with involuntary admiration, and the women found themselves reluctantly responding to the charm Aldebaran well knew how to produce when it was called for. It had been rather casual of Miss Flood, departing into the garden like that with Henry Tollemache !—but that was probably the way one behaved, if one was a celebrity. They murmured greetings which were swept away in the torrent of Aldebaran's apologies.

"I simply couldn't resist—Ruth, you'll never forgive me—it was shockingly rude of me, but this entrancing place goes straight to one's head—and I haven't swum by moonlight for years."

"You don't say you've been in the pool? " Ruth was smiling, but her eyes were anxious.

"I'm afraid we've made a most terrible mess of your dressing-room." She paused to allow the pronoun to sink in.

"Where's Diamond ? " demanded Don.

"Gone upstairs to tidy herself." She accepted a drink from Lenwood.

"You've both been swimming ! " howled Don. "Say, Morton, what do you know ? They've been swimming ! "

"Oh you couple of meanies ! " roared Morton.

"Don't tell me Henry joined you?"—Ruth's laughter was light with relief.

"Isn't he in?" She gave a glance of surprise round the room. "He showed me the magnolias, and took me to the pool, and then, I think he took Tanner for a walk"—that disposed neatly of the time-lag, with the minimum of direct lying.

It was annoying of Diamond not to come down again. Ruth sent up her maid Barbara, who came down with the news that Diamond was tired and had gone to bed. The boys departed, crestfallen; Henry came in; the Corts and the Lenwoods made their farewells.

It was two in the morning when Aldebaran dragged her exhausted limbs up the stairs.

III

She was back in Cone Street. Queerly enough, the street was silent. There was not a living soul in it but herself. Somebody had swept up all the garbage but dust lay in a thick powder across the sidewalk. As her feet scuffed in the dust it rose in a cloud about her knees and clung to her clothes like an infection. She tried to shake it off and it came at her again. She was walking up some steps. Inside was a room like Marie Adkins' cabin, with a piano in it. Lee looked up. His face shone like a pearl out of the dust, his red hair was ruffled down to his eyes. His shoulders were hunched and the lids of his eyes were swollen. The eyes themselves looked raw. He had his hands on the piano. She looked down at his hands. They weren't there. Just two stumps.

She was back in Paris. Under the glass roof of the atélier the heat was stifling. She felt herself suffocating. Her body was flattened out like lead under the pressure of the heat. Tishy was there—because it was her studio, and she had been very kind. But she would not open the window and let the air in. And Naimbanna, in a bright yellow shirt that threw reflections

into his throat of polished ebony, was trying to hide a bundle
And there were bitterness and quarrels and reproaches—from
which she awoke with sweat in the roots of her hair.

Then for a little while she lay in the darkness, listening to the
thin whine of a mosquito and the cracked note of a nightbird
An argument between the boys and Diamond had been part of
the evening : Morton, who was a swing fan, had brought a
new record and insisted on their going into Diamond's sittingroom to play it over before dinner. They came back arguing.
The best piano record of the last ten years, said Don, grandly
asserting his seniority over the other two, was Pax Hathaway's
" Jehovah Blues." It wasn't Pax Hathaway's, corrected Morton.
Then whose was it ? Don had heard Pax Hathaway's band play
it at Palm Beach. Everybody played it ; but Morton, the
specialist, was able to inform them that it was composed by a
fellow whose name he happened to have forgotten, but it was
the only thing the chap ever wrote. Morton had the original
recording at home ; he could go back and get it, if they liked.
Jiminy Peter ! They didn't want to listen to an old thing like
"Jehovah Blues."

. . . Lee's white face came again out of the dark. It isn't
true, is it ? She found herself battering at him. It isn't true,
it isn't true ! The smile was wiped across his face like a sneer.
They were in a room with a bed. Lee made as if to pull her on
to it. First she resisted. Then she did not resist. The moon
shone on the smooth white bone of Lee's shoulders. She was
crying, crying . . .

When Ruth came in softly, about eleven of the following
morning, Aldebaran was lying flat on her face. An untouched
breakfast tray was pushed down to the end of the bed, on which,
and flowing to the floor, was scattered an unopened mail.

Drawing a curtain, Ruth let about an inch of light across the
room. Her experienced eye recognised more than ordinary
exhaustion in the flattened lines of Aldebaran's body.

Who were these Andersons, anyhow, who had sent her
tearing all over Charleston yesterday ? and why was she so
cagey about them ? Ruth was shrewd, and her instincts more

often right than wrong. Perhaps they weren't the kind that is supposed to do credit to a famous author. So what? The British are queer; they've spent centuries working up what they call class distinction, and it sticks to them closer than a bug. They despise snobbery, and practise it on a scale inexplicable to the average American . . .

As though her presence communicated itself to the sleeping figure, Aldebaran raised herself on her elbows, pushed back a falling lock of hair, and turned her head.

" Hallo."

" I'm just going to order you some more breakfast."

Ruth dropped the curtain and the room darkened again. She knew what it felt like, to be taken at a disadvantage after a white night. Aldebaran's voice, thick and dry, intercepted her move towards the bell.

" No—don't do that—ugh! I feel muzzy. What time is it?"

" Getting on. But take it easy. You can have lunch in bed, if you like."

" Jesus!" Aldebaran flung back the covers and stumbled to her feet; she crawled to the dressing table and peered into the glass. " Sweet Jesus, talk about ' one of the ruins '!" She whistled the tune as she dragged a comb through her hair.

" Well, if you insist on getting up, I'll send Barbara to fix your tub," said Ruth presently, and closed the door quietly behind her. To her surprise, Diamond was loitering on the landing.

" Hallo, honey; do you want me?"

" I was going in to tell cousin Aldebaran good morning."

" Uh-huh." That was good, in its way; Ruth wondered what methods Aldebaran had employed to make friends with her antagonistic daughter. " If I were you, honey, I'd lay off for a while. She's had a bad night; she's not feeling so good."

" Okay." But she lingered discontentedly.

" You'd better go practise your *étude*, Monsieur Ralli is coming tomorrow," Ruth reminded her, and closed the door of her own room on Diamond's grimace. This maternal business was tough. But it was better, she told herself, than it would have been in Cuba, with Jim's relatives all spoiling the child and filling her up with notions of her own importance as the heiress of the Rodríguez fortune. Now, at least, that danger was out of the way. Jim and Maria would have sons, and Diamond's portion would be insignificant beside theirs.

The soft, scented water had revived Aldebaran : she was back on the chaise-longue, a brew of black coffee beside her, the envelopes of her mail scattered on the floor, when Ruth returned to the room.

For no reason, she found herself telling Ruth about Orlando.

" But, honey, why don't you accept him ? You're crazy about him, and it's a good match, isn't it ? " said Ruth seriously. " You'd make a cute peeress. Most of the ones I've met don't look the part, but you're as cut out for the strawberry leaves as old Queen Alexandra was for the crown of England."

" It takes something more than a good figure to get into Debrett."

" Poops ! What about the chorus girls that marry earls ? If it comes to that, look at the earls who've married Americans with no more qualification than poppa's dollars."

" It's not that," said Aldebaran slowly. " You see—Orlando's first wife didn't give him a son. I'm supposed to repair the omission."

" For crying out loud, don't tell me you're scared of bearing children ? "

" I'm scared of bearing the heir to Paragon."

" How do you mean ? "

Aldebaran shrugged her shoulders.

" In point of fact, I'm not—eligible."

" You mean," said Ruth, after a pause, " you've had an affaire."

Aldebaran blew a smoke-ring and spoke through it.

" Listen : I'm twenty-nine ; I grew up through the war——"

" Sure." Ruth's voice was steady.

" As a matter of fact—it was an American boy."

" He didn't give you V.D. ? "

" No—not that ! "

" Well—hell——" Ruth's laugh was a little forced. " Were you crazy about him ? "

" One is—at sixteen."

" As early as that ? "

" Well, that's when I fell for him. Actually, it happened after the war—in Paris."

" Gee—Paris——! " She laughed again, softly. " I'm beginning to get the layout. This is where the Andersons come in, is it ? My, my ! They're bred-in-the-bone Quakers—purer than driven snow ; all the girls marry without knowing the facts of life, and the boys are brought up to look on females as something holy—but now I think of it," broke off Ruth, " I never heard about any of the Anderson boys going to Europe. They certainly weren't in the fighting, though I think Charley ran the Red Cross and was on the list for overseas——"

" His name wasn't Anderson." She interrupted the flow of conjecture. " That was a married sister—and they couldn't possibly be related to your friends. I know hardly anything about them, but I think—I'm sure—Lee came from quite obscure people."

" You know how it is over here : you're ' obscure,' as you call it, today, and in the headlines tomorrow," was the easy rejoinder. " Still, the Andersons—they're Henry's friends, not mine, though I happened to be at school with Mercy— they've gotten themselves into the Social Register a couple of generations ago. So where do we go from here ? What's eating you, honey ? " asked Ruth gently. " You're not still in love with him, are you ? What we fall for in our ' teen-age ' generally turns out pretty dim when one comes to years of discretion ! " She flung her arms suddenly round Aldebaran's shoulders. " Did it have consequences ? "

" If you mean, have I got to present Orlando with a bastard —No," said Aldebaran in a dry voice.

" Then, for goodness' sake—drop it ! You can't rub out a stain without it leaves a ring : but who's going to notice the ring unless you draw attention to it ? " Ruth got up from the

L

deep chair in which she was seated. "I'm going down to quarters to see how they're coping with Marie. I'll be back for lunch——"

"Let me come! I've only got to slip on my dress," said Aldebaran.

The sun was at the zenith when they were half-way down the tidy row of cabins—tidy so far as walls and roofs and porches were concerned: the vagaries of Negro temperament scattered the immediate surroundings with household detritus, mussed the interiors, and drew no more than a smile of toleration from Ruth.

"It's their life, not ours," she excused it. "None of our people has got less than a couple of rooms and every cabin has its own privy. When we came, they'd just got holes, with a board clapped across them; there wasn't even an attempt at decency. And the water was carried from the swamp. We had thirty cases of typhoid and twelve deaths, our first summer. Jim put in a pipe line and every cabin's got a tap. It's no use cussing people out for being dirty unless you make it tolerably easy for them to be clean."

In the middle of the row they came on a shack so dilapidated, so obviously disreputable, that Aldebaran averted her eyes; far, however, from being embarrassed, Ruth burst out laughing.

"You know the 'Before' and 'After' advertisements? Phil's always nagging me to pull that down. It's one of the things we don't happen to agree on: isn't it, Alger?"

The youth who sauntered at their heels smiled faintly. Aldebaran wondered what, on her first morning at Hammock, she had found attractive about him. His dust-coloured hair was faded by the sun, and his shoulder-blades poked out the thin shirt he was wearing. From a distance, riding his horse along the rough lane he had looked like the young Phoebus. In the fierce, midday light he had the jaded and unhealthy look of a city youth, with a background of saloons, crude lodgings and dubious women. His skin was a thin yellow web over the fine bones of his face; there were purple circles under his heavy-lidded eyes. Something of this seemed to strike Ruth.

"Goodness, Alger, you look all in! Did you get any sleep last night—with Peppermint?"

Under its tan, his face went ashen; he hitched his shoulders and muttered a disclaimer of her solicitude. Ruth turned again towards the disgraceful cabin.

"It's old Smyrna. She's the mother of Diamond's mammy. Come in and see her—but hold your nose!" she cautioned.

Out of a bundle of rags stuck a head so small, so dry and wrinkled, it appeared to be mummified. A grizzle of grey wire went over it like a cobweb. Like an old owl on a branch, blind as an owl, lids and lips lost in the innumerable lines of the face—the bundle squatted, motionless.

"Hallo, Smyrna," said Ruth.

The lines of the eyes cracked unwillingly open; two slits of amber gum filled slowly with filmy pupil. A strange sensation went through Aldebaran: the eyes were blind, yet they could see; the pupils were a blur, more blue-ish than black, yet filled with some obscure and antique enmity, that struck at her with the exhausted venom of a dying snake.

"It's a fine morning, Smyrna. The boys ought to put you out in the sun." Ruth dropped a little package in the old woman's lap. "There's some more tobacco for you, and I'll send Perry to fill your pipe. Smyrna was born a slave," she said, as they emerged, to Aldebaran's relief, into the hot, spiced air. "Nobody knows how old she is—she's been on the plantation longer than anyone, white or black, remembers. Phil thinks she must be over a hundred; Mammy was born when she was over forty."

"A hundred—but——"

"Yes. I thought of that too."

"She might be one of the slaves who came over in our ships——"

"It's possible," allowed Ruth, "but not probable. Rodríguez and Flood weren't the only traders, even in 1830. I got Jim to look up the books, and we found Smyrna and her mother were bought from a Texas dealer and brought to Hammock in '37." She opened her parasol and tilted it between her face and the sun. "You'd like to see the records, wouldn't you? They'll interest you—more than they interest me."

"Yes. I've got a fancy that we—Floods—are paying for all that."

"You're not the only ones." Ruth turned to the youth who continued to lope at their heels. "That's all, Alger; go get your dinner—and you can get the books out afterwards; I'll bring Miss Flood to see them, some time this afternoon. There's no answer to the colour problem," said Ruth, as he strolled away. "I used to think there was. I've tried to find my own personal solution—and I'm pretty sure I'm damned for it. I'm what they call 'a do-good-er'—which means I'm as unpopular with the Negro high-ups as I am with the whites. I try to give our people a square deal, but I can only afford to keep a given number. The surplus ones have to get out. They find themselves paying taxes, and getting nothing for them. They're told they have a vote—and get shot if they insist on their privilege. They're told they're equal with whites in the eyes of the law, and God help them if they believe it. A white man commits a crime, and a Negro's framed for it. You can't blame them if they're bitter because here, on Hammock, they're brought up to believe such things 'don't happen any longer,' and a coloured boy has only to behave decently and honestly and he's given an equal chance with a white. Why don't you tell me to put a sock in it?" Ruth's smile was drawn tightly across her small face. "This is boring you to death; you don't have a colour problem in England, do you?"

Don't we? She thought of the *Obango*; she thought of Orlando's letter that she had left in her room, of Uncle Joe struggling with the complications Purcell-Flood left behind them, in the relentless drive for the prosperity of the Company and the shareholders. Colour problem: it was like an open sore on the face of humanity.

One of the house boys was loping along the plank walk.

"What do you want, Tom?"

"Mistah Henry, ma'am. He say, yo' please come'n de libery. Yo' please come quick!"

She waved the boy away, smiling dryly as she linked her arm
into Aldebaran's.

"Come and listen to me being put through my paces by
Henry! It may amuse you."

"Why should it 'amuse' me? Has he any right to 'put
you through your paces'?" asked Aldebaran, as they turned
towards the house.

"If you mean, am I going to marry him—No. I'm still
quite a lot in love with Jim."

"In spite of divorcing him?"

"I was the one to blame," admitted Ruth. "When we
took Hammock, the arrangement was, we were to go back to
Cuba for four months of the year. It worked out while Diamond
was a baby : Hammock in summer is no place for a little child.
I put up with it on her account, but I guess I wasn't meant
for Spanish family life. When she was about five, I suggested
Jim should take her back and leave me to look after things
here."

"That wouldn't be popular—either with him or the family,"
she suggested.

"There was practically a civil war about it. I went back to
fight the matter out and they treated me like a leper : I'd outraged
all the conventions. We were stopping at the summer place ;
Rodríguez from all over the island converged on us like a flock
of crows ; at one time we had seventeen stopping in the house,
and as many more parked out in the local hotels. I must say
Jim behaved mighty well ; he stood by me from start to finish,
and did all he could to stop them bullying me. But I was just
poison by then. To start with, I was a Protestant, and that's
the same as criminal to the Cuban Rodríguez. And I was acting
like a Protestant and a loose woman, wanting to stop here by
myself for four months."

"How did Jim take that?"

"Well, he was kind of staggered. He was fond of Hammock,
but it never meant to him what it meant to me ; he wasn't
shocked, the way I was, by how the place all tangled itself up
when we weren't here : and he never saw how I was trying to

build something up, and getting more and more discouraged,
each time we came back, to find all the work undone."

" So what happened in the end ? "

Ruth laughed.

" I came back with a duenna ! One of Jim's old cousins,
told off to keep an eye on me, while Diamond and her father
stayed on the island. And that, of course, was the beginning
of the end."

" So I should say. I don't see you settling down with a
female policeman."

" We managed to keep the peace until Jim came back. Then
she started in. There was nothing she didn't accuse me of—
from extravagance to immoral relationships with poor Phil.
Of course Jim told her off; he was used to the first and didn't
believe the second. We sent the old bitch back—but things
weren't the same, between Jim and me. Next year there was no
argument; I was left behind, and Diamond—I had a hard
fight for this—was sent up to Catholic relatives at Cape Cod.
Jim came back once more, and then—we both knew it was the
end. It's not easy for Catholics to get a divorce."

" I expect Rodríguez money smoothed that out."

" If I'd given Jim a son it wouldn't have been so simple.
Diamond—didn't matter ! There's Henry waiting for us," she
interrupted herself. " Goodness, his face is pink, even from
here. I warn you," said Ruth, deliberately slackening her pace,
" when Henry's agitated, he's apt to be quite discourteous.
Ah, but I'd forgotten : you had a sample of that, didn't you,
last night ? "

IV

He slammed the door behind them, and turned the key in
the lock. His face, Aldebaran observed, was not pink, but a
mottled crimson, and crowded with such a complexity of emotions that it would have been embarrassing to look at him, had
Henry Tollemache not been past embarrassments.

"At last—at last!" he stammered. His lower arms were jerking, the hands performing odd little movements of futility: betraying, thought Aldebaran, the weak, fussy creature under that monument of dignity.

"I left word we had gone down to quarters." Ruth settled herself coolly on a couch and picked up the cigarettes. "Why didn't you have the bell rung, if there was any special hurry?"

"And advertise to all and sundry that there was trouble up here? There's quite enough ado already, with the sheriff's visit——"

"Jameson's here!" Startled, she put down the cigarette unlighted. "Whatever for?"

"Cort rang him, and he came right out, expecting, naturally, to see you."

"Naturally! Well—really——!" She gave a little laugh of annoyance. "Who told Cort to ring?—and why didn't he mention his intentions to me? I don't want to get nasty, Henry, but at this rate I'll pretty soon be obliged to define my own position as mistress of Hammock!"

"That is not necessary," he was beginning, when she cut him short.

"Well, where's the sheriff?"

"He's gone; he was on his way to that shooting trial at Skeeterville. Barbara went to look for you; it was ten minutes, at least, before we discovered you had gone out."

"If his business was important enough to bring him right up here, you'd think he could have waited a little longer," said Ruth crisply. "Well, you saw him, I suppose——?"

Tollemache's face had returned to its natural pallor; he sat down, swung one leg over the knee of the other and placed his fingers delicately tip to tip; looking at the two women, he appeared to forbid them to remember his former agitation.

"I showed him the letter."

Ruth turned casually to Aldebaran.

"That paper Alger handed me last night when we got in; do you remember? Of course you had to chatter about that last night!" she accused Tollemache. "As though it were anything more than a silly and rather nasty joke! You know perfectly well the boys round here have been playing that trick for ages—whenever they're at a loss for something to do——"

" The sheriff happens to agree with Cort and myself that that note is not a piece of boys' fooling. It was most unfortunate—although not, perhaps, from his point of view—that Alger also was out of the way."

" Leave off sniping at Alger ; he was walking round quarters with us," snapped Ruth.

" Jameson appears to think that he knows something about the person who threw that note in through the office window," said Tollemache evenly.

" How should he ? The window opens on the swamp and there's no way round, except through the water. Whoever brought that letter waded neck-deep through the swamp, and by the time Alger got to the window there wasn't a soul in sight. Naturally there wasn't! Whoever it was had only to drop back five or six steps and duck in the reeds and he'd be invisible."

" That, I suppose, is Alger's story——"

" He told it to you himself, didn't he ? "

" He made no attempt to go after the fellow."

" He didn't drop out of the window into the swamp, if that's what you mean. He got Phil's gun and loaded it, and waited far enough back not to be seen from the water. He waited long enough to be sure the person had got away. After all, there's alligator in that water! Nobody would hang around longer than he had to. And Alger would have fired if the reeds had stirred."

" Personally, I doubt that he would have taken the risk of shooting," sneered Tollemache.

Ruth sighed impatiently.

" Look here : if what you and the sheriff are hinting at were true, he needn't have given me the letter."

" I have never accused him of neglecting his obvious duties."

" You've never given him credit for loyalty ! " she retorted.

He looked at her with exasperation.

" Very well; I'd better tell you what the sheriff says. If

you get rid of Alger Dunnock, he can handle this business in such a way that no one will be the worse for it. If you don't— well, he can handle it; but it will not be good for you, or for Hammock."

She gave her short, contemptuous laugh.

" You could have given him my answer to that. How often have I to tell you, Henry, that I won't be bullied or ordered about in my dealings with the people who work for me ? " She turned back to Aldebaran. " Sorry about all this mystery ! "

" The letter was a threat of some sort, I suppose ? "

" We've had them before." Ruth shrugged her shoulders. " Three years ago the schoolhouse was burned down. It didn't matter, because it was old and disgraceful ; it never ought to have got that way. Jim rebuilt it——"

" What's this, anyhow, about Alger ? I don't seem to follow you there."

" A pretext," said Ruth, before Tollemache could speak. " Alger's been given more authority since Phil went away, and certain people don't care for it ! Alger has to do business for me in town and act as my liaison officer in various ways on the estate. Since Phil was away, he's never stopped working ! " she cut short Tollemache's attempt to utter. " Why should he spend the whole of last night up with Peppermint ? That's Jake's job ; if he doesn't attend to it, that's just too bad—for Jake. I'm capable of dealing with slackers—whether they're black or white," she concluded.

Henry Tollemache said,

" You make it very difficult for people to help you."

" Henry dear : I know it sounds ungracious, but when have I ever asked for help ? "

" You will never ask," he retorted, " until it's too late."

" And not even then ! " she defied him. " When you've worked hard to build a person up : when you've received in return the most perfect loyalty, the utmost devotion to your interests—you don't suddenly throw the person out, on account of the objections of people who are only actuated by vicious prejudice."

"*Do you want to get me killed?*" The scene by the swimming pool swam back into Aldebaran's memory. If Ruth knew about that, would she still support Alger? Knowing the little she did, was it her duty now to betray Diamond? Ruth was obviously waiting for her to speak.

"Well, it wouldn't seem to be their business——"

"They imagine it is. You didn't realize, did you? I didn't tell you because I wasn't sure if it would alter your attitude towards him; I never tell people who come here as guests. Alger's a Negro."

She heard herself say,

"It's—not—possible"—and heard Ruth's laugh.

"Several generations back, a great-great-grandmother, or something, was black. According to our law, that makes Alger a Negro. There's not a thing to show it—not even his nails. He's as patently white, in looks, manners and character, as you or I. Even I, who am pretty sharp about colour, hadn't a suspicion until he told me.

"That's one of the things that make me stand by Alger," Ruth continued. "I respect him for not 'passing.' You know what that means? Coloured people who hide their origin and live as whites are said to 'pass.' Nothing would be easier for Alger; anywhere north of the line he'd be accepted as a white boy, and enjoy all the privileges of the whites."

"Then why in God's name not let him go?" burst out Tollemache. Ruth looked at him quietly.

"You're very fond of the South, aren't you, Henry? Its customs and its traditions are knitted into your blood. How would you feel if you were suddenly ordered to go North? to pull up your roots and set fire to your Southern traditions and live and act like a Yankee for the rest of your life? You know you'd die sooner than submit to conditions that went against all your sentiments and your upbringing."

"The comparison is outrageous. I refuse to accept it!" he returned icily.

"Do you suppose your class has got the monopoly of feeling for the South? Alger would sooner put up with all the humilia-

tions his colour brings on him than quit the land where he was
born and bred."

"Then let him put up with them! Send him back to the
job he was doing when you pulled him out of it and brought
him to Hammock."

"Let him keep a news-stand or clean windows or drive a
garbage truck? Make him say 'sir' to any white trash he
meets and step off the sidewalk for fear of touching a white
woman?" said Ruth scornfully. "Put him back in a com-
munity where he's as much despised by the blacks as the
whites? You call yourself a humanitarian, Henry Tollemache:
do you seriously suggest I send Alger back to all that?"

"If no other argument will avail "—his voice rose above
hers, beating it down, "what about Diamond?—what about
your daughter?"

Aldebaran's heart thudded at her breastbone as she watched
Ruth's face sharpen and lose its delicate colour.

"You're being absurd, Henry. Diamond's a foolish child.
Don, Morton, Alger: they're all one to her—male specimens
on which she's bent on sharpening her claws."

"The Frasers would not be flattered to hear their son's name
coupled with that of a coloured youth!"

"I'd as soon trust Diamond with Alger as with Morton,"
said Ruth stubbornly. "And rather not trust her with any
young man at all, at present! I allow she's going through
a very trying stage, that they probably handle better in Cuba
than we do here. Still, I've got my plans—and they've got
nothing to do with the subject we're discussing. What else
had Jameson to say?—or did he exhaust the whole of his
ingenuity on the notion of dismissing Alger?"

Their voices blurred; Aldebaran curled in the corner of the
sofa, saw a fine, neat profile, a little sharp and bird-like; jutting
nose with thin nostrils; a thin-lipped mouth. Straight hair in
untidy flakes of dusty tan over a high, flat brow. Rather flat
grey eyes pushed in like discs of tin between puffy eyelids. A
slack, graceful body. How closely, without knowing it, she
must have observed the youth, Alger Dunnock, who, without

knowing it, now confirmed the truth against which she had struggled so long.

Suddenly Ruth's voice soared from the low altercation with Henry Tollemache.

"What sort of a hypocrite do you take me for, when my daughter, my own daughter, according to their reckoning, is a Negro?"

Chapter Eight

I

THE TWO women bent over the document Ruth had spread on the table between them, the broad page, unfolded, but retaining the stiff rectangles of the folds that fitted it between its leather covers.

Slowly, from the imposing Rodríguez genealogical tree, going back into the twelfth century, Aldebaran Flood plucked the lines and brackets referring to her own people. Her eye travelled from step to step, down from that seventeenth-century Hercules Flood, from whose eldest son Jonathan she was descended, until it reached John Flood, b. 1877, d. 1900, under which, in pencil, someone had added her own name : Aldebaran, b. 1901.

Then, in a parallel column, starting again from Hercules and Hercules' youngest son, James, came Matthew, b. 1734, m. *Sheba, a Negress* : and, down from them, María Cayetuña, who married de Lorcha, and her daughter, María Pia, who married Carlos Rodríguez, and their children.

Two more generations down from the third son, who married his cousin, came Santiago Maria Xavier Jaime Mateo de los Flujos Rodríguez y Torrevelludo Baviera.

" That's Jim," put in Ruth. " Isn't it an ungodly name ? —and he inherited—I don't know whether you know ?—nearly a quarter of a million from one of your ancestors, an old boy called Quentin : there he is, away to your right—when he was a child of seven. Have you lunacy, on your side the family ? Nobody except one of Jim's great aunts had ever heard of Quentin Flood, till it boiled up her mother had had some sort of a flirtation with him, back in the dark ages. Mark you, I say *flirtation* ; it's all you'd expect the Rodríguez to admit ! But may be Diamond's more closely related to you than we know. Well, here you are : Jim married me, Ruth Harland, and we had one daughter, Diamond——"

" Did you know, when you married Jim ? "

" Do you think I'd have—Yes," said Ruth slowly. " I would have married him. But I'd have taken darn good care we had no children. The Rodríguez don't make anything of it, of course ; there are very few of the old criollo families that haven't got a touch of colour somewhere. I understand now the fuss made by my family when we cabled them Jim and I were married. I was holidaying with some friends in Cuba——"

" But how did you find out ? "

" I saw this, just by an accident, about the time Diamond was conceived. Jim couldn't understand the state I was in ! "

" I should say it was enough to bring on a miscarriage ! "

Ruth smiled faintly.

" Things don't solve themselves as easily as that. I'm as tough as a horse. Well, then we had to come back to the States, because my mother was very ill, and I made Jim swear he wouldn't tell a soul. We planned to go back to the island as soon as Mother was better, but she died, and I was pretty ill—her death, and the shock about Jim, and Diamond well on the way. It was years since I'd been in the States, and I'd forgotten how much I loved it down here——"

She began slowly to fold the sheet, pressing down each fold with her small, capable hands.

" Well, then the doctors said I mustn't travel, and there was nothing to do, while we were waiting for Diamond, but read and ride around, looking at places. That's how we found Hammock. It was Jim, first, who took a fancy to it ; he was like that about houses. I can't remember offhand how many places we've bought and got rid of after a few months—when the bloom, for Jim, had worn off. There was the palazzo in Venice and a lovely house in the old quarter of Pekin. We owned a Moorish place near Marrakesh for about six months, but they wouldn't get on with the alterations Jim planned, so we just got out and left it to them. May be it was because I was tired,

and feeling ill with Diamond, that I felt I wanted to settle down.
Hammock was so quiet and shut away ; summer, you know, and
steamy hot. All the other plantation houses shut up and the
families gone to the beaches. We never saw anyone for months
except the Negroes, and I used to look at their faces and listen
to their voices and think of my baby."

Aldebaran's hand shot out, caught Ruth's and held it tightly.

" Poor Jim. I gave him hell. He couldn't understand my
panic, or see why we make such a fuss about colour in the
States."

" But—Ruth—all those generations back——? "

" Of course; but I was raised on old wives' tales and I daren't
ask any of the Charleston doctors ; I didn't even dare ask our
family doctor in New York."

In the long glass opposite Aldebaran could see herself, see
her white dress spread calmly along the couch on which they
were sitting. She forced herself to think of Diamond—of the
lovely child, proud, wilful, full of the allure of her youth and sex.
Diamond—rated as a Negro.

" Diamond doesn't know, of course ? "

" Nor ever shall, if I can help it. That's one reason I want to
get her abroad, before this marriage business comes to a head.
May be," said Ruth sadly, " I'd have done better to leave her in
Paris. Candidly, my child just scared me. Every man we met
—young, middle-aged, elderly—went for her ; her head was
completely turned before we'd been there a week."

" But wouldn't a good finishing school have taken care of
that for you ? "

Ruth shook her head.

" Nothing would hold Diamond Rodríguez, if she made up
her mind to break away. It wouldn't feel so good, to get a
cable to say my child had bolted with some visiting fireman
who'd caught the eye that was supposed to be riveted on the
Nike of Samothrace. She's moderately fond of me—and that's
the one ray of hope on the situation. That's why I decided to
keep her home till I'd found some sort of solution. And I've

got to find it quick! I guess you've seen enough to realize that."

" Alger ? "

Ruth shrugged her shoulders impatiently.

" Alger's the least of my headaches. Diamond's a thorough little snob, and for all her devilment, she'd never go for Phil Curtis's underling. But there's young Don Fraser—over heels in love with her, and the Frasers all for it. There never was a nicer boy than Don, and the Frasers are our best friends ; how can I open my mouth and tell them why Don and Diamond can't marry ? You just can't live in these parts if you've got one drop of coloured blood in you."

" But Ruth, there must be hundreds like Alger——"

" So there are," said Ruth grimly. " Sweeping sidewalks and washing pans. Those who succeed in ' passing ' live their lives in mortal terror of being found out. Plenty go north, and find themselves worse off than they are down here. As many as can afford or can wangle it quit the country. Hundreds of them joined up with the forces for the sake of getting to Europe, and never came back——"

" I know all that ; but surely, in your position, you can protect Diamond from that sort of thing ? "

" No position can save you, if somebody makes it his business to crawl up your family tree and finds colour somewhere among the top branches ! " was the bitter reply. " I guess you British just can't imagine the hell of being piebald in this country of ours—how all of your life turns into mean little subterfuges and evasions, and you don't dare be intimate, or even make friends in a casual way——"

Both women turned their heads quickly as Henry Tollemache entered the darkening room.

" Ruth, where is Diamond ? "

" She went down to the laundry with Mammy. What's the matter ? "

" Ah—that's all right ; though they should be back." He consulted his watch. " It's getting dusk."

"Mammy won't let her stay out late. Has anything happened, Henry?" She rose to lay her hand on his arm.

"One of the boys has found something painted up on the end of the schoolhouse." He was trying to control his breathing.

"Sit down," said Ruth calmly, "and give your heart a chance. Ought we to ring the police?"

"I've done so already; they should be on their way by now. I've also put a call through to Washington. Phil has promised to be on the night train."

"Oh Henry, I wish you hadn't!" She tried to conceal her irritation. "If something's planned for tonight, he can't possibly be back in time, and if Lucy has another of her hysterical relapses it will burn Phil up to leave her!"

"It's his duty to be here. Dunnock can't handle the situation if the people panic. I've sent word to the Frasers, and Alec and Don are coming; they'll probably pick up Cort on the way. And we'll have to put a guard on the farm and the stables."

"But that's a job for the police, surely?"

"The police can't get here for an hour—at the earliest, and you must realize these devils may be somewhere about the place already. No doubt they'll wait for darkness, but they've got plenty of cover. Look there." He pointed from the window; two of the houseboys were scudding furtively across the space between the house and the outbuildings. Out in the lane stood a mule-cart, half-toppled in the ditch; there was something disquieting about the deserted vehicle—mule and driver vanished—toppled there in the dusk, its shafts raking the last pale yellow band of daylight that ran along the horizon.

"I suppose you can shoot." Ruth turned to Aldebaran; she might have been assuming that she could play a game of Bridge.

"Not with any certainty of hitting the target," Aldebaran admitted. "We don't get much practice in England. But I'm not scared of firearms and I don't mind carrying a gun—if it's likely to make an impression."

"This is hardly a time for flippancy." Henry Tollemache was scowling at her.

M

"Who's being flippant?" Ruth cut in. "You say the police can't be here for an hour, and long before that it will be dark. By then, with luck, Alec, Don and Chandler will be here, and there's us, and there's Alger. We can manage to cover the farm and the stables, the garage and quarters; the out-buildings will have to look after themselves. Somebody'll have to be responsible for the house—though I don't fancy they'll have the gall to come up here——"

"It would be foolish to count on that." Tollemache rang the bell, and a scared butler appeared. He tried to smarten himself under Tollemache's irate eye, but his hands trembled along the seam of his white trousers. "Pete, you are to load the guns and lay them on the gunroom table."

"Yah-yassuh!"

"Don't be an idiot, Henry!" said Ruth as the door closed behind the quivering figure. "Don't you see he'll blow himself to pieces? Come along, cousin; we'd better do the loading—and you can find Alger," she added to Tollemache. "He'll be in his office, unless somebody's told him——" She halted to look at the sunburst clock over the door. "They ought to be back by now—Diamond and Mammy. I think I'll run the car down and pick them up; it will be practically dark under the trees."

"Why can't I do that?" She grasped with relief at an opportunity for action. "The laundry; isn't that the building behind the schoolhouse? You pointed it out to me yesterday when we were coming home."

"No, that's where we keep the ploughs and things. The laundry—you turn off to the right, just before getting to the schoolhouse bend, and there's a narrow track, and the laundry's at the end, close to the creek." Ruth spoke absently; she was looking for a servant, but the hall was empty. She opened the door herself, and a curious light flowed in, almost like an invasion of water, pushing the shadows down the long hall towards the door that cut off the servants' quarters. Usually that door was closed, but today it stood wide, and the white-tiled passage beyond gaped like the throat of a snake. There was not the least sound down there, from whence usually came the occasional peals of laughter, the continual gurgle and grunt of darky voices. "No, honey, it's mighty sweet of you, but I'll go find somebody; both Pete and Jake can drive, after a fashion——"

"But if they're panicked it's likely to be quite a fashion, isn't it?" Aldebaran pointed out. "I can be there and back while you're finding them. I like driving and I don't mind the dusk——"

Ruth smiled faintly and shook her head.

"Look, that's my car—the one I drive myself; it's the easiest starter. Lucky Joe's not back from town or it would have been put away. See, honey, get in and start the engine while I tell Henry where we're going, or he'll be agitating like an old hen turkey. I think you're right about the darkies; we'll go together." She turned in the archway of the door. "I shan't be more than a minute—and we'll give Alger a honk as we get down near the creek; he'll hear it and know he's wanted. Do you want a wrap or anything?"

"Goodness, no—it's stifling!"

She waited for Ruth's figure to be swallowed in the dusk of the house, and ran down the steps.

While waiting for the engine to settle into its steady purr, she occupied herself by letting down the windows; a sweaty, scented heat—unseasonable for the time of year—poured in, and, gasping, she wondered whether to wind them up again or to depend on the draught of the movement. The faintly illuminated dial of the clock told her the time: twenty of seven. (Three months ago she would have called it "twenty *to* seven.") As the minute hand crept slowly towards the quarter, her sense of suffocation increased; the gigantic liveoaks with their cascades of moss enclosed her as in the heart of a petrified waterfall; yet water carried the suggestion of coolness. She found herself worrying over the simile. The soundless and unlit house stood there, sucking in the advancing dusk. Where could be Henry Tollemache?—where Ruth?

At ten to seven her nerves cracked. She thrust open the car door, ran to the foot of the steps and called, " *Ruth!* "

Her voice sounded dead; no answer came. Time was slipping by: down the avenue it would be almost dark. Suddenly she took the decision: loosened the brake, let in the clutch, and the car slid down the carriage sweep, across the grid, through the gap in the ring fence and out into the lane, into the difficult twilight. She tried the headlights and found them confusing, the sidelights equally so; her eyes would soon accustom themselves to the semi-darkness, from whose blacker patches shone the tiny torches of beetles. It was good, to be driving away from one's thoughts. Orlando's attempt to make her promise not to drive a car while she was away brought a smile to her lips.

So complete an emptiness and peace lay on the shadowed woods that disturbance was unthinkable. Tomorrow, the train, and Agnes, recovered, waiting in New York, and perhaps a night in a hotel—Agnes would have all the plans in hand—and then the ship, and escape.... In the tops of the pines the motionless buzzards were carved against a darkling sky, already faintly pricked with stars. Escape, and sleep—the ship's doctor would surely have some kind of drug to purchase the oblivion so long denied ...

It was only when she found the schoolhouse on her left that she realized that somehow, in the dusk, she had overrun the turning to the laundry. She put on the sidelights and peered over the bonnet, seeking some place to turn the car. She decided she could take it between the schoolhouse and the front of the barn. As the tyres lumped over the uneven ground, the lights picked up something on the clap-boarded end of the school building: K.K.K.

A little stream of coolness ran down her spine. Did anyone outside the States believe in the Ku Klux Klan—except as an ingredient in a slightly improbable thriller? After recovering from the momentary shock, her professional brain took charge of the incident, began mechanically to weave it into a story. She brought the car back on the road with a lurch and again put out the lights, because here was a clearing, and driving, in the English fashion, on the left of the road, she was less likely to miss the turning when she came to it. It might be as well, now to sound the horn for Alger. Her finger hovered over the button, when a shot cracked out beyond the fringe of the low bushes that bordered the swamp.

II

Bored by Mammy's procrastinations, Diamond loitered near the doorway and at last slipped out. It was an exquisite moment of evening : a sky of pink and golden brocade slid down to the purple line of the swamp and flung salmon-coloured flakes into the waterway which, a hundred years ago, had been the reservoir for the old rice plantation. In that stretch of onyx water were mirrored the flowering shrubs planted by her father—one time when he thought of making Hammock rival its great public neighbours, Magnolia and Middleton : the azaleas, the iris, the lilies Mammy had picked and made into garlands for Diamond as a little girl. Then Jim tired of his project and abandoned it, as he abandoned everything that ceased to engage his errant fancy. But it was still lovely there, behind the laundry, beside the creek across whose bend, a purple rectangle against the sunset, stood Phil's—for the present, Alger's—cabin.

Originally a field hand's shack, Phil Curtis had taken it over, patched up its tumbledown walls and roof and established his office there, for the sake of the outlook across the swamp. From its window one could pick off wild duck, gallinule, an occasional swamp fox or otter ; one could observe, unseen, the grace of ibis and heron, or mark, by upheaval among the rushes, the blundering progress of alligator in the breeding season.

Diamond was forbidden, by her parents and by Phil, to go to the cabin. It was strictly a man's hide-out—and Lucy Curtis was a jealous wife. At the age of twelve, Diamond was already engaging the jealousy of women twice her age. Phil laughed at her and teased her, and managed, all the same, to scare her away from the cabin. His most effective line of persuasion was the fact that the narrow path beside the creek was swarming with moccasin.

All her life, Diamond had been terrified of snakes—a terror fostered for their own purposes by those whose duty it was to look after her. A moccasin, she was assured, would follow for miles, and get its victim in the end ; the rattler could launch its lethal blow from a distance twice the length of its own body. These useful myths prevented the child from wandering off into the swamp, or straying into long grass after too-beguiling butterflies. Every inch of brushwood and every yard of marshy ground, according to Mammy, was invested with the peril of snakes : and if the spectacle of a couple of piccanins charming an adder raised doubts of Mammy's veracity, Diamond was told that little black children were different from little white children, and the snakes knew the difference.

She stood there, looking poutingly across the loop of the creek, at the dull orange blur in the window of the cabin which meant that the lamp was lighted, that Alger was there.

She despised Alger. His failure to rise to the challenge of her charms made her scornful of everything about him which once, in a casual way, she had found tempting. She was not used, when she gave people encouragement, to having them hold off ! Just on this account, and no other, Alger had come recently to occupy quite a disproportionate share of her thoughts. Unlike Don and Morton and the people she met in Paris, he was difficult, and this was tantamount to throwing down the gauntlet to one who had prematurely learned to regard herself as irresistible, so far as the opposite sex was concerned.

She was not in the least in love with Alger ; her vanity and his humble situation on the plantation put him outside her consideration as a suitor. But he was male, and this was enough to render his apparent invulnerability intolerable. How long did he mean to keep up this silly pretence of not being interested in her ? And that ridiculous night, when she teased him until he chased her to the swimming pool, and, just when she had *almost* got him to kiss her, had flung her away ! " Do you want to get me killed ? " What a stupid thing to say ! Who ever got killed for a kiss ?—and how many knights of the olden days would have considered it a privilege to perish for a kiss from their ladies !

Of course, being a Negro made a difference. If people looked white, why couldn't they act white ? Plenty of the children she played with at Grandmamma Rodríguez' looked like little niggers, although they had Spanish names ; at one of the island weddings, the bride had been, in everything but her name and the silken straightness of her black hair, as like Mammy's youngest daughter as possible ; and several of the most fashionable families in Havana were so dark they would never get by in the deep South, in spite of their being absolutely Spanish for generations.

She would !—she would run along the path now, and knock on the cabin door and make Alger come out. She would say she was scared to go home alone in the dark—and see what he said. At this time of night the snakes would be sleeping. Mammy would get into trouble for letting her out of her sight—and serve her right, for dawdling to gossip with Lavinia and Jacinth in the laundry.

Sprays of Cherokee roses caught at her hair and a few frightened small birds flew out of the branches in which they had been dozing. She went on tiptoe, gathering her skirts closely, between towering golden rod and black-eyed susans drained of their colour in the dying light. Her heart beat fast. She gasped when a tough loop of grass caught in her shoe-buckle, tried to kick her foot free and was obliged to bend and untangle the green loop before going on. While she stopped, muttering, to break the grass, she heard, almost at her ear, the small, dry, unmistakable rattle that had stood to her for terror since childhood.

It was as though a bolt, driven through her from head to foot, nailed her to the earth. She was not more than twenty paces from the cabin, but she dared not move ; looking wildly to right and left, she opened her mouth to shriek, and caught the scream back ; it might make the rattler strike at once. She could not see it ; it must be behind her. Would a leap save her ? She tried to remember how long it took for the poison to work . . .

Alger put the account book into Phil's tin safe, looked round to see if he had forgotten anything, and turned down the lamp. He stood for a moment, looking towards the pale square of the window through which, yesterday, the note had been thrown : the note, addressed to Mrs. Ruth Rodríguez, but without seal or envelope, that said " Get rid of your nigger overseer," and followed it with a paragraph of such obscenity that he had been sick and ashamed at the thought of putting it in Ruth's hand.

All day fear had been biting at his intestines, but he had struggled with it, reminding himself that he was responsible, in the absence of Phil Curtis, for the safety of Hammock, and that Ruth trusted him, and, above all, that she had repeatedly assured him that nothing evil could happen to him on Hammock. But the sheriff's visit, its unexplained object, had increased his terror, and he had barely been able to concentrate on the accounts it was his duty, in Phil's absence, to keep. Excellent as he was at mathematics, he had been obliged to go over the columns again and again before he was sure he had not made any mistakes.

He stood there, wiping away the sweat which kept beading his cheekbones. He felt weak with hunger, but he had not been able to touch food all day. His thoughts were disconnected—now concerned with the business of the plantation, now with his own danger, now, with a shudder of horror for the peril he had escaped and of dread for the future. Christ Jesus, couldn't Mrs. Rodríguez see, didn't she understand, the dance Diamond was leading him ? Oh sweet Jesus Christ, to get away just for a while : a long way off—over in England—where one could enjoy a woman and not die for it.

As he stepped out on the path, his heart leapt into his mouth. He clutched his throat and gulped, realizing that what in his first moment of shock he had taken for a ghost was Diamond Rodríguez. Oh the tramp, oh the hell-fired, kissing-sweet, double-crossing little tramp : pulled up there tight in her thin dress that showed her legs and her breasts and all a man wants. He suddenly saw that Diamond's attitude was not natural ; that something was riveting her ; and, a second later, saw what she, from her angle, could not see—the big rattler, swinging gently against the light, taking its time.

Inside the cabin was Phil's perpetually loaded gun. If the girl did not scream—if the rattler did not see his movement out of the corner of its eye and launch its venom out of panic——

The shot was the one heard by Aldebaran at the opening to the laundry track. Diamond subsided gently with her face in the golden rod.

Alger put the gun back in the cabin, locked the door again, and, after a brief hesitation, strode across the dead snake and, rather gingerly, touched Diamond with his boot.

"Get up. Can't you hear me telling you? Get up."

But the faint, although brief, was genuine enough. After a few despairing shakes and jolts, he managed—for all her slimness, she was no light weight—to hoist her in his arms, and began to stagger along the darkling path. They had gone almost half-way to the laundry when Diamond recovered. When she gasped, "Oh, Alger!" he dropped her so suddenly that she almost fell flat, and clutched at him for support. "Oh you great, clumsy pig!" Recollecting their whereabouts, she thrust him away and looked guiltily towards the laundry door, which was shut. She gave a giggle of relief. "They must have run away when they heard your gun!"

"Who run away?" He shook her off him.

"Mammy and the girls; they were all in there, buzzing about the sheriff's visit. That was a mighty sweet shot of yours, Alger," she was gracious enough to tell him. "Another second —just one more second—and I guess I'd have been dead of fright. Right now I'm feeling pretty weak. You'd better give me your arm again."

"You don't want my arm." He tried to avoid hers, which linked itself into his with remarkable vigour for a young lady feeling, on her own avowal, "pretty weak." "What the heck are you doing here anyhow, Diamond? You know Phil don't let you in his cabin."

"You don't suppose I'd bother to come way down this old track to visit Phil?" she mocked him. "You've surely been acting peculiar, Alger, this last few days, and I thought I'd give you a chance to explain what you mean by it."

"I don't have to explain anything to you. I say," he repeated on a note loud with resentment and inexplicable fear, "I don't have to explain anything to *you*! I don't know how you mean 'acting peculiar' and I don't care. How I act's got nothing to do with you and you got no business to come here pestering me."

She gave a wriggle of satisfaction; this was beginning to be interesting.

"You know I like you, Alger, and most boys would take that as a great compliment——" The words were torn from her lips by the sudden blare of a car horn. Diamond leapt as though it had been a shot.

"Gosh—that's the Buick! What on earth's Mother doing down here at this time? I suppose she's looking for me." Two beams of light shot down the leafy funnel beyond the laundry building. Diamond looked wildly round. "We'll have to hide. We mustn't be found here—there'll be a fearful row——"

"You get on and hide. May be I'm wanted." She clutched him again as he tried to thrust her aside.

"You're not going to leave me hide alone in the dark?" she hissed indignantly. "There—over there behind the pines: they'll never see us if we stop quiet." She started to drag him with her, and short of knocking her down or doing her an injury he could not break her grip.

They stood in shadow, close to the immense trunk of a pine, he stiff with resistance, she shivering with excitement and pretended fear, which gave her the excuse to press herself closer to his reluctant body.

The horn blared again; the car had come to a standstill in the opening to the track; its twin shafts of light, brilliant under the tree-darkness, paled out in the clearing, which still held the afterglow from the western sky. A shrill whistle sounded through the tree-trunks, followed, after a pause, by "Diamond. Coo-oo—Diamond!"

"Gee, it's my cousin!" gasped Diamond. "Do you think Mummy sent her? Gee, this is fun!" She giggled and thrust herself into the unwelcoming curve of his arm. " Gee, isn't it getting dark ? I'd be *paralysed* if you weren't with me, Alger ! "

He ought to shout out—give them both away—but fear held him silent. Even Ruth—even she might be suspicious of a thing like this : of him and Diamond alone by the swamp at nightfall. And Henry Tollemache—his enemy—and no Phil at hand, a man to stand up for a man. Phil knew all about this little bitch.

Aldebaran's white dress flashed across the clearing. They watched her, tall and slim, her thin skirts blown back by the breeze from the swamp, rush to the laundry door, drag it open —and fall back from the empty darkness inside. They saw her take a step forward, into the darkness, and heard her call " Diamond," once, doubtfully, as though aware no one would willingly stay alone in that dark hiding-place, with possibly bats or rats to keep her company ; saw her come out, leaving the door ajar, and take a few hesitating steps about the clearing, then start to run back down the channel of light made by the headlamps.

With a sudden impulse of mischievous triumph, Diamond flung her arms round Alger's neck and glued her lips to his.

The light of a torch smashed full on their joined faces. Before Diamond had time to scream, a blow sent her staggering back against the tree trunk. There were men—how many she could not see, nor whether they were men or boys, for they all had scarves or handkerchiefs tied across their faces. Some one shouted, " We'll teach you to lay your hands on a white woman, you dirty dinge ! " and heard a long shriek of intolerable anguish.

III

At the sound of the shot, Aldebaran said to herself, Whatever it is, I must keep my head. The reflex of her foot on the accelerator had sent the powerful car leaping forward, and before she could correct its course she was jammed, half in, half out of a hidden ditch. In her nervousness, she mistook the gears, and, instead of backing, drove the car farther forward, so that, while the bonnet was tilted steeply up the bank, one of the back wheels slid into the ditch which, under its clumps of weed, was filled with slime. She felt the wheel spinning helplessly in mud, while the other held on a crumbling surface. She felt, This is the end! as the engine raced and the wheel refused to gain purchase in its treacherous bed. She could not drive forward for the undergrowth that formed a web like steel wire in front of the bonnet.

By the time she at last manœuvred the car back on the road, she had lost, she reckoned, at least ten minutes—it felt like as many hours—and she dared not speed along the narrow track whose opening she had found at last. Even more disconcerting was the discovery that the flounder in the ditch had disconnected the horn; she had gone some way along the track before she was able to take her attention from the steering long enough to grope for, and find, the old-fashioned compression horn which was located, as though ashamed of itself, under the dashboard.

By now her mind was utterly blank and empty. Every now and then trivial thoughts raced across its surface, like clouds across crystal : as why should not someone be shooting wildfowl on the swamp ? why had it not occurred to her that, while she was reversing down by the schoolhouse, Diamond and Mammy had come out of the track and walked calmly home along the high-road ? For some reason, these eminently reasonable suggestions were too simple to carry conviction. Her palms filled with sweat, and she had to wrap her handkerchief round the driving wheel to prevent its slipping under her hands.

When at last the clearing showed ahead of her, she drew a breath of sheer relief. Calm and faintly golden, after the intense darkness of the track—nothing sinister could possibly have taken place in that flowery opening, beyond which stretched the still swamp to the yellow edge of the sky. She called, and no one answered. Whistled, and still no answer came. Of course ; in over-shooting the track, she had missed them. But she would just run down to the laundry and make sure, and,

incidentally, see if there was a place to turn in, instead of having
to back all the way down the narrow and twisting path.

The empty darkness of the laundry for some reason revived
her fear. The steamy hiss of the swamp grated on her exacer-
bated nerves. She suddenly felt she was watched. She cried
out again—"Diamond!" and shuddering at the sound of her
own voice, ran back to the car. If she meant to make the turn
up here, in the clearing, she must do it before the last of the
light went. And then came the scream.

She stood for a moment petrified, one foot in, one out of
the car. Then she dragged herself in, and performed, purely
mechanically, for she did not think about it at all, the actions of
putting the car in gear and letting in the clutch. The Buick
jerked forward against its brake; she flung the gear out again
and raced the engine. Then, in the thin, high shriek that
followed the first, she recognized Diamond's voice.

Diamond was running, her mouth wide open, one side of
her face and the shoulder of her dress covered with blood, down
the path of the headlights. Aldebaran threw the door open
and dragged the weeping and distracted girl into the car; she
fell forward with her face on the driving wheel, apparently
unconscious; Aldebaran pushed her head down on her own
knee, and waited, trying not to hear the sickening noise of blows,
the more sickening cries of a human creature taking more punishment than human flesh and blood can stand.

From the start, she never doubted it was Alger. She heard
herself gulping, heard the breath pumping loudly through her
own teeth. It was Alger. It was Lee. Alger—Lee: two of
them, but the same. In the figure that broke from the bush and
weed to her right she recognized, more by instinct than vision,
Alger: a fluttering, human rag, trailing its blood weakly across
the path to plunge into the thicket on the opposite side. Three
figures clambered after him—three hunting dogs, beastly against
the sky which briefly silhouetted their figures.

A bloody fury burst in her as, regardless of Diamond's head
lolling on her lap, she let in the clutch and drove her foot
down at the same time on the accelerator. The heavy car leapt

like an animal; she had a spasm of triumph as she felt the
bumper thud into a stumbling body. She knew the glory of
murder, as her hand groped for the brake.

One of the men was screaming and swearing, the other lay
still, completely still, somewhere under the front of the car.
Somewhere in the undergrowth the third, escaped, was blundering and shouting on the track of his quarry.

I have got to get out of this car. I have got to look at what
I have done.

As she pushed Diamond gently aside, lifting her head to lay
it against the back of the seat, she felt the girl's blood soaking
into her thigh. What had they done to her?—shot her? She
could remember only the one shot; had that, intended for
another, found Diamond? Her knees were trembling as she
got out; then, suddenly, she was obliged to vomit. She hung
on to the wing of the car, retching helplessly. While she
stood, wiping her lips, there was a loud shout, followed by a
gurgling splash. I can't move, she thought. I can't move ever
again.

She found Diamond beside her. She had wiped her face on
her skirt; it was white like wax, and all the blood had come
from a few deep scratches and a small graze on the cheekbone.
She was clutching at Aldebaran and crying noisily, like a child.

" Come on—come on—let's get back home ! "

" I think that man's dead." She felt completely calm about
it. The second man still screamed and groaned, clutching a leg
she guessed to be broken.

" I don't care. I want to go home ! "

" There's Alger."

" Oh—damn Alger; take me home," screamed Diamond,
pulling at Aldebaran's skirts, trying to drag her into the car.

Her brain felt very clear. The first thing of importance was
to get the car turned and rush Diamond back to the house
before the arrival of the police, but the bodies of the two men
were in the way. To back all the way down the track was too
slow, too dangerous; it could only be a matter of minutes—if
Henry was right—before the police were there.

"Come on, you've got to help me." She bent to grip the shoulders of the dead man.

"Oh no—I couldn't!" Diamond shuddered back as Aldebaran motioned her towards the feet. There was no use in arguing ; she tried, by hooking her nails into the stuff of the coat, to gain purchase on the body. Her nails broke. She let go, panting and shivering. All right ; let that one lie. As she bent over the other, he screamed behind the black rag bandaged across his face,

"Lay off of me ! Lay off, you bitch ! "

She suddenly saw what he was trying to do, and snatching at the hand which was groping in the direction of his hip, she doubled it under at the wrist, felt the hand break open, and heard him scream like a rabbit. She pulled the pistol out of his belt. The curtain of her hair dropped over her face, blinding her, and she felt the bloody wetness of her skirt. She gripped the collar of his coat and yanked at it, feeling him throwing his weight against her effort. She heard herself gasp,

"By God, I'll run the car straight over you if you don't let me shift you."

And she heard him groan,

"I'll see you pay for this ! "

Something crashed through the thicket at her side : something that dripped water and blood, and snatched the pistol out of her hand.

"Oh, Christ—oh, Alger——"

She was deafened by the report and dragged down, as the body she was gripping sagged over in the dust. Everything was darkness and blood, and out of the darkness and blood loomed the travesty of Alger's face, mouthing something she did not understand. Diamond, her fists pressed to her mouth, was whimpering like a frightened baby. That helpless whine was what brought her to her senses. She staggered to her feet and, clutching Diamond, stumbled into the car.

From then on her movements were automatic ; her hands performed the necessary actions, her feet smoothly played their part. The car rolled forward, back a little, rolled forward again

until the turn was completed. Suddenly it roared into the track.
Tree-trunks flashed past. Several times Diamond shrieked and
clung to her arm. The headlights plunged ahead of them like
spears.

It was Diamond who gasped,

" There's something coming—we're going to meet it—it'll
catch us at the turning ! "

At right angles, flashing between the black columns of the
trees, travelled twin bands of light, pointed towards Hammock
Hall. It could be the Frasers and Chandler Cort ; it could be
the police. In the latter case, they were done. There was no
point in stopping, in switching off the lights : they must have
been seen—yes, the other car was slowing down. It was waiting
for them at the opening on to the highway.

" Diamond——"

" It's the Frasers' station wagon ! " shrieked Diamond.
" Oh mercy ; what are we to do ? Can't you shoot past ? "

Don, knitting his brows in the glare of the Buick's headlights, stuck his head out of the window and called a doubtful
" Hey ? " A pang of relief stabbed Aldebaran when she saw
he was alone.

" Keep your head and leave this to me. Hey, Don." She
was surprised at the steadiness of her own voice as she ran the
Buick in beside the Fraser wagon.

" Say, is that you, Miss Flood ? "

" It is. Don, there's trouble."

" There sure is. Mr. Tollemache telephoned my father, and
he's gone to pick up Mr. Cort. Are the police here yet ? "

" No—I mean, I don't know. Listen, Don : I want you to
take Diamond and drive like—like hell." She turned to the
weeping and shuddering girl and shook her slightly. " You're
to do exactly as I tell you." Don had got out of the wagon and
round to the door of the car ; she saw him start at the sight of
the dark patch on the bosom and shoulder of Diamond's dress.
" Don will put you down by the pool and drive straight up to
the house. You're to take off your frock and fold it up in a towel.
Put on one of the robes, as if you'd been swimming. Put another

towel round your head, and pull it down so the side of your face
doesn't show ; if anybody sees you, you can say your cap came
off when you were diving. Stop a minute. Don must wait for
you to give him your dress—and do what you like with it,
Don : you know this place better than I. When you get in,
rush upstairs as though you were frightened of being caught——"
She paused ; was the girl, in her state of panic, capable of
following these instructions ? The chance had to be taken. She
pushed Diamond gently out of the car, and helped Don to pull
her into the wagon. " Look after her, Don—and don't pay
attention to anything she tells you ; she's had a scare and she's
feeling jumpy."

She backed the Buick and waved them ahead. The lights
of the wagon diminished down the tunnel of liveoaks.

Would Ruth's chauffeur be at the garage ? If so, how to
explain the condition of her dress, ripped into ribbons round
the hem and patched with Diamond's blood ? Only Diamond's ?
A shudder ran through her. Her knees were quivering and
her foot slipped on the clutch ; it was difficult, holding the car
straight ; it wove from side to side along the fortunately broad
high-road, now and again lurching into pot-holes that nearly
flung her out of her seat.

The garage doors were shut and padlocked, but a light
burned over them ; she wondered how far the light shone, and
who might be observing her from the dark beyond its radius.
As she switched off the engine she sat for a moment, to regain
her breath and still the thudding of her heart. She must find
something to cover her dress : hadn't there been a dust-sheet
in the back of the car, the day they drove to Charleston ? What
about bloodstains ? And fingerprints ? Once again, panic took
possession of her. It was not safe to turn on the light in the roof,
but she had pushed her handbag down in the pocket beside the
driving seat. She found and opened it with trembling fingers ;
groped for the lighter—Orlando's parting gift—and spun the
little wheel.

So far as she could see, there was not, on the pale buff
upholstery, the faintest trace of blood. The spread of her gown

had prevented Diamond's face and shoulder from coming in contact with the felt. She caught up a piece of her skirt and rubbed carefully all over the driving wheel and the inner handles and all parts of the coachwork Diamond might have touched.

She slid out of the car and stood for a moment, shivering and listening. The bonnet, of course—the bonnet! She slipped between the headlights and the white-painted garage door which reflected them back on the chromium and paintwork. On one side the wing was badly—and obviously freshly dented, where she slid into the ditch and up the bank; there were small marks on the bonnet and bumper that might be attributed to the same cause; and the number plate and bumper bar were out of true.

All these things might easily happen to someone driving a strange car after dark down unfamiliar roads. No trace—she built up her quivering confidence—of blood, or hair, or textile —then it occurred to her that the blood—if there was blood— would be on the tyres.

Away beyond the yard a glow appeared, spreading and strengthening, then blotted out, then lifting again. The long wooded approach to the plantation house deadened the sound of engines, but here, at last, were the police cars.

Between the garage and the back of the house she remembered a swampy stretch, skirted by the highway, but easily enough mistaken by the stranger, short-cutting towards the lights of Hammock through the dark! Aldebaran got in again quickly, started the engine—and drove slap into the swamp.

She almost laughed, as she realized her ruse had succeeded beyond her own intentions. She felt the wheels sinking, squelching, skidding, revolving helplessly. When she judged there was no hope of driving out, she stopped the engine, opened the door, and stepped out—far over her ankles. That took care of the hem of her dress, she thought. But the blood—Diamond's blood—had gone higher; up to her waist, almost to the bosom of her gown. Drawing a deep breath, she let herself sprawl . . .

The round lamps were lit at the top of the steps; moths whirled round them—a cloud of silver petals in the glow. She called out "Ruth!" as she reached the door; wondering if her voice sounded natural, if her laugh would convince them. Ruth and Henry Tollemache came quickly out of the drawing-room.

"Where have you——" began Ruth : and stopped. "My God," she whispered. "What has happened to you ? "

Aldebaran listened to her own laugh ; it did her credit. She had her story ready, but at that moment Don Fraser leapt the steps behind her.

"They're here—Dad, and the police, and——" He stopped, as Ruth had done, his jaw dropping, at the spectacle before him. "Jimini-Peter—Miss *Flood* ! "

Ruth, the first to recover, pushed her towards the stairs.

"For heaven's sake, go get a tub. I suppose we'll all have to face up to the police—but I'll get you out of it, if it's at all possible. Cousin—I'm terribly sorry——"

Aldebaran put her arm round Ruth's shoulders. Suddenly she felt very strong, very secure.

"You don't have to worry. Diamond's in, isn't she ? I'll be down as soon as I've made myself decent."

Chapter Nine

I

"WE'VE GOT to wait until they send for us."

Henry Tollemache's roughened hair lent an odd air of clownish distraction to his agitated face. The three men turned sharply.

"What for?"

His frown ("Remember the women!") flicked Diamond, shivering and clinging to her mother's arm; her head was tied up in a scarf and she had on the crumpled cotton frock she had worn in the morning. Stripped of her sophistication, she was a frightened schoolgirl, perilously near breaking-point. Aldebaran looked at her steadily. She caught the look and sank her teeth into her lower lip.

"Only a matter of routine. I'm sure we are all agreed we owe Miss Flood an apology. This is hardly the kind of reception that Hammock is accustomed to offering its guests!" He made a little, artificial half-bow, half-smile in Aldebaran's direction; she accepted it without emotion.

"Give her material for a new novel," grunted Chandler Cort.

"Don't talk nonsense. What's the matter, Henry?" Ruth lifted her face sharply. "Out with it; we're none of us children—not even Diamond, if it comes to that." She took her daughter's hand firmly in her own. "What have the police found?"

"Two men—dead—at the back of the laundry." Tollemache spoke after hesitation. Chandler Cort whistled softly; Diamond gave a wail—"Oh, Mummy!" lost in Ruth's cry.

"Not Alger?"

He reproved her indiscretion with a furious look.

"No one belonging to us."

"Then where *is* Alger?" she persisted. "I suppose we'll all have to account for our movements in the last few hours? I don't imagine anyone will have much trouble over that!"

After a silence—the silence of innocent people, aware that a slip, or an accidental misstatement, might involve them in an abominable situation—Alec Fraser, the father of Don, said,

"So far as I'm concerned, Chandler's household can vouch for me; can't they, Chan? And we caught up with the police car not fifty yards from the main road. What about you?" He swung on Don, sitting on the fenderstool, looking at the clasped hands which dangled between his knees; the tips of the fingers worked in between the bones, backwards and forwards, as though trying to make grooves in the flesh. His face, like Diamond's, was grey and very young; he did not lift his eyes to reply.

"I came right here after seeing you. I—I didn't see—or hear —anything—out of the way."

"You didn't hear the shooting?" put in Cort.

"I guess I wouldn't notice." As though Cort's eyes dragged up his own, he shot a resentful look at the elder man. "There's plenty shooting on the swamp every night," he muttered. Anyone, thought Aldebaran, would know he was lying.

"You'll have to tell them about your swim, honey." Ruth spoke calmly to Diamond.

"Oh, Mummy, must I?" Terror stared from Diamond's face.

"May be this will teach you a lesson." Ruth patted her daughter's arm, trying to be robust about it. "Well, I'm all right! I've been in ever since lunch, and, until you came back from quarters, Henry, I've been trying to talk some sense into these scared nitwits in the house." She suddenly remembered and turned to Aldebaran. "Oh—my—God!"

Aldebaran felt her lips curving into a smile as she took a cigarette from her case and felt for the lighter. As Henry stepped forward with his own, she remembered where she had left it, and thought, with a calm that astonished herself, That's the kind of thing that hangs a person!

"It's all right; I haven't been shooting people round the laundry! I wasn't going to tell you what a fool I'd been, but —if anyone likes to look, they'll find my wheelmarks round behind the schoolhouse!" She went on, outrageously calm, embroidering the scene. "They'll find the awful dunt in your off wing where I hit something, turning round. And, to top all, I've left the car in the swamp. No, not the big swamp"—as everyone gasped—"the little one, behind the house. I wasn't expecting to have to own up to all this in public, but it's a useful rehearsal for what I'll presently have to tell the police—and it's my own fault for not telling you to start with that I'm a shocking driver, and my last act before leaving England was to pile a friend's car up on a stone wall outside Southampton. Ruth, I'm sorry; I was lost ten minutes after I got outside your ring-fence—and for God's sake send me the bill for the Buick."

There was hardly time for her to wonder if they had swallowed it; for Ruth to say, "To hell with the Buick—it's my fault—I shouldn't have let you"; for Henry Tollemache to make his stiff little speech—"I hardly think anyone will accuse Miss Flood of implication in this unpleasant incident!"; for her to frown aside Diamond's wide-eyed stare; for Fraser and Cort to avert their eyes from her face—when a voice from the door said,

"Mrs. Ruth Rodríguez. The Chief wants a word with you, Mrs. Rodríguez"—and Ruth, with a squeeze of Aldebaran's wrist in passing, went quickly out of the room.

She wondered what she looked like. She had slipped, after her bath, into a plain grey linen shirt-frock, with some idea that it was less likely to strike a note of antipathetic frivolity than any of her evening gowns. Would that in itself be considered suspicious? Ruth was in evening dress; would her guest be expected to be? Between it and the dank curtain of her hair which, in spite of brushing, clung to her temples and the line of her head, her face looked like a bone: like a scraped and polished clavicle, on which someone had painted the black brows and exaggerated scarlet mouth. It was a face, she told herself, to suspect; the blank mask of an adventuress, rendered deliberately empty by the elimination, not merely of emotion, but of sex. So that—the thought had come to her before her mirror—was how a murderess looked. Her own reaction was academic, rather than emotional. She felt the thing taking place again inside her : the breaking from cover of the hunting figure, the welling up of rage—the bitter, heart-breaking rage of sympathy with the hunted ; she felt the downward drive of her foot and the forward leap of the car—suddenly become a lethal weapon—and the shock of the impact of chromium and steel on human flesh ; followed by one instant of pure and quivering triumph . . .

There, opposite her in the glass, was the mask that covered all that ; and was not a mask in itself an object of suspicion ? Was she to go through the rest of her life, wearing a mask through which nothing could penetrate—hate, or love, or fear, or any of the small, tender emotions that redeem the living face from clay ? She felt herself struggling behind the mask which, before anything else, would betray her to the trained and watchful eyes of her questioners. She tried to imagine how one ought to look, on being examined by the police ; obviously not panic-stricken, and not aggressive ; but decently nervous, candid, dependent on the goodwill of the questioner. Not hard-faced, not indifferent, not . . . oh, my poor, my poor Orlando.

She did not notice Ruth's return until the latter's hand fell on her shoulder.

" They want you, honey. Go on—it's all right. They're awfully nice."

She did not realize until she was half-way across the room that her eyes were swimming in tears. There was just time to use her handkerchief before she was looking up at a big figure in uniform, its thumbs stuck in a belt to which—incredible feature to the British mind—were slung a couple of holsters. The shape of the guns hypnotized her ; she could not take her eyes off them.

. . . . It had been too easy.

It was natural a stranger, particularly a celebrity like Miss Aldy-bairan Flood—she forbore to correct the pronunciation ; the questioning, in any case, had almost broken down when it transpired that the speaker was a Flood fan ; had read *Bells on her Fingers* twice and seen the film four times—should lose her way on a plantation the size of Hammock. Folks ought to have their estates sign-posted—what, by the way, was she doing in the car?

Fetching Diamond—as she imagined; not knowing Diamond was in the pool. They thought she might have gone over to the Frasers' (this, by pure chance, was corroborated by Don's saying, when it came to his turn, that they had expected her at tea-time). No, Diamond had not heard about the threat to the plantation. They were anxious when she did not turn up at dusk.

Yeah; but didn't Mis' Rodríguez have a chauffeur? Seemed more likely he'd have been sent to look for the girl.

Oh yes, certainly; Joe; but he was somewhere on an errand. It was getting dark, and Diamond was not supposed to be out alone after nightfall.

" If she'd been at the Frasers' somebody could have brought her back, couldn't they? " put in the one of the two questioners who was the less amenable to the glamour of a famous author.

No doubt they would. The point was, no one knew for certain she was there. Mrs. Rodríguez might have rung up—Aldebaran could not say; in any case, if the Fraser plantation was the size of Hammock, it might have taken them some time to find her. It was simpler to go out and look.

" Now, Miss Flood "—the more friendly one of the two policemen resumed the questioning—" did you happen to hear any shooting when you were riding around? "

Yes, she had heard shooting, but had not made anything in particular of it. There were a great many wildfowl, weren't there, in the swamp? And buzzards; she didn't know much about buzzards, but she had an idea she had read somewhere that buzzards were usually hunted at night. Laughter greeted this statement, in which Aldebaran felt it was safe to join. She knew the overseer shot sometimes from his cabin. (Was this a dangerous admission?) And by then she had begun to realize she was lost, and she was getting anxious about Diamond. Her anxiety was increased by meeting Don Fraser, and learning that

Diamond had not been to their house. She begged him to hurry on and let Mrs. Rodríguez know. And after that—well, she would have to admit she lost her head; she found herself right off the hard road and into the swamp at the back of the house. Yes, indeed—it was too bad! Laughter again was in order. They would have thought so, if they had seen the spectacle she presented when she got back to the house!

"Just one more question, Miss Flood"—when the laughter subsided—"How come none of you went to look if Diamond was in the pool before you set out on this trip of yours?"

"Because she had been forbidden to go there by herself in the evening."

"Any particular reason?"

Aldebaran lifted her shoulders, and let them drop.

"I suppose Mrs. Rodríguez was uneasy. It's rather a long way from the house."

"And she's the sort of kid that does as she's told?" The tone was sceptical; it invited another smile.

"I think I must leave you to form your own conclusions about that—after you've seen her."

That was all okay, and she was thanked a lot, and accepted the loan of a fountain pen to autograph the Chief's note-book: "With best regards, Aldebaran Flood"—a fair specimen of a Flood signature, in spite of the unsteadiness of her hand. It was only when she handed the pen back that it occurred to her that it had given them her fingerprints; she noticed that the Chief did not accept it, but signed her good-humouredly to lay it down on the blotter. They shook hands; the younger and stiffer of the two walked ahead of her into the drawingroom and called out, "Diamond Rodríguez!"

Diamond rose like a ghost, swayed past her with her eyes fixed in terror on the policeman, and vanished behind the closing door. Now—God help them all.

II

Diamond was much better than could have been expected under examination. She was white as crystal and all the bones stared in her face, so that her eyes appeared to have sunk into the depths of her head. She was not beautiful at all. But she answered the questions briefly, and rarely faltered.

Yes, she had been in the swimming pool. No, she wasn't supposed to go there alone after dusk; there'd been a row about it only the day before. Then why did she go? She guessed, because she wanted to.

" What made you come in ? "

" I was scared."

" Go on ; what scared you ? "

" I heard a gun. I was out of the pool by then, and it made me run into the trees and do this." She touched the scars on her face. The two men exchanged looks.

" Who saw you come in ? "

" No one ; I didn't want to be caught ; I went up the servants' stairs."

" What did you do with your swim suit ? "

She faltered for the first time. The younger man shouted at her.

" You heard what the Chief asked you. Where's your swim suit ? "

" If you want to know," blurted Diamond, " I swam naked ! "

Ten minutes later she was sobbing in Ruth's arms—" I want to go to bed ! I want to go to bed ! "—and Henry Tollemache was describing how he walked over to quarters with Joe the chauffeur, who had got back from Charleston shortly after Miss Flood left the house—to calm the people down and tell them to stop indoors whatever they heard ; how while he was there Diamond's Mammy and the two laundry maids arrived in a state of panic, having heard something. His questioners groaned ;

they knew what it was like, getting information out of niggers. All this was only routine work; it was as clear as daylight who'd done the killing—in one case by a clean shot behind the ear, and in the other—well, time would show; it was a mighty hit had driven a man's ribs into his intestines, so he bled to death inside. They'd get that dinge, sooner or later. By then, may be the Rodríguez dame would have had her lesson.

Ruth had gone with Diamond to her room, and, feeling herself an outsider in the conclave between the Frasers and Chandler Cort, Aldebaran went upstairs. There was evidently demoralization in the household; her bed had not been turned down, her bureau set in order or the odds and ends she had scattered in her hasty dressing collected and taken away. She had purposely left her muddied shoes and stockings for evidence in the swamp story; the dress and petticoat, with their tell-tale stains, she had bundled into an attaché case—the only piece of her luggage which boasted a combination lock.

In the adjoining dressingroom her half-filled cases stood on the trestles, in a flurry of scattered tissue paper. Barbara had begun to pack for her in the morning, then the shock of the sheriff's visit, the rush of panic through the servants' quarters, had blown everything out of her woolly mind. Apparently she would have to finish the packing for herself. She began vaguely to fold a few garments, but soon gave it up. She dragged off her clothes, put out the lights and got into bed.

The lights of coming and going cars fanned across the ceiling. The sweep was like a busy intersection on Fifth Avenue. Cars and motor-bicycles were stacked against the tea olives. There was a continual tramp of feet up and down the steps and along the porch. The countryside had emptied itself into Hammock. The moon had risen and silvered the moss, and the noise of engines and brakes drowned the sound of escaping steam which was the swamp; even the frogs were silent.

This is the kind of thing one reads about in stories of the Deep South, in novels on the " Negro problem." It boils up sometimes in short paragraphs in the Press. It has " nothing to do with one "—then suddenly it breaks out, drags one right inside the lives of people like Alger Dunnock, like Janet Jackson, like—Aldebaran pressed her hands down on the soft place between her ribs, where something went on fluttering, making her feel sick. Somewhere in some snake-infested spot, a lost boy was bleeding, perhaps to death—with no hope of escape.

I've killed a human being, thought Aldebaran. A human brute. Somebody will have to carry the blame. *Alger*: the realization went through her like a knife. Alger, if he is caught, will have to suffer, not only for shooting the only witness to what probably no one but I, and possibly Diamond, realizes was a deliberate crime—but for the other as well. And the third man—the one who had got away in the bushes? Did the shout and the heavy splash in the reed-bed mean that Alger had dealt with him too, before returning to finish off his confederate? Alger's face, running with blood, swam before her on the darkness. She flung herself over, crushing her face into the pillows. Alger, who would not run away from the Deep South, which he loved—and Lee—who had run——

Lee, who had loved and deceived her—out of fear. The deep core of fear which lies deep in his unhappy people and is the essence of their un-belonging. Fear that has nothing to do with physical courage, but rises to betray them in their most need.

Imagination, unwinding like a spool of silk, helped her now to trace it all. The Deep South—the little she had seen of it—painted for her the picture that had formerly been a blur: of the little red-haired boy, son of a white father, and perhaps high yellow mother, growing up in the No Man's Land of the half-breed, with the resentment swelling inside him that eventually resolved him to run away from home. Lee had told her as much as that. " I ran away when I was twelve." It sounded like Lee, with his tuft of flame, his strange cat's eyes, his grin and the thrust of his square jaw. It sounded real—like Lee's halting descriptions of how, as a boy, he had played the piano on the river-boats and got himself jobs, now and again, in saloons. He had told her these things unwillingly, because she asked ; she did not ask much, because she felt his reluctance, and felt

that he was suspecting her of prying. But, sitting in the wheel-
chair on the terrace at Paragon, he had talked readily enough of
how, when the war in Europe broke out, and it looked as if
America was not going to come in, he and another boy made
up their minds to hike up into Canada and join up with the
Canadian forces, for the sake of getting to Europe and " joining
the circus " !

That did not frighten you, Lee : not the tear-gas or the mud
or the sight of men's torn bodies or the possibility that you too
might hang one day, like a ragged bird, on the barbed wire.
None of those frightened you. You and Orlando used to joke
about it—in the high rooms at Paragon which were all turned
into hospital wards ; and Cat and I, too young to be V.A.D.s,
were supposed to "amuse" you. Draughts and dominoes
and cards and your brown hands and your eyes and something
growing between us that made me shy and terribly excited and
afraid of anyone guessing. And the day you were lifted to the
piano and played "Jehovah Blues."

Then came the time when you did not have to be lifted and
sometimes you came through to the Medallion Room and once
or twice we were by ourselves. I made you play to me because
we were both shy and talking was difficult.

" Do you see pictures, Lee, when you play ? "

You knitted your brows at me, wondering what I meant.

" Nope," you said, when I insisted. " I guess—it goes kinda
this-a-way. First I start off with ' Honey Boy,' or ' Joe Turner,'
or one of those old Pace and Handy numbers ; and I'm hotting
it up and tapping it out with my foot—then—it's like something
starts inside me. Yeah, right in a roomful of folks, all laughing
and shouting and dancing, I'm as lonely as hell. Right with
guys hitting me on the back and women giving me the green
light—I'm scared like I could fall through my pants. I got a
grin on my face—I can feel it there—and there's tears running
down the back of my throat and filling me up inside—right there
while I'm shouting the words and the folks are laughing fit to
fall down—and then my mouth's open and nothing's coming
out—because all the scarey feeling and the loneliness has gone

down in the notes. I can hear it—and I'm wondering how the hell folks can go on dancing the blues, blues, blues ! "

I can hear it all, Lee, as though you were saying it now : it was the only time you really let me inside—and the next moment you were angry with yourself and with me, and you slammed the lid down on the piano and limped out of the room.

You ran away, Lee, and Alger didn't ; and if you hadn't, you might have been dying tonight in a swamp with your enemies trying to get at you.

Then there was the last night, the night of the dance— " Valencia " and " Alexander's Ragtime Band " and the old " Destiny " waltz—when because you couldn't dance much yet, you and I found ourselves alone together in the Œil de Bœuf. I wasn't used to drinking, but I suppose the one Martini I had had went to my head. I started to show off. I pointed to the painting of *La Incognita* in the corner, and said, " She's supposed to be an ancestor of mine. She had an affaire with one of the Saxes and nobody ever mentions her ! " As you did not seem to understand, I added, with a foolish giggle, " They say she had nigger blood in her ! "

And you—after a pause,

" D'you mean—you got *colour* ? "

And my sudden, inexplicable fright, and your arms round me, and your mouth on mine—

Oh Christ. Oh Lee.

III

It was four in the morning. Ruth came in. She had not taken off her clothes. The contrast between her neat, dark hair and the aged, disordered lines of her face struck a fresh blow at Aldebaran's heart, as she sat up and switched the bed-light on.

" Ruth, you haven't been to bed ? "

" Diamond's told me everything." She sat down on the end of the chaise-longue. For a moment or two she looked vacantly about the room, as though trying to recognize her sur-roundings. "I came to help you pack. There won't be over-much time in the morning."

"But——"

"It's all right. Henry's squared the police. You'll be head-lines in the news and they'll probably chase you to New York —but you've had plenty of experience dealing with reporters, haven't you?"

She pulled a dressing-gown about her shivering body.

"Ruth, listen. I can't go. If they get that boy—Alger—he'll be charged with both murders, won't he?"

"One's enough—more than enough—to hang him." She made a dry noise, like a laugh. "I'll look after Alger—if there's anything to look after. Your job's Diamond."

"You want me to take her with me?"

"We've told them it was all arranged previously: that Diamond was going back with you, to school. They don't want this blown into front page news. You ought to have locked your door." Ruth crossed the room and turned the key sharply. "We've got all the Press here, including one of the best-known sob-sisters from Skeeterville! They're busting themselves to plaster the name of Aldebaran Flood, in connection with the Hammock murders, and you'll have a rough time if they get in."

Aldebaran looked for a moment through the screen down on the still lighted porch, on the crowds seething in and out of the open doors, and turned away with a shudder. An ugly eagerness ran from man to man; a shouting group was clustered about Henry Tollemache. In a little while it would be dawn.

"I don't know how much money you have," Ruth was saying, "but I've given Diamond a cheque; they'll cash it in New York. If there's any trouble about her passage, twenty bucks will take care of that——"

"There won't be; I've got a two-berth, and my secretary's got a single, next door. I'll have the single and push the two of them in together——"

"I feel kind of—stupefied!" Ruth pushed the heels of

her palms up against the roots of her dark hair. "Alger—and
Diamond. They went for him because he was kissing her
Because he, a Negro who looks white, was kissing my daughter
who, according to their laws, is a Negro——"

"For God's sake, Ruth——!"

"No, of course they don't know. But if they get him,
I might have to tell them."

Aldebaran caught Ruth in her arms.

"Ruth ; you can't do it."

Ruth loosened herself quietly and went back to the chaise-
longue. She sat there, resting her brows on her hands.

"I don't expect I'll have the chance. If any of them get
hold of him—If he's caught by the police, they may get him
safely into jail. There may even be the pretence of a trial—
though there's no evidence, unless they find the third man.
Anyhow, there's no real trial when there's a killing, and a coloured
boy mixed up in it. Diamond says Alger pushed the third fellow
in the swamp. The alligators may have taken care of him. But
if he turns up, and says they went for Alger because he was
meddling with Diamond—well, I'll have to tell them ; it's his
only chance." She let her hands fall, palms upward, on the
couch each side of her. "However it goes, we're finished—at
Hammock." She looked up at Aldebaran, her lips stretched in
an unreal smile. "You look awful. Have a drink. By this
time tomorrow you'll be out of it all——"

"Leaving you with all the horrors. *I've* done this to you,
Ruth ; you must hate me for it."

"Look after Diamond. You don't understand us down
here—we're tough about this sort of killing. The man you hit
with the car, he's been had up for rape ; he got off, with graft,
but they're after him for another case—one of the Frasers'
coloured girls. They'd never have got him, so nobody's inclined
to make a fuss about that. The one Alger shot did time in
Alabama for killing a policeman and got off with a life sentence
by giving away the gang. That's the sort of people who are
against us because we treat our darkies like human beings ! It's

part malice, part fear and perversion. You don't want to feel guilty, honey, about anything you did to a brute like that."

She wondered what violent blood she had inherited, as she reflected that, although she felt disgust and horror, she had no sense whatever of guilt.

A very much reduced Diamond accompanied her on to the train the following morning; occupied the sleeper next to hers; met her eye apprehensively across the breakfast table.

"Do you suppose Mummy's all right? Can we phone her from the hotel?"

Aldebaran was not disposed to relieve the young woman's anxiety; she returned laconic answers to Diamond's questions.

"What'll it be like in England?"

"You'll be obliged to behave yourself," said Aldebaran, and had the satisfaction of seeing Diamond wince. "Do you realize" —she leaned forward to speak the words deliberately—"that because you've been misbehaving yourself, somebody's going to die?"

"You mean—Alger?" Diamond started. "Oh—well— he mightn't—might he? He might get away."

"I should say the chances are ninety per cent against it," said Aldebaran dryly. Diamond wriggled her shoulders.

"Well—Phil's back. Mummy won't be by herself."

"We're talking about Alger, not Phil."

"Black and white people oughtn't to have children," burst out Diamond. "It's always happening, to people like Alger. It would probably have happened—anyhow."

"And don't you care?" The attitude was incredible: even from someone as frivolous as Diamond.

"Of course, it's horrid!" Again she writhed her shoulders. "I want to forget about it. I want to go back to Cuba, to Father; I don't want to see Hammock any more."

Aldebaran closed her lips tightly and lifted up her magazine between herself and her companion.

You met me at the Gare du Nord—her mind raced back against the throb of the train—and it was the first time I saw Paris. You looked different, because, up to then I'd only seen

o

you in hospital blue and khaki. The war was over, and I was
two years older and so were you. You were different in yourself
I pretended not to notice. I pretended not to see you were taken
aback by my coming, by my determination to make you live out
the dream I'd lived, all through the end of the war, and the
Armistice, and the months that followed after. We quarrelled
and then you made the best of it—oh, poor Lee. You made the
best of it. We made the best of it in bed together, in those hot
summer nights—that wasn't part of my dream, but it was yours.
For me it was " growing up "; it was crossing a bridge between
romantic adolescence and a sharp-edged, adult existence of
which my reading had made me dimly aware.

IV

Aldebaran pushed the door open into the stateroom, and
found Agnes on her knees before a half-filled wardrobe trunk
" Where's Diamond ? "
" I wouldn't know. We've just had a dander of a row and
she went out on the promenade deck about ten minutes ago."
" Leaving you to do the packing. Get on your bunk, you
idiot ! I'll find Diamond. I'll make that one work her passage
or my name's not Flood."
" Your name will be printed up on a nice chunk of marble
if you don't look out." Agnes sank, however, with relief against
her pillow. " Do you happen to have taken a look at your
self—— ? "
" Don't hold with looking at myself on shipboard," grimaced
Aldebaran. " Lowering as it is, as a Flood, to admit it—I'm
not at my best off dry land."
" Seriously, will you take a rest when we get back ? "
" Seriously, I might—for a week or so. I expect Lady
Carlyle would have me at Petersham."
" Full regalia every night and Bridge until three o'clock in
the morning ? That's not a rest."
" Or I might wander round a bit with Mother. It gets me

occasionally, you know—*nostalgie pour la boue!* There's something, say what you like, about theatrical digs in, say, Nottingham——"

" You're cuckoo."

" I've got a slight conscience about Mother. I've only heard from her twice, and I've an idea she's been getting into trouble while I've been away. And I must spend a few days with Uncle Joe."

" That can come later. What about a fortnight in Cornwall —some place where nobody knows you and you can slack around in an old sweater ? "

" The sooner I'm back on the job again the better." She picked up one of a pile of magazines which Agnes had stacked, with old letters and theatre programmes, on a corner of the dressing table, leafed it over absently and dropped it again.

" My God, you've had four months ' on the job '! Can't you ever take a let-up ? "

" I want something to read," said Aldebaran discontentedly.

" Oh, do you ? I've just taken the books back to the library. You can have my McKenna, if you want."

" That ? I've read it. Never mind. I'll go and find Diamond and send her in to do her own packing."

Diamond, for once, was engaged in the innocuous occupation of a game of poker dice, which there was no good reason for interrupting—particularly as Agnes had the peace of her own stateroom, and had probably settled for a nap.

Somebody waved to her from the bar ; she drifted over indifferently, not caring, but not wishing to leave an impression of " celebrity snobism " on the transatlantic crowd with whom she had struck up the casual acquaintances of a voyage. Shipboard clothes had given place to mink and tailormade ; carefully made-up eyes stared through voilettes at her turtle-neck sweater and slacks.

" *Darling* : aren't you coming to *Paris* ? "

" No ; I've got to go right through."

Everyone was drinking champagne cocktails ; a glass appeared at her elbow.

"What I say about Paris is, it's *civilized*." A stout character with a rubicund face was beaming at her with the aimless good nature that prevails at the end of an Atlantic crossing. "What you have to do"—he leaned towards her confidentially—"is, dodge the tourist places."

"Naturally," said Aldebaran, recognizing at a glance the type that makes life worth living for the professional guides.

"Now—I'm not putting on side: but I *know* Paris. Wait till I show you the Goutte d'Or."

"I'm not getting off at Le Havre."

"You're not . . . ?" Incredulity gave way to assertion. "You've *got* to come to Paris! I can show you——"

"I expect you could show me a lot. I haven't been in Paris for years. I don't suppose any of the places I knew exist."

"You don't know La Cabane?"

"That must be a new one since my time."

"You wouldn't hear of it. It's not what they call a 'chic' place. It's one of those little *French* places——!" There was no need to look, to be aware of the dropped eyelid, the sly satisfaction of the foreigner who "knows Paris." She said politely,

"It sounds attractive."

"*Vie de Bohème*—mixture of white and coloured. They were putting on a nigger floor show last time I was there—about six weeks ago. Pooh—we've got nothing like it in London. They'd got a chap at the piano——" He caught the eye of the hovering bar man. "Let's sit down, shall we, at one of these tables? Same again, George."

"I'm a bit of a connoisseur of jazz." He broke a lighter under the tip of the cigarette she had pushed between her lips. "You don't often get it well done in Paris. The French haven't caught on to it, outside the smart cabarets and two or three places that cater for Americans. *Chaqu'un à son goût*—what? You don't come to Paris for what you can get in London and New York."

"But in this place—La Cabane——?"

"Of course, it's no good, if you want to *dance*. You know those Left Bank joints: a couple of square yards of floor space packed stiff! But there's some deuced amusing customers and the champagne's all right. What I like's sitting and watching the fun. Listening to that chap teasing rag-time out of an old tin piano. Sure you won't stay off at Le Havre?"

She shook her head.

" Sure ; I've got work to do, at home."

" Well, I'll tell you what. I'll give you my telephone number. They keep me a room at the Meurice."

" Thanks. But I'm not very likely to turn up in Paris. It's off my beat."

" There it is "—he finished scribbling—" and there's the address of that place—La Cabane ; it's close to St Germain des Prés, you know : Quartier Latin. Glad to take you there—any time." He stared at her with a glassiness of innumerable cocktails in his eyes. " S'funny ; I was trying to think of that chap's name—the red-haired chap that played the piano. He was a Yank, you know——"

She told herself, This is just plain crazy. I'm daft. I've got an obsession. Her hand was shaking and she had suddenly to put down her glass. She swallowed twice.

" One of those rum names—those American names—like you get on the movies. Dammit, it's slipped my memory."

She heard herself say,

" Marion. Lee Marion."

. . . You cross the Atlantic, and you play sweet hell all over the States and you wear yourself and other people out and waste your own time and theirs, and you come back, and the answer's *here*. . . .

Agnes, still stretched on her bed, finishing the last chapters of her novel, gaped at the apparition of Aldebaran in a squirrel coat, velvet hat and gloves. Wondering if she could have fallen asleep—if they could possibly have been into, and out of, Le Havre—and were half-way across the Channel—she dropped the book, swung her feet to the floor, and was thrust back on her pillow by Aldebaran.

" Stop where you are, and don't scream. I've decided to take a day or two in Paris."

"Taking Diamond with you, I assume?" emerged at last from Agnes's inarticulacies. "If that one knows you're going to Paris, she'll fling herself overboard and swim ashore."

"It's your job to see she doesn't," said Aldebaran sweetly.

"Thank you. Oh, for the sweet love of heaven, A. F., be your age! What do you expect me to say to Orlando? You know he's coming to meet us at Southampton."

"I think you can safely leave the saying to Diamond. The magic of Landy's charm, plus his title, will relieve you of the necessity of making any conversation between the docks and Park Village West."

"It's no business of mine," said Agnes, slowly, "but the way you treat him is bitchy—to put it mildly."

"As you say—it's no business of yours."

She's like a man; a sullen and indifferent man, thought Agnes, with her eyes on Aldebaran's fingers, smoothing her gloves.

"I suppose you want some things packed."

"Don't bother; I've got all I want. If Diamond comes down, keep her with you, if you can. I'd rather she didn't assist at the *débarquement*. It might be difficult to get the captain to put her in irons. One hates to admit it," said Aldebaran reflectively, "but Americans—when they're chivalrous—are apt to overdo it. Any of our skippers would have had that young one under control before we were past the Statue of Liberty."

"Well, don't leave her in my charge too long; that's all." Agnes reached for her handkerchief and wiped a beaded brow. "What *are* you going to do with her? It isn't often I accuse you of biting off more than you can chew, but you've got a pretty mouthful this time. I hope she won't bolt before you get back."

"You can tell Landy that's his homework, and I expect him to earn full marks."

"She'll scare the living daylights out of him! Or else she'll find him too old, and be rude."

"It's not so easy—being rude to Landy. Let Nature take its course. My old school, The Lodge, will look after Diamond, when I've had time to fix things up. I may be prejudiced, but

I back Miss Colin against any Spanish-American flapper with nymphomaniac tendencies ! "

The trouble was, avoiding those members of the boat-train crowd—in particular her acquaintance of the cocktail bar—who would greet her change of plans with whoops of delight and absorb her into the company she was most anxious to avoid. She manœuvred this by lingering until the last passengers were off the ship ; having no luggage but a light case, she was able to make a last-moment rush for the train, and fortune favoured her, in that the end compartment into which she was thrust by an impatient porter was empty. She twitched down the blinds between herself and the corridor and settled into a corner. Past advertisements, etc., etc.

Past advertisements of Byrrh, and Eau de Javel, and Michelin the train lumbered towards Paris.

Only a little while, and I'll have all the answers. A little while, and then Goodbye—this time with no arguing. It's been wonderful, although I knew all the while it was only a schoolgirl obsession that turned putrid in the end—I've never loved anyone but you. See, Landy : I'd got to make sure the magic wouldn't work again. I'm sure, now, there'll be no magic, ever again, for me. But I've got to make it safe for you as well.

For the last few years I've been hating Lee : hating him because he spoiled my life, made it impossible for me ever honestly to love again. And hate's dangerous, darling, because it can so easily switch back to the other thing. If Lee and I had met, before, the switch-over might easily have taken place—at least, on my side. I expect he's forgotten, but I don't believe any woman can meet the man who first taught her about physical love and feel *nothing* : unless the parting took place in some terrible fashion that paralysed the whole thing. And Lee and I didn't part that way. I was crazy for him, for years. (Is this a terrible way to talk to you, Landy ? It will make it easier for you in the end.)

There's got to be no argument, this time, and it is you who have to put a stop to it. There's nothing left of my feeling for Lee except pity. (They say pity is akin to love ; that's the damnedest thing to say.   It doesn't mean a thing ; it's just a curtain-line, invented by the cheap dramatist, the hack writer.) All that dialogue of mine about the difference in our outlook and background—that was hot air as well ; we both knew it. There's no earthly reason why we shouldn't get married, darling, except—it's impossible.   That's why I'm here now ; to make sure that it's impossible.   I'm sure, already, in my heart, but I've got to get the whole of the dossier.   When we've got that, there's no more danger of weakening, for either of us ; the whole thing's out of our hands.

Oh God, how'll I ever tell you . . .

When I was last in Paris, they had a song :

> La maison de mon coeur est prête ;
> Dans la chambre du souvenir
> Il n'y a plus rien à regretter—
> Amour nouveau, tu peux venir !

I love you, darling.   Darling, it's too late.

Chapter Ten

I

HER FRIENDS said to her, " Let's run over to Paris and see the dress shows."

They said, " Let's make up a party for the Prix de Drague."

They said, " You must take a look at the Pitoëffs—at Sacha's new piece—at the Monte Carlo ballet."

She had an engagement, or she was rushing some proofs through for the press, or one of her editors was clamouring for an article overdue. Any excuse but the real one : I don't want to go to Paris.

Her Paris had been blanketed with summer heat, the dusty grass speckled with shrivelled leaves, the trees like swollen, dark green tents, shabby and devoid of freshness. Parties of tourists, listless as cattle, slogged stoically in the wake of the guides. Many of them were taking in Paris on their way back from the battlefields ; most of the women wore black and the men black arm-bands. Their faces were crimson puddles under their dusty hats, their eyes glassy with weariness and incomprehension. All day the sun glared down and at nightfall the city became a furnace.

It was with something like relief that she looked out on skeleton trees hung with the mist that swallowed the long perspectives of the boulevards, on pavements thinly skimmed with ice, on windows with lights behind the curtains—although it was near midday. Faces were bluish white and lips drawn thin in resistance to the cold ; people no longer dawdled but hurried along the pavements cleared of their iron tables and chairs. This cold grey Paris held no pangs of recollection ; it was hardly to be recognized. Wiping away the steam that collected on the window of the taxi, she peered out, wondering at the emotionless curiosity which was there, in place of the anguish she had expected.

She went to the Crillon, because it was the only hotel that came to her mind; also because its situation and its luxury alike would help to emphasize the gulf between past and present. She checked in her baggage and took the taxi on to the rue St Honoré, where she managed to find a pair of flat-heeled shoes that fitted her; to try them out she walked the length of the rue de Rivoli to the Palais Royal—and found that she was hungry. There was a restaurant here—or wasn't there? Somewhere under the colonnade at the end she turned into Vefour's. As she made her choice from the carte she saw through the print herself and Lee, anxiously seeking a place where they could get some beer to drink with their cheese and rolls.

She found another taxi and told the driver to put her down on the Place Pigalle.

This was it. She shivered slightly as she stood on the curb, looking left and right along the boulevards Rochechouart and Clichy. This was it. A thin blade ran down inside her, turned, laid open the old scar. The Moulin Rouge, its wings dully scraping the dull sky; the façades of the night places, closed and dingy; steam on the windows of the cheap eating houses, and a smell of food. La Cigale, Bruant, the Boule Noir; L'Enfer, Le Ciel, Le Rat Mort. They had a shrunken look, a look barely of survival—innocuous relics of the " night-life " that Monsieur Chiappe had cleaned up on coming into office. There was a smell of poverty in the air; Montmartre, a derelict slut, perishing at last of her own vices.

Aldebaran shuddered, crossed the Place quickly, and started to climb. In a few minutes she was panting. What a fool, not to have taken the taxi on. She stood still for a moment, her breath hung before her mouth in a thin cloud. She stood still, to wonder at the sameness of it all: the plunging pavements, the climbing stairs, the sloping walls that rose into sudden cliffs penetrated by innumerable windows, or dropped to little, shingled roofs. She went on, until the winding street broke into the cobbles of the Mairie : until she saw the green dome of the Sacré Coeur rising coldly above the ramshackle roofs.

An almost irresistible desire to run away—to leave it alone swept over her. What was the good ? She *knew* ! What was the need of coming back here, stirring up old dust ? She drove her clenched hands deep in her pockets, and, after a moment, turned into the little bar they had all of them known and ordered herself a cognac. She looked at the patronne from the corners of her eyes, wondering if she would be recognized ; but the woman's eyes looked back without interest. If she remembered a thin girl with golden plaits round her head and a cheap cotton frock she was not likely to associate her with this fur-coated stranger who had the eccentricity to climb to the Butte on a day to freeze the stones.

It was silly, of course, to imagine that they would still—Tishy and Naimbanna—be in the old studio, but one must start from there. Strange heads were shaken from the door. The concierge —not knowing her—said, Mademoiselle and *le grand noir* had left years ago. There were some new flats on the rue Cortot (flats on the rue Cortot !) ; some of the foreign painters had moved in there.

She trudged for an hour—climbing upstairs and down, penetrating into courts muffled in the dry trunks of wisteria, which had not known existed—before it occurred to her to ask at the art dealer's where Tishy, occasionally, took some of her work. She stood among the frames and the canvases in the corner shop where, ten years ago, they were selling Utrillo for a hundred francs.

The proprietor came out to see her ; she looked just the same as ten years ago. Aldebaran stammered,

" Tishy Morgan and I were friends ; do you remember me ? "

" *Oui, mademoiselle.*" The eyes calculated, the lips spoke dispassionately. The French are wise, thought Aldebaran ; they don't squander their emotions ; they don't spill sentiment right and left, the way we do, until they're sure they've got something to make out of it.

She learned that Tishy had earned "*un peu de galette*"; that she was "*partie en Maroc*"; that she was making "*un petit tour de paysage*"—just what Tishy had longed, and never had time to do, when board and lodging depended on the cheap little Montmartre sketches that the tourists bought, and she could run off like a line of knitting between her serious painting.

"And her friend——?"

"*Le grand noir?* He occupied a room in the rue Lepic. He is much in demand as a model. The great artists send for him from the *rive gauche*; even from their properties in the country."

It was growing dark when she toiled up a staircase in the rue Lepic; it grew darker as she mounted from floor to floor —until she remembered, and stretched out her hand to the light switch. A faint bulb illuminated a closed door—and went out as she bent to read the paper which was pinned to it. She groped again for the switch, and the light glimmered again. She read:

Parti pour la campagne.
Retour vendredi.

It was Monday evening. She resigned herself.

II

"——Naimbanna?"

"Yes: that is my name—mademoiselle?" He showed polite surprise. He too had not altered; perhaps a little thicker, and his clothes—a turtle-necked sweater knitted in cable-stitch, covered by a plaid mackinaw and a woollen scarf in stripes of rust and red—belonged to him, instead of lying uneasily over his broad shoulders and narrow hips. They, alone, signalized Naimbanna's acceptance of his European status, which had established itself during the last ten years.

"Don't you remember me—Barry Flood?"

First there was silence; then some slow movement took place behind the ophidian eyes. Yes, he had known Barry Flood; because of it, he had read a very boring novel, called *Les Petites*

Cloches, which had left him a little sad and disappointed—because, although it was very smart and slick, and no doubt deserved its great popularity, it was not at all the kind of thing he had expected Barry Flood to write.

" Bar-ry." He said it slowly, separating the syllables.

" Naimbanna, how marvellous ! " She was laughing, quivering, clutching his hand.

Then they were in a room, long and empty, almost like a studio. The next ten minutes passed in recognizing pieces of furniture which had belonged to the atelier off the Place.

" Tishy left me this—she gave me that." His voice, like hers, was trembling with excitement; in his excitement he tutoyer-ed her, as in the old, light-hearted days. " *Tu te souviens de ça ?—c'est son chevalet ; je le garde pour son retour.*"

" And the canvases ; have you any of her canvases ? "

He laughed happily.

" There are not many canvases to keep, these days ! Everything is sold, almost before the paint is dry," he told her triumphantly. " She too is successful—Tishy." His look dwelt upon her with sweetness, as though it made him proud to be associated with the pair of them, Barry and Tishy, whom he had known in all the anxious uncertainty of the past.

She went to sit on the divan, remembering, as she did so, how she had lain there, in Tishy's studio, and how good they had been to her, both of them. It was a long time before she braced herself to speak the name of Lee.

" I do not know anything about Lee."

" You know more than I do ! " she accused him.

" No—really."

" You needn't duck it; I know everything," she told him steadily, and saw his eyes flicker.

" We never saw him again, after you went home," said Naimbanna, after a pause. " I do not think he can be in Paris——"

" Yes, he is."

" You have seen him ? " She had startled him. She shook her head.

" How do you know ? "

" I happened to hear—on the ship, when I was coming over. He is—or was at a place called La Cabane, rue du Dragon. Do you know it ? "

" We have been there, sometimes. We don't go much— Tishy and I—to those places. La Cabane—it's a *sale bôite*," he grimaced.

" But tourists go there."

" That's why," he told her, with a grin.

" Is it—coloured ? "

" Of course."

" Then Lee——"

" They have white turns, sometimes."

" But—do you mean Lee has never been to see you, since—— ? "

" It was you we cared for," said Naimbanna simply, " not Lee. For him we were only sorry."

" Then you knew—— ? "

" Of course we knew." The question appeared to astonish him. " We thought, at first, you knew as well ; then, when we began to realize you didn't, it was very awkward. That was why Lee and Tishy quarrelled."

" I never knew they quarrelled."

" Oh yes. That is why the portrait never got finished." He flashed his teeth at her. " A pity—no ? "

" Have you got it here, now ? "

" Perhaps I could find it." He hesitated. " But do you really want to look at it ? It is really—too good."

" Please."

She turned her back while he silently fumbled among canvases, and, at last, hoisted one on the *chevalet*.

" You may look now, if you want to."

Remembering, she walked to the far end of the room, where the criss-crossed flakes, and seemingly casual squares and rectangles of Tishy's brushwork composed into the beauty of the living whole.

Lee. It was not fair that a man should have all that beauty :

eggshell-coloured skin drawn over a compact design of bone, of short, blunt nose and square brow, across which the hair, like burnt corn, drew a parallel line with golden brows ; clear-cut chin, almost too perfectly in proportion with the other features ; long, muscular neck, like that of a Greek athlete. All was faithful to the Lee she remembered : the broad lips, rather flat and pale, closed—in the painting—over teeth so white and even that only a minute speck of gold in an incisor redeemed them from artificiality. And the curious eyes : grey, with so much yellow in them that they appeared to be green . . .

It was when she was quite certain that this painted Lee, or its original, had no longer power to quicken her heart, that Aldebaran turned calmly to Naimbanna.

" I think, if he'd been plain and insignificant, I'd have fallen in love, just then. At sixteen one's crazy to love and be loved. The way he was—it was too easy."

" And if you'd known—— ? "

" Yes," she said, after a silence. " I think—I'm sure—that would have finished my loving."

His face was like a mask in basalt.

" Then he did the right thing."

" To run away from me ? "

" What could he do about it ? His life was much harder than ours—who have our race written in our faces. It is bad, to grow up with a secret for which you are not responsible, knowing that, if it is discovered, you will be an outcast wherever you go. That is a kind of bitterness you cannot understand." She made a movement of painful deprecation. " How should you ? " asked Naimbanna calmly. " What Lee did to you was wrong—but it was part of his trying to make himself belong to your people. Then he got scared. He knew you were too young and inexperienced to carry the burden of loving him, after you knew the truth. He knew someone, sooner or later, would give him away ; there are too many coloured people in Paris. So he tried to put it right by running away, as once before he'd run away—don't you remember ?—from his adopted people in Great Rock."

"Did he tell you that?"

"No. It was Tishy thought of it. She never believed Lee's story, about hiking his way into Canada because he wanted to fight the Germans. Lee never cared about the Germans; why should he? He never cared about anything but his music. It wasn't likely, was it, he'd risk death, or mutilation—perhaps the loss of his hands—to fight in a war that didn't mean anything to him?"

"Then——?" Her mouth felt dry.

"Something else drove him out of Great Rock; something to do with his colour. There wasn't anything to do but run— the way he'd run, as a kid, from his home in the South. Lee was running all the time. You didn't know he was making you run with him. Then he found out you couldn't run fast enough. And that you'd expect to get somewhere in the end. There's no end for anyone like Lee. He's got to go on running until he hits the wall, and owns himself beat."

She found the tears running down her face. Naimbanna moved across the room with his movement of a big tiger and lit an oil lamp, that slowly sent a glow of orange round the shabby walls.

"I didn't pay the light last month; I guess I forget," he apologized, smiling.

III

The room was long and narrow, and solid with smoke between the table tops and the low ceiling. Up by the band there was a minute floor space, on which couples, clamped bosom to bosom and thigh to thigh, obeyed the rhythm of the drums and saxophone without stirring from their square foot of floor. Coloured men danced with white women, coloured women with white men—if it could be called dancing. It was different from the *bal nègre* she remembered—the old *bal* down in the rue Blomet: where there was space and gaiety and wholesome pleasure, and, though in those days they were dancing the Black Bottom and the Java, a quaint air of respectability pervaded the scene. Very few white people went there; a coloured woman who accepted the invitation of a white was viewed askance by those of her own race; no coloured man would dare to approach a white girl.

They found, with difficulty, places at a table at the back of the room. The table was slopped with the remainders of other people's drinks, and a woman's cheap handbag, two glasses and a bottle of champagne staked out occupation of the opposite seats. Behind them there was a narrow bar, with some coloured street walkers hung on the end of it, and a party of youths, white and coloured, who leaned with their shoulder-blades against the bar and watched the dancers indifferently. There was a table of English tourists, with a guide; the tourists looked glum, looked the way they look when they think someone is taking advantage of them. You paid nothing to go in, then you found you were expected to order champagne. A bottle of champagne was the price of sitting on a hard chair, in a corner of a stuffy room, with nothing to look at but couples shifting about a few feet of floor space.

Naimbanna had American cigarettes; she lit one and tried out of the smoke to conjure the illusion of twelve years ago. It didn't " take." *Then* one was a beglamoured schoolgirl, seeing Paris for the first time; *now*—the highly-paid novelist, with an acquired taste for—for what? A sudden nostalgia swept over her, for the simple years, the years when pleasures were measured by the purse, and sharpened by inexperience. This was sentimentality, and, like the rest of her generation, Aldebaran scorned and feared sentimentality. Because of that scorn and fear she forced herself directly to stare at the man in a pale, flashy suit who leaned on his folded arms at the end of the bar : with rings of discoloration under his light eyes and a tic that jerked his head intermittently towards his left shoulder. Barely recognizable as he was, she had no doubt it was Lee. She wondered if he would know her. Naimbanna's head was down, she could feel his discomfiture. He had not wanted to come, but he would not let her be alone. Suddenly Lee's eyes met hers. His

P

were curiously glazed: she knew the look that goes with "junk": with what, in Paris, they called "le coco." She forced herself to look at him steadily, until the glaze cracked, almost imperceptibly, and something flickered behind the green glass of Lee's eyes. She saw him look over his shoulder, as though calculating the distance between himself and the door. The narrow gangway was clogged with people. She found herself being terribly sorry for him—sorry for Lee who, for once, could not run away.

Then he was hitching himself between the tables. He was standing above them, looking down, with a smile, stiff with bravado on his lips.

"Hello, kid."

Naimbanna looked up, and looked down again. It was he who muttered "Hello." She said, "Hello," and discovered how easy it was to smile. Lee remained there, as though not sure what to do next; his smile touched with irony, his eyes —she could feel them—fixed on the diamond spray on the lapel of her gown; on her squirrel coat; on all that marked the difference between Barry Flood of 1919 and Aldebaran Flood of 1931. His eyes returned to her own, with bitterness and antagonism in them.

"You stopping in Paris?"

"Just for a night or two. Have a drink."

He hesitated, nodded at the waiter, and slumped into a chair. The waiter brought pernod. Lee sank it at a gulp.

"Funny—you turning up here." He scowled at her.

"Why? It's quite a place, isn't it?"

"Yeah—sure." He lapsed into silence. The noise of the band beat round them. Naimbanna got up suddenly and left them. Lee started to follow him, sank back, and looked at her from the corners of his eyes, like a distrustful animal. Crushing the stub of the cigarette into a saucer, she wondered whether to suggest they should dance.

"I looked for you in New York, and in Detroit." No need to mention the other places; no need to let him know, by speaking of Charleston, that his secret was no longer his own.

" Yeah. They said you was over there."

So he had deliberately avoided her. She forced a laugh.

" I'd forgotten about the publicity." It was hard to imagine Lee—this Lee—reading anything that had not to do with show business. He was not looking at her : scowling at the glass he held in his hand. " I never thought of our meeting in Europe. You must have left soon after I was in Detroit."

" Yeah. Soon after."

" How—how did you get over ? "

" Swam. What's this third degree line, anyhow ? "

She shrank before his sudden, furious antagonism.

" Why, Lee, I'm just—interested," she faltered.

" Listen, baby." He set his elbows on the table ; she saw a pool of liquor beginning to stain the pale, flimsy stuff of his sleeve. " You got noth'n on me, have you ? "

" Of course I haven't." Her cheeks had started to burn ; she could feel the people behind them listening. " I'm sorry you should take it that way. It—it was nice meeting you again ; that's all ! "

" Okay." His brows were knitted, as though he still mistrusted the motive of her visit, and was prepared to repudiate it. " But you don't have to trail me around . . ." His voice faded away in uncertainty.

" Gosh, who's trailing you ? " she sighed. " I'm going in a minute, but I'd have liked to hear you play before I go. What time do you come on ? They say you're terribly good ! "

" Sure I'm good." He echoed her with irony, but his ruined beauty broke into a smile as though, at last, he had made up his mind that she had no intention of making trouble. " You look pretty good yourself, baby ! I guess those books of yours musta made you a packet." His eyes had slid again to her diamonds, and it went through her like a knife : He wants money. Can I offer it to him ? Would he take it if I did ? And he looked up suddenly and she saw on his face an incredible expression ; incredible, yet not to be mistaken. Sly, confident, prepared. It told her in a flash that women like herself—not yet past beauty, discontented and plainly well-to-do—had come to be part of Lee's calculations, his design for living. While still she sat frozen in a horror of realization, Lee bent a little towards her, and said, hardly moving his acidly smiling lips : " It's still waiting for you, baby."

The wave of nausea that blurred the lights and drove sweat into the palms of her hands was swept back by pity. She made herself look steadily at this dingy and damaged framework, this coffin of the boy who had loved and taught her to love.

The band finished on a blare of saxophones and people came back to the tables. A blue light bulb shone out over the piano. A coloured woman grabbed at the bag she had left on their table, sat down and started to make up her mouth, staring across the top of her mirror at Aldebaran. Then she flashed a smile at Lee, who slouched to his feet, muttered, " I'll be seeing you," and pushed his way through the crowd and the smoke to the piano. There was a little applause, and some scrambling for chairs.

She found Naimbanna in the doorway, and pushed him towards the rain-striped darkness of the street.

" You'd better stop here while I look for a taxi."

" No, I don't care." She let him take her arm ; they bent their heads to the rain and walked down the pavement like wet oil-cloth ; she felt the water from the puddles splashing up on her ankles. The long, secret-feeling street was empty but for an occasional lighted car short-cutting towards the boulevard that glowed at the end of their tunnel.

" You are getting wet," said Naimbanna, with concern.

" I don't care. So are you." His thin coat was less capable of holding out the rain than her grey squirrel. The cold and wet belonged in some way to her mood. Because it was raining all the taxis were engaged.

" We can take the Métro."

" I don't care."

" Some people are getting out of that one ! Wait here— I'll fetch it."

He left her on the pavement and plunged out into the traffic.

She stood, watching the rain drip from the awning of Les Deux
Magots : thinking of all the weeks on the divan in Tishy's
atelier ; of Naimbanna, coming every day to model for Tishy's
picture—always with a book, or a handful of pears, or a flower,
always kind, always gentle. Naimbanna, who was there when it
started—Naimbanna, who knew——

The taxi made a great arc and swung in, squelching the
liquid mud from the gutter over her feet. When she got in,
she found she was shivering. Chauffage, a hot bath ; no—
Tishy's divan, with the Turkish shawl pulled over it and the
stove making a little red heart of heat in the middle of the room ;
and the iron pipe that climbed to thrust its way through the
sloping ceiling . . .

" Naimbanna ; my baby."

She saw his eyeballs gleaming in the darkness by her side.

" It was coloured, wasn't it ? "

She saw him nod slowly.

". . . Very ? "

After a brief hesitation, he lifted his hand and touched his
own face.

" Thank you," said Aldebaran, " for being honest."

After a long silence, they were crossing the Pont Royal ; then
the Concorde was a black sea reflecting the stationary lights of
great ships at anchor and the small swift lights of the night
traffic. As they stopped at the Crillon, she said,

" Won't you come in for a drink ? "

He refused smilingly, and, as she crossed the foyer, she was
glad, and ashamed of being glad, not to walk with a black man
into a white people's hotel . . .

IV

The sound of the taxi braking woke Joe Prior from his nap.
He pushed himself out of the chair, catching at his stick, lifting
his shoulders, letting them down sharply and flattening his back.
To the day of his death Harcourt Flood had never fallen into

such dotard's habits !—and here was himself, Joe Prior, only in his fifties, acting already like a slippered pantaloon.

When the doorbell rang, he rubbed his hand hastily over his ruffled hair. The woman who " did " for him had gone to bed : yes, he'd been letting her get into slack ways, but he wanted no waiting on, and why should two lonely people sit in separate rooms, yawning and watching the clock, until a foolish convention set them free to go to their beds ? He had wondered about having her in to sit with him, but felt Harcourt would not have approved of it ; with Harcourt's money he had inherited, perhaps, some of the old man's formalities.

" Hallo, Uncle Joe."

Half stupefied, he received her kiss ; a glow of joy illuminated his heart—as it was illuminated each time that Deb, as a child, came to spend part of her holidays with him in Bristol. Somewhere inside this tall, graceful woman, behind the artificial beauty time had laid on her face—behind all the fame and flattery and success which made him a little shy—was Deb. He reminded himself of it as, withdrawing the arm she had flung round his shoulders, she slouched ahead of him into the dining-room, let her furs fall in a dust-coloured heap round her feet and poured herself, without invitation, three fingers of Scotch. Leaning back against the sideboard with her ankles crossed, like a boy, she let him pick up the coat, and lifted her glass to him.

" The prodigal's return. Chin-chin."

" But what's this, Debby ? What are you doing here ? we all thought you were in Paris," he chuckled delightedly. His glance went up and past her to the portrait of Harcourt : the copy he had had made from the bit oil in the Board-room. Yes, you ; you who looked down on women ; what do you make of this one ?—and back to her proudly.

" Do I have to show my papers, or can I have my baggage fetched in ? "

" You—you've come to stop ? "

" You don't suppose I'm going to crawl into a bed at the Royal at this time of night ? "

The taximan had put her bags in the hall ; impatient, at such a moment, of economies, Joe thrust a ten-shilling note at him and clapped the door on his heels.

"Where's Agnes? Who's looking after you?"

She flung her head back—Johnny's trick—and laughed.

"Do you think I still need looking after, you old fool?"

"Ay, that I do." He came out with it stoutly. "What's come over you—streaking off to Paris—with all of us waiting for you at Southampton?"

"Oh lord—the reception committee. I'm sorry—but it serves you right for fussing. I've only been away a bit under five months——!"

"Ay, little enough, I know, at your age. Polly was right-down upset." He would not confess to his own "upset," which she saw shrewdly in his eyes.

"Was Mother working Southampton?"

"She took the trip specially to meet you," said Joe, "and it was a rare disappointment to find no one but Agnes, and the American young lady. Couldn't you have sent a wire, love?"

"It's the first time in her life Mother's come to meet me." Recollection of the many times she had hoped to be met, of the humiliation, among scenes of rapturous reunion, of having no one to meet her at Paddington on the first day of the holidays sharpened Aldebaran's voice. "I suppose Orlando was there." To get it over, she threw the name out defiantly.

"He drove Polly down from London."

"Then they had a pleasant trip, and that made up for the rest. Now have you finished scolding me?"

"Deb, love," he slipped his arm round her, "you forget the way folks care for you. Do you want some supper?"

"No, I ate on the train." She turned, however, and refilled her glass. She had grown thin, and sharp as a razor-blade; there was probably no colour under that stuff she put on her face. Racketing, like the rest of her generation.

Disregarding her fretful disclaimer—"All I want is a bath, a rug and a mattress!"—he roused the housekeeper and ordered her room got ready: the room with its Regency furniture and cherry-striped chintz which he had furnished for a neglected and lonely little girl whose home ought to have been with him. When she was a baby there was no help for it, but Polly, with all her well-meaning, had done wrong keeping Deb with her through all those changes that robbed the child of any feeling of a settled home.

There she sat stubbornly, refusing to go to bed; drinking whisky; her face draining itself more and more of life and colour until it was almost green, the dead fall of cinnamon-coloured hair accentuating its strange colour that reminded Joe of a painting he had seen by one of those modern fellows whose one idea seemed to be to get as far away as possible from human nature. Abandoning at last his efforts for her good, Joe lapsed into silence and puffed on his pipe. She said at last, constrainedly,

" Thanks for all your letters, Uncle Joe. It was good of you to keep me in touch."

" Huh. I 'spose you've been hearing from Landy."

" Landy ? " Her heavy lids lifted for a moment; the use of the " little name " indicated a familiarity which Joe would not previously have claimed. She smiled a little. " You and he seem to have been getting on pretty well, while I was away."

" He's a right good lad, is that," said Joe heavily. " Yes, love; you've picked a right one——"

" I ? What's Landy Sax got to do with me ? "

He took the pipe from his mouth and stared at her. Lifting her head, Aldebaran pushed back her hair.

" Let's cut that out for now."

" Didn't you get my letter, about three weeks ago, about the mess ? " asked Joe slowly.

" What mess ? " She laughed. " I thought things were going on pretty well, considering; you'd talked the Avonmouth men out of the strike, and you were in the thick of investigating passports, and you'd succeeded in proving that four of the coloured hands on the *Obango* were entitled, as holders of British papers, to the same rate of pay as the men they'd replaced : it all sounded as though you were succeeding in giving Purcell Flood plenty of headaches ! "

"There's no need for anyone to go round looking for headaches with more than two million tons of shipping laid up," muttered Joe. "But you must have got the one about— well," said Joe, "it must have been the middle of last month the tale got around Purcell-Flood was on the rocks. It wasn't as bad as all that, but the folks that were talking had got something to go on." He stretched his able leg towards the fire, and looked up at the fierce painted eyes above him for inspiration.

"You know, Deb, as well as I do, Purcells are shippers; they've never been venturers, like us—not in the proper sense of the word. They're a young firm—in comparison with Floods—that started when the big venturing days were over. They got a few factories dotted here and there, but somehow they never seemed to find the right fellows to run them. It takes quality to make a district agent."

"That's their look-out."

"Ay; and the shareholders'. It ain't so pretty a look-out for them, is it?"

She nodded gravely.

"Uh-huh. The old yarn of muddle and loss——"

"And the Malayans coming in with ribbed smoked sheet; who wants our lump rubber now? And there's been some ugly dealing with the blacks. It's a bad thing when a firm loses credit with the natives."

"What are they going to do? Pull out?"

"This isn't the time for pulling out." Joe scowled. "It's thirteen years since the Armistice. Trade's just starting to pick up. We've got to consolidate, not crumble away."

"I suppose Purcells have got the wind up." The Flood lip curled.

"Ay—and well they may. There's chaos out there on the Coast and hell to pay at Liverpool." Joe chuckled unexpectedly. "The morning our shares hit rock bottom I had Lord Mildenhall on the telephone. He's a very fine old gentleman, Lord Mildenhall," said Joe scrupulously, "but not what you'd call a business man. I'll not forget the time we had after Landy told his old man what was cooking up at Liverpool, and I spent the best part of an hour trying to put it in words of one syllable why he couldn't pull out every penny he'd put into the Company. Well, there he was—ramping and roaring and raging to sell out, with our shares not worth a spit in the cinders ! "

" Why didn't you take him at his word ? "

Joe looked at her ; looked at the cold and implacable face which was the Flood face, down the centuries.

" Nay, I couldn't do a thing like that. The slump's over, nearly. This time next year—with luck—we'll be showing dividends——"

" Then I will," she interrupted him. " By God, Uncle Joe, we owe Saxes nothing ! I'll ring the bank in the morning ; I'll buy up every share old Mildenhall's got ; I'll get myself on the Board, and I'll show them what Flood stands for ! "

" You're too late."

" What do you mean ? " Her lips had whitened.

" Landy's done it. Landy's bought up his father's shares."

" I don't know how to forgive you," she whispered, after a silence.

" But, Deb, I thought you'd be pleased. Look." He reached to the desk—Harcourt's desk—that stood in the angle between the chimney-breast and the wall, and handed her a sheet of paper ; she looked down at the Company's imprint, at the list of directors' names, at the line which ran through the name of Joseph Prior, and the new name that stood in type under it : The Honble. the Lord Orlando Sax. " That's stopped the shareholders panicking and hung a smile on Purcell's face—even if it's a sour one," commented Joe.

Strangled with bitterness, she was silent.

" I never thought but it would please you," said Joe miserably. She gave a short laugh.

" I'll take your word for it. Jesus ! I'd like to see the face of old Harcourt ; I'd like to see the faces of all the Floods, back to the first Hercules, if they could see the name of a Sax on the scrip of the company ! " Closing her fingers on the sheet of paper, she crushed it into a ball and flung it into the heart of the fire. " Am I crazy, or you ? What good's Landy to you ?

What does he know about shipping, or trade? It's simply your damned old-fashioned reckoning: I, because I'm a woman, don't count! I'm a Flood, but I just don't count—though I know, and care, more about our ships and our people than anyone—except you, Uncle Joe; except you." Her voice broke on the words.

Joe faltered,

"I never thought . . . It was on your account I didn't buy up the shares. I thought you'd sooner Landy . . . He only acted on my advice——"

"Landy—who doesn't know palm oil from gasoline!" Abruptly she dropped her head in her hands. "If it couldn't be me it ought to have been you. It ought to have been a Flood. Oh, come off it, Uncle Joe:"—as he started—"do you think I don't know you're the old boy's son?" She pointed to the portrait lowering down on them. "If you want to lie low about your parentage, you'd better get rid of that! You've inherited all our principles, all our passions; you've stood for Flood to Bristol ever since the old man died. What on earth does the name of Sax mean in our world—the world of shipping? What authority can Landy carry—with that title and everything!—when it comes to the last trick?"

"He's learning. He's been coming to school here, once a week, and he's putting his shots very nicely, just where I tell him. Ay, say what you like, Deb, Purcell's missing his dummy! Landy's my mouthpiece; through him, I've got as much control —nay, more than I ever had."

"Oh—if all you wanted was a parrot!"

"Why, love—it sounds like you're jealous."

"What if I am?" she flung at him. "You'll surely admit I've got something to be jealous about? It was bad enough when we had to sell out to Purcells, but I could take it—more or less— so long as you were on the Board. But Landy—with his fancy directorship——!"

"How'd you have found time to be a director, with all the jobs you've got to do?" he rallied her mildly.

She tried chokingly to gain control of her anger, jealousy,

resentment and bitter disappointment : but she suddenly realized that this was what she had been counting on : that this would have been the answer to the question that had tormented her all along the journey from Paris—how am I to fill my life ; what am I to put in the place of marriage, and love, and children ?—the things writing does not make up for, because writing—novels—turns round and round on those very things, so there is no escape from them in one's thoughts : all the lovers will be Orlando, and all the children——

"You've cheated me, and I'll never forgive you," she muttered.

A log dropped to the hearth ; as the thin flame flickered and died an acrid scent of smoke rose to their nostrils. Neither moved to throw it back in the grate.

"Deb," said Joe painfully, "aren't you going to marry him ? "

V

She caught the crumpled yellow dressing-gown round herself and crept up the stairs to the attic. It was years since she had been up there, yet, as she held the candle above her head and waited for the flame to steady itself, all seemed unaltered.

There were the old trunks and wooden chests she had played " house " in as a child ; a battered Gladstone bag with J. F. in almost illegible lettering on its side ; a shabby wooden writing desk which, also, had belonged to Johnny Flood. An immense saratoga trunk, strapped with leather, held, she guessed, all that remained of Uncle Joe's mother—whom, as a child, she had bitterly resented, because her unforeseen return from " abroad " had dispossessed her—Aldebaran—of all she had ever looked upon as " home." The imponderability of human sentiment : for fifteen long years the one-time Kitty Prior had led her son a dog's life with her petulance, her inebriety, and her demands on his money and his benevolence. Now, her remains—her showy, food-stained gowns, her dreadful hats and bonnets, all the shabby detritus of a woman without taste or fastidiousness, lay there sanctified.

Before her coming the attic had been kept as a spotless playground for a lonely child ; now dust lay thick—her fingers shrank from it. She felt her way across the uneven floor and sank on her haunches in front of the wooden chest in which, as a child, she had kept her " secrets." She assured herself it was locked before she groped in the pocket of the dressing-gown for a bunch of keys. (" What's this old key on your ring ? " asked Agnes one day. " Oh—just an old box." " Shall I take it off ?—there's no point in carrying extra weight." " No ; leave it alone.")

The lid creaked back on its rusty hinges. She peered at the piles of childish manuscripts : scribblings of her schooldays. Some day I'll destroy them. But she found herself touching them with the tenderness one keeps for the things of one's happy youth.

That which she sought lay on the top : an envelope, marked " Tenerife " and a thicker parcel : sealed in brown paper : the two tied together with tape. She knew what was in the envelope : the manuscript of " The Sad Dove." She slid her thumbnail under the flap and lifted it. How much her handwriting had altered since those days !

THE SAD DOVE

by

ALDEBARAN FLOOD

On the fly-leaf, in purple ink, she had printed out the *folia* :

> *Yo soy la paloma triste*
> *la triste la desconsolada*
> *que bebia en agua turbia*
> *y no puede beber clara*

and followed it by her free translation :

> *In turbid streams dipped I my foolish wing*
> *and mourn my folly now alas too late.*

No more for me the crystal of the spring
I the sad dove—the sad—disconsolate.

I the sad dove. The candle flickered in the draught. And mourn my folly now, alas, too late.

She leaned her bosom on the sealed packet as she turned the yellowed pages, wondering what they had meant to Janet Jackson, and to Janet's listeners.

When she crawled into bed and pulled the hot-water bottle up into the angle of her cold knees, she saw the glorieta on a long, flat roof, where she waited for Uncle Joe's return from the Gold Coast, and, to wile the hours, wrote and wrote until she had written the poison out of herself. And she saw the narrow cabin on the Flood liner where, stretched on her bunk, she had tried to bring herself to drop what she had written overboard, and could not, because to do so seemed like a kind of—suicide! She saw herself making up the packet with trembling hands, sealing it, and stamping the wax with an old seal she had discovered in Uncle Joe's writing desk; then bringing it home —always in terror of its being mislaid, of its falling into alien hands—and hiding it on the top of her wardrobe in the flat, until the opportunity came of taking it down to Bristol and laying it, like a corpse, in her old " secrets " box where no one could touch it—not even Uncle Joe's mother, whose prying curiosity led her everywhere—because Uncle Joe, when he had the box made for her, had given her the key. Strange, that the childless man should so understand childhood's craving for privacy. Polly had never understood; to Polly, hiding things stood for deceitfulness. She remembered the many times she had been accused by her mother of being " deceitful," as a little girl.

She remembered how, having locked the box, anxiety made her open it again, to take out the parcel, and write in blotted capitals between the sealing wax and the string: " In case of my death, to be destroyed unopened. Aldebaran Flood." And, even then, how many times she had trembled for its safety, and, on each of her visits to Bristol, would make some excuse to

rush upstairs and reassure herself that her secret was untouched :
until, as time went on, she ceased to worry, for who would
break open an old box, on the lid of which was painted her
full name ?

She lay there, remembering lines, and paragraphs, and
chapters. Feeling sorry for Orlando and trying to beat back
sorrow, because of the way he, with Joe's connivance, had
tricked her : thinking to make sure of her ! That's finished it,
Landy ; that's finished it. She shut her eyes tightly and drove
her nails into the palms of her hands.

Chapter Eleven

I

ORLANDO SAT on the edge of the divan, his elbows on his knees, staring at his own clasped hands. For more than an hour he had been trying to follow the intricacies of her female reasoning, to go with her in pursuit of what seemed to him insignificant shadows; what, after all, signified except their mutual relationship—that poor, exhausted thing which he saw, with an unusual flash of imagination for Orlando, stretched naked between them, helpless, and, unless he could find the means of saving it, dying. It gave him the same sense of angry injustice he had experienced, years ago, while watching his mother die.

Now and again, listening to what she was saying, he found himself being surprised; once he was shocked by finding himself perilously near to boredom. He rebuked himself by reminding himself of the strain through which she had come, but his direct mind could not entirely avoid the impression that she was dramatizing herself.

As a soldier, the act of killing in the way of duty had deprived Orlando of the civilian's horror of violent death; to kill in self-defence was a rational thing, in peace or war—though only to be resorted to in extremity. As a man and as her lover, he did his best to imagine how the taking of human life—even of worthless human life—must affect one of her sex and temperament; he tried patiently to disentangle "literature" from fact in the wild jumble of description, of self-accusation, of nightmare imagining, which for the last hour she had been pouring out: more like a patient exteriorizing herself to a psychiatrist than a woman talking to her lover. And all the time, to Orlando, it seemed as though they were moving at a tangent, far, far away from the only thing that mattered—but his love helped him to understand that she must get all this out of her before she was ready to come to the things that mattered to himself, and to her.

" And did the fellow get away ? "

She shook her head behind the lattice of her fingers.

" How should I know ? I suppose I'll hear, one of these days. Ruth's bound to tell me."

She wandered on, in her voice of a somnambulist.

" Crawling and crawling. Always a little weaker. You know : from loss of blood. Or it might be hunger. They'll hunt him more viciously, because of what *I* did. Not quite daring to use the gun on himself, because—well, you know better than I : don't people cling to life—even beyond the edge of hope ? Don't they ? When you're young, there's so much of life to live. And you've got to die, because of something that isn't even your fault. You've got to die, because of somebody's lust, way back before you, or even your parents, were born. You've got to die—because of the vast, inchoate fear of a million guilty men."

He muttered something which she disregarded.

" Or else you've got to run. And keep on running. You've got to trick your way out—if you're lucky. Then you've got to find some place to live. Some sort of slum, where they don't care what you are."

" Listen, darling : you've got to stop this."

" Stop—— ? Can't you understand ? If I hadn't done what I did——"

" I'd probably have done the same, if I'd had the wit to think of it. Actually, I suppose it would have come more natural to me, as a man, to go for the fellows ; they would probably have beaten me, but I'd have held them back long enough to give the other chap a chance. I don't see what else, as a woman, you could have done ; dam' few women would have had the courage to do it."

" Courage ? I didn't need any courage. I *wanted* to kill."

" Of course ; in defence of the weaker."

" No. In defence of Alger. In defence of—Lee."

Q

"*Lee?*"

"Lee—Marion."

In his confusion, he began to wonder whether her mind had failed. Lee Marion?—who pulled him off the wire, after Messines; whom they—his father mostly—had managed to wangle into Paragon, which was a hospital for officers, but it was the least they could do, considering that he—Orlando—owed his life to the Yank. The fellow who played the piano?—who composed that infernal thing, "Jehovah Blues," that sounded on every dance band and came with sickening reiteration over the wireless. The past resurrected itself dimly—Cat and Barry, a pair of flappers, hanging around the wards and being chased out by Matron—and refused to join up with the present. Impossible, after all those years, to accept Lee Marion as his shadowy rival! She was infecting him with her nerves. Poor dear, she was just a little crazy—and no wonder.

"Look here." He got up suddenly. "You're worn out. You must go to bed, and I'll come back in the morning."

Her eyes met his, and switched away.

"No; don't do that. It's finished."

"What's finished?"

"I suppose you thought, when you went on the Board, that you'd got me? It was clever of you, and Uncle Joe, but not quite clever enough."

His face, under its sudden flush, was cold.

"It wasn't intended to be clever. I believe in what your uncle told me: that a firm like Purcell-Flood can't crash—can't be allowed to crash—in times like these."

"And you're going to save it?"

"I don't know that I've done anything, in particular, to invite you to jeer at me," said Orlando, after a pause. "I know nothing about shipping: that I don't need to tell you. I don't pretend, as a member of the Board, to be anything but a mouthpiece for your Uncle Joe."

"If he went back, he wouldn't need a mouthpiece."

"Try making him," was the short reply. "You ought to know he's the last person on earth to haul down his colours."

She pushed her hands up over her face and hair.

"All right. I hate to push you out, but I'm going to see if Diamond is asleep. That one has a happy trick of smoking in bed. I'd as soon we didn't go up in flames before morning."

"When is she going back?"

She looked at him speechlessly.

"Haven't you listened to *anything* I've told you, so far?" she said at last. "Diamond can't ever go back to the States; I thought I'd made that clear when I explained about her connection with our family."

"Oh, don't be ridiculous—as though you'd all got black blood in you! If you want my opinion—you're taking a great deal too much on yourself. Both her parents are alive; they can't foist the responsibility on to you!"

"There's no question of 'foisting'; and the responsibility's there—whether I accept it or not."

"But it isn't. You're inventing it."

"I suppose you'll say next I 'invented' the slave traffic?"

At last he lost patience.

"All this thing about colour—you've let it grow into a mania! I know—I'm trying to be reasonable—that you've just come up against it, in a particularly horrible way, but so far as I can make out, you've completely lost your sense of proportion. That particular headache belongs to the Americans, and I wish them joy of it! But as for raising that old bogey about the slave-trading Floods—God, it makes me think you're just looking for a pretext to get rid of me. As for that unfortunate little cousin of yours—I couldn't care less; I wouldn't care if she were as black as, according to the Ku Klux, she ought to be! If you think you've got a mission to the blacks, I can't help it—and I won't interfere with it; but I'm damned if it shall interfere with us. If you want to, you can turn Paragon into a head-quarters for a society for coping with the colour problem——"

"There isn't a colour problem," she interrupted him wearily, "except what we whites have worked up, out of our fear, and our personal doubt and our shame. That Matthew Flood—down there in Bristol, on the Parade—who got conversion and finished up as an Abolitionist: he knew that, in the end. I know it. The very words 'colour problem' are only a synonym for fear. What makes the difference, if a person's black or white? He's got the same need, hasn't he, to make a living, and put food in his mouth, and the mouths of his family? Then why do people have to be classified as 'whites' and 'blacks'? Why can't they just be 'people,' with equal rights: not to be granted favours or made to endure penalties on account of an accident of pigmentation? Why can't you understand that the thing that bothers Uncle Joe—and me, because, in spite of all this writing, I'm just a trading Flood, when it comes down to fundamentals—is, not 'colour problem,' but how to make more trade, so there's employment for everybody regardless of colour: and the same money for the same job, and the same chance of getting the job, and of holding it down."

God, thought Orlando; I came to ask her to marry me, and this is what we've arrived at. I love her, and here we are, launched into this infernal subject——

In the pocket of his dinner jacket lay a velvet box. Because he had heard it was unlucky to buy the ring before " popping the question "—an argument which hardly held good in his case since he had " popped " it times without number: still, it was wiser not to trifle with superstition—he had brought with him, in earnest of the jewel they would choose together, a little ring of white enamel on gold, bearing the inscription " *Tu.es.ma.mie*," a diamond between each word, which had been his mother's keeper.

He made a strong effort to control his temper and to clear his mind.

" Well, all right; I grant you everybody's got a right to have a chance of making himself a decent living. It's only what I'm trying to do myself—but you appear to resent it."

" What *do* you mean? " Her smile was so coolly tolerant that he could almost have smacked her face.

" You know as well as I do that our days are numbered. I mean—families like ours; places like Paragon. You said yourself we're as obsolete as pterodactyls! It isn't we ourselves who are obsolete; it's the régime we represent. But after the régime's gone there'll still be the necessity of living—won't there? And even when there's no more privilege, and no more authority, and no more leadership—I can see no reason why a person like myself shouldn't become a useful member of whatever kind of society rises from the ruins of the one I happened to be brought up in."

"Poor little rich boy!" she mocked him.

"Rich? While Papa's alive, we may have a few more years of enjoyment of the old standards. The death duties will put paid to all that. By the time the Government vultures have done with the carcase, there'll be no Paragon and no Portland Place—so far as we're concerned."

"I suppose not. And it would have been rather tiresome, wouldn't it, to have set up house in the Burlington wing, and be faced with *déménagement* at almost any moment?"

Her smile glittered at him. Orlando's lips tightened; she should not, for the present, force him into losing his temper.

"That was why I was glad of the directorship. It might —well, just check the landslide for a month or two; it means I shan't be quite a parasite. And I must say that it didn't strike me as unreasonable that you would be pleased about something in which you've always taken an interest——"

"An interest!" She laughed shortly. An interest.

"My obligations to Paragon won't finish after we cease to live there—any more than those of your family did when the company ceased being Floods. For God's sake, darling, can't you see I'm practically asking you to keep me, as things stand—at any rate, to keep yourself—until I've found that job which is to put food in our mouths and make it reasonable for us to start a family."

As her hands flew to her ears he saw with satisfaction that he had got through her guard.

"Will you for sweet heaven's sake stop talking as though we were half-way down the aisle, with all your friends making a book on how long it will be before I walk out on you—or vice versa?" she cried shrilly.

It was Orlando's turn to flinch.

" I sometimes wonder whether you've got any heart at all, or whether all your heart and all your imagination is given to the damned blacks," he muttered.

Her hands dropped slowly, and pressed themselves against her thighs.

" On the whole, wouldn't it seem to you that the whites are more likely to be ' damned '—as you put it ? "

" I don't care which it is ! " he burst out. " I only know that you and I are quarrelling, like a pair of children, over something that doesn't matter. Doesn't matter ! " He almost shouted it. " You've treated me pretty badly, but even that doesn't matter—for the present. I suppose I've given you the right to use me as a doormat—and you've certainly taken full advantage of the permission ! Now for the last time, will you marry me ? "

She made a slight, negative movement of the head.

" Why not ? "

There was a deadly stillness. He wondered if it was the clock, or the sound of his own heart ticking. Then—as though something—some virtue—had gone out of her, he saw her reel : leapt towards her and caught her in his arms.

" Why not ? " He whispered it with his lips against her hair. He wondered what gesture of supreme humility to make, that would break down her pride.

" Do you really want to know ' Why not ' ? "

As her head dropped for a moment against his pounding heart, he thought he had won her ; then she thrust him away.

Stunned, a little giddy, for his body, as well as his soul, ached for her, he watched her cross the room, the dust-coloured velvet of her dress dragging back like a serpent from her narrow hips. When she turned, she had a packet clasped to her bosom ; his eyes went involuntarily to the beauty of her crossed arms and long white hands that clutched the upper edges of the packet.

" I want you to take this home and read it. It was written a long time ago—only for myself. There are things in it—about your mother—that perhaps you won't like "—she saw his slight

stiffening, not in antagonism to her, but in defence of the dead—
" but you must try to make allowance for a child's impressions :
a very self-conscious, rather unhappy child. I'd probably feel
quite differently, if she were still alive."

" What is it ?—a diary ? "

" I suppose you'd call it an autobiography—*not* for publication. I wrote it when I was about twenty-two. You know how
important one's own life seems then—and full of all kinds of
things that no one understands ! " She was talking quickly,
nervously, smiling at him across the space between them.

" Couldn't you—tell me about them ? "

She shook her head so violently that the hair swung in a bell
about her narrow face.

" When you've read it, you'll know all sorts of things it
would take too long, and be too—too shy-making, to tell you.
You'll find it rather long-winded, and bits may be boring, but
please read it all—especially the first chapters, about when we
were children, because they help to explain what happened.
Explain : not excuse. I don't hold with making excuses."

" You have nothing to excuse, to me."

She pushed the parcel towards him, and he still held his hands
off it.

" I'd so much rather not——"

" You've got to."

" All right," he said reluctantly, and took it from her. " But
—whatever it is won't make any difference."

Looking down at the parcel, he saw it had been sealed, but
that the seals were broken. She answered his unspoken question.

" I opened it to add something—one little sentence—last
night, at Uncle Joe's. Something I went to Paris to find out.
Something I had to be sure of, before seeing you."

Obeying an overwhelming instinct, he cried out,

" I won't read it ! Whatever it is belongs to the past, before
we cared for one another ; it's got nothing to do with the
future, for you and me." He knew he was being cowardly, that
what he wanted—most passionately—was not to be hurt.

" My poor dear," said Aldebaran, in a voice of pity and

wonder, "do you really think you can get rid of the past as easily as all that ?"

II

Orlando put the light out. He had read steadily, to the end, to the four words scribbled in pencil at the foot of the last page. As the reading lamp blinked out, a pale fold of dawn lay down an edge of the drawn curtains. The window was open, he heard a taxi brake on the corner of Cavendish Street.

At no moment had sleep visited his eyes. There had been moments when he caught himself smiling at evocations of their childhood—seen through the eyes of Cat's gawky school-friend, the "odd little creature" (so his mother had called her) whom Cat had insisted on bringing home for part of the holidays : stiff, ill at ease, too visibly impressed by the "grandeurs" of Paragon. "Not *quite*"—another of his Mother's phrases ; but she had, of course, a prejudice against Floods. Cat, mulishly insistent on the newly formed friendship, was, however, quite as stubborn as her Mother, and Barry's visits became an institution. She was called Barry in those days, because Aldebaran was too fine a name for schoolroom use. Barry sounded better than the old-fashioned Deb, which, on her introduction to The Lodge, Aldebaran was at pains to conceal.

But presently there was no more smiling. *Childe Roland to the Dark Tower Came.* By the poignancy of her writing she swept him into the Dark Tower. Once—in some let-up of the pain— he found himself thinking, "This is the best thing she has ever written. She will never write the like again."

With his eyes on the dawn gleam, he forced his mind back to this aspect. Her best writing. The only other time she had captured anything like its quality was in *The Sad Dove*. If I don't appreciate her as a writer, everything else fails. That's the first thing I've got to accept : the waywardness of the creative artist, the thing that's more powerful in her even than her obstinate blood. I'm not an artist, and I'm not creative, but I suppose

I must have inherited something of the disposition that made one Sax a painter, and most of them write poetry—of sorts. You cannot be born and brought up in Paragon and remain indifferent to all that. If this were published, it would put her in the category to which she would like to belong. If this were published——!

His thoughts, alarmed, went galloping off like a scattered flock of sheep. He was back in the Long Gallery—which, some time in 1914, had been cleared of its cabinets, its couches and its Old Masters, and filled with a double row of hospital beds, to one of which, through some blessed dispensation of providence, aided by his father's wire-pulling, they had brought him back with the tube in his leg. In the next bed—also by grace of the authorities—was the one they called The Yank (not understanding this was an insult to a Southerner), to whom he, Orlando, owed his life. The Yank's wounds were not serious, and it was not long before he was out of bed, beating the piano which had been brought in from Cat's old schoolroom—now a mess-room, or something, for the nursing staff.

Or in the Medallion room—one of the few reserved for the private use of the family—with the girls dancing, or, more often, hung in rapture on the end of the Steinway : because that kind of music was new to Paragon—new to the majority of British, who had hardly had time yet to get used to the red-hot " ragtime " ushered in by the blaring of the saxophone, which had roared through the country in the last few years before the war. The Yank's music was different ; it got one in the guts. It had a misery in it—yet it held fascination for those boys in hospital, for whom misery had an interpretation of its own. It collected it some way all their disillusionment, all of their dim apprehension of the future in an altered world ; reminders of the girls they had loved when they themselves were " different " and of the girls they now loved easily and forgot easily, because they—the girls themselves—were different, were easy : like—Lydia ! Lovely Lydia, lifting her head in the dawn, as she had lifted her mouth one night in a dark passage. *Take it, take it, Orlando : take everything that comes easily.* Why should not the all-pervading mood infect a wide-eyed schoolgirl, dizzy with unfamiliar rhythms? "Jehovah Blues"; that god-damned tune which, in future, whenever he heard it—which was, on the average, a dozen times a week—would strike chill to his heart, and leave him wondering what it meant to her; whether it was evoking the old magic . . .

"Jehovah Blues"—da da de dah—"Upon the mountain Jehovah spoke"—down the years—down the centuries——

Orlando flung the blankets aside and leapt out of bed. Somewhere across the room was a syphon. He blundered in search of it, forgetting about the light, groping, until he found it, and found the trigger, and the water hissed out, splashing his wrist. As he tipped the glass, something wet and cold nosed at his naked ankle.

"Sorry," said Orlando, mechanically and groped for the rug to fold over the basket, which, at Laura's request and the annoyance of the housekeeper, he had brought up in the car from Paragon. There were some squeaks, some creaks, a glutinous noise of licking, and a heavy flop, as someone fell out of bed, and, instantly wide awake, began a snarling and snapping attack on Orlando's bare toes.

"Stop it, you little bastard." He hoisted something warm and fat and thrust it back in the basket; submitted to some finger-chewing, terminated it with a cuff and went back to bed. The marks of Laura's shame—he ought to have got rid of them; but the silly bitch was so pleased.

III

"'The contrast is evident from the moment of one's arrival,'" dictated Aldebaran. "'The slowing-up of the emotional tempo——'"

"Hey!" Agnes lifted her head to reveal an expression of disconcertion. "You can't use 'emotional tempo' for readers of *The Daily Liar*!"

"Oh—put 'pace.' What's it worth, anyhow?"

" Roughly speaking, a thousand a year," was the dry rejoinder, as Agnes continued her scribbling.

" When's the contract up ? " Aldebaran asked abruptly.

" I'm not sure ; do you want me to check up on it ? "

" It doesn't matter. They'll notify me from the office. I'm not renewing—that's all."

Agnes regarded her employer steadily.

" Then I take it you're not renewing the car hire, or the account with Lacon and Ollier, or your table at Biri's."

Aldebaran stared.

" What's the matter ? Are you nuts ? "

" *I'm* not. But you can't keep a Rolls on the doorstep, turn up at all the first nights and continue to feed your friends two or three times a week at one of the most expensive joints in town, if you've suddenly made up your mind to drop a third of your income."

" Okay," snapped Aldebaran, " I won't—feed my friends. I'm going into the country to write a book."

" What sort of a book ? "

" A *nice* book ! " bluffed Aldebaran.

" Sales round about two thousand five hundred, I suppose," murmured Agnes. " Well, thanks for letting me know. I'll tighten my belt. Have you any particular plans for Diamond ? "

" I don't need to have any ; The Lodge will look after her."

" She says you were taking her to Lillywhite's this morning, to get her sports kit," Agnes reminded her.

" Oh—*you* take her."

" How can I ? We promised that typescript for noon today, and the letters you gave me this morning will take me every minute up to post time."

Aldebaran hitched herself out of the chair, and, hands in pockets, went to look across the leafless trees at the ice-skimmed surface of the Regent's canal. It was a bluff about the book ; she had not an idea in her head. Since waking, she had been in the grip of the terror that overcomes, at intervals, all creative workers : that she was finished, that she would never write a line again. No editor in his right mind would accept the

article she had just dictated to Agnes. To succeed in journalism
—as in any other form of writing—one must believe in what
one was doing, and she had lost her belief. She had reached
the end of her run—the brief, glorified run of unworthy success !

There had been a letter from Bob Winter in the morning's
mail, and a royalty statement. " It looks as though you'll be
able to live on *Bells* for the rest of your life ! " Bob had written
—thinking it would please her. She would certainly need to
have something to live on ! The bank manager had been
courteous, but not over-encouraging, when she telephoned to
know how her balance stood. The answer had shaken her—a
little. How, in so short a time, could she have got through so
much money ? Naturally, she had not made a penny out of
the lecture tour ; no one does. But she had expected to find
enough in the current account to pay off all the " accounts
rendered " which had accumulated through her absence ; and
it had been a shock to discover that, even had she been advised,
she could not have raised enough to buy up the Mildenhall
shares, as she had boasted to Joe she would.

In all her life she had never known the meaning of financial
insecurity. The decline of Polly's earnings had synchronized
with her own entrance into the world of " big money." It was
desperately disconcerting to discover how much of one's assurance depended on the ability to write a cheque. She realized,
with an access of panic that, unless she could break out of this
numbness of uncreativity, she would not be able to pay Agnes's
salary. It was something to do with her nerves !—flustered, she
tried to rationalize it ; something for which she should see a
doctor. Can medical science kindle an extinguished spark ?
Has anyone, since Jesus, succeeded in raising the dead ?

A shriek from Agnes made her turn. The door opened.
Something small and amber-coloured executed a splattering
prance across the floor. Agnes, down on her knees, scooped up
a spaniel puppy, which slobbered and struck with fringed paws
of velvet at her face. Agnes caught the paws, with their hard
little horny crescents, in her unoccupied hand.

" Laura's love—and *no* apologies."

Orlando was standing inside the door; his face was pale —almost dust-coloured—but he was smiling. She turned on him furiously.

"Who let you in? I simply won't stand for this sort of thing; you know perfectly well I'm working." She made a lunge at the desk and dragged a pile of typescript towards her.

There was silence. Then the sound of the door, quietly closing. Agnes—taking the puppy with her! Just—common— treachery. She found herself looking at Orlando's hand, planted on top of the page she was pretending to read.

"It's—unforgivable of you, to do this!" Her eyes were wet with anger.

"I like your autobiography. It's most beautifully written. Nearly as beautifully as your poems."

Had everyone gone crazy this morning? She found herself speechless.

"It's much more sincere than you were last night," he was saying calmly. "Perhaps most authors write better than they talk. As a matter of fact, I think it's "—he paused—"*great* writing. It made me very proud of you."

She could not control the tears now; they gushed over. Groping for her handkerchief, she muttered,

"No one could accuse you of being personal!"

"One ought to be impersonal in one's approach to any work of art," said Orlando, as though he were repeating a lesson. "Even I realize that!"

"So now, I suppose, we publish it!"

"I'm naturally disposed to admire anything you do, but— well, I suppose there's no harm in saying, now, that I never cared much for *Bells on her Fingers*."

"No?"

"I always knew you could do better," said Orlando calmly. "It's nice, you know, when one's opinions are justified."

"Have you ever," said Aldebaran carefully, "thought of going in for publishing?"

"No, I can't say I have." He took her seriously.

"Then that's all right. Don't," was the crisp retort.

"Seriously, that manuscript you gave me to read last night. I think it's the best thing you've ever done. Naturally, I wouldn't set my opinion against yours—and I don't know a thing about writing—but how much of a thing would it be, to translate all that from the first into the third person, and, of course, take out some of the more personal passages——"

Has anyone, since Jesus, succeeded in raising the dead?

She came back from some dark cavern of the mind, to stare at a bulky envelope Orlando had laid on the desk.

"What's this?"

"Look at it."

She gave him a suspicious look, put out her hand, and drew it back.

"No."

"Please look at it."

She knew the stiff shape and feeling of Company scrip. Orlando's face was very grey, there were pouches under his eyes, but he was smiling.

"I will *not*!" She brought the flat of her hand down hard on the table—Harcourt's gesture—and defied him with her scowl.

"As a favour to me. It's your wedding present," he said coolly. "At least, one of them."

"I won't marry you!"

"Why not? Are you afraid of loving Lee Marion again?"

"My God, no—not now!" burst from her.

"You mean, since finding out he was coloured?"

It was like a fighter, entering on another round.

"Do you *like* the idea of marrying a woman who's had a coloured child?"

"Candidly, no," he told her. "But I don't know that colour has much to do with it, in the circumstances. If you told me you'd deliberately gone to bed with a black——"

The laughter came out of her in sobs that sounded as though they were broken out of her, and left her bleeding.

"That would make a difference, wouldn't it?"

"It certainly would, to me."

" I know it would ! "

" And you—you wouldn't "—for the first time he sounded uncertain—" carry your—your principle as far as that—— ? "

" No. No, I wouldn't ! " Losing control, she beat her hands on the desk like a child. " Why do you have to keep on at me —to cheapen me : as though I didn't feel cheap enough already ? Don't you see what it's like—not to be honest ? Not to be true —to you—or to Lee—or to what I *believe* ? Oh, Jesus ; you've read the book. Why can't you let me alone ? "

" I suppose the answer to that is—I love you," said Orlando slowly. " I love you in a way over which I've got no control, and I don't believe there's anything that would alter it. I tried this morning to imagine how I would have felt, if you had come to me with that unfortunate baby in your arms——"

She looked up at him haggardly.

" Yes ? " she said, and waited.

" Well," said Orlando, and smiled a little, " perhaps I'm not a very imaginative person. I just couldn't see it. All I could see was you——"

" Let me help you," she said with gentleness. " Supposing my baby hadn't died. Supposing we had had, together, to take care of him ; be responsible for his happiness ; look after his education——"

" Let's throw away 'thinking' and 'supposing' and 'imagining' ! " There was no smile left on his tired face. " We aren't living in a world of ghosts. This is you, and this is me, and we've done what thousands of other adults have done in a world disintegrated by war. You've paid for it more heavily, because you're a woman ; but if you stand logically by your own opinions, the other thing doesn't count. What was it you said to me last night ?—' They're just *people*, with the same rights as ours ; not to be granted favours or made to endure penalties '—something like that. I don't say I'd have been able to keep up this objective attitude if—oh my God. I suppose, like most people of my sort, I'm conventional : which—I suppose again—means I've got my share of the fear, and guilt, and shame our race has inherited.

"This is you and this is me : two people who care enough about each other to make the gamble of spending the rest of their lives together worth while. On my part, it goes beyond caring ; I do most definitely need you. I'm not complete without you . . ."

There was such a strange, far-away look on her face that he wondered if she was listening. He waited, then took the envelope she was unconsciously clutching out of her hand. He slid out the stiff sheet of paper it contained, and flattened it before her. Then he picked up her pen, removed the cap and held it out to her.

"Agnes should be here, to witness this."

She blinked at him confusedly, automatically accepted the pen, and laid it down.

"I'll never write another *Bells*."

"No, you probably won't."

"Something in me's dried up. I'm not ' a great writer.' "

"I never thought you were," said Orlando calmly.

"But—but—" stammered Aldebaran, "you said—I mean, I shan't be able to pull my weight."

"Darling," said Orlando, "will you just sign here ? "

She read, slowly, and at first incredulously. When she lifted her head, tears were streaming down her face.

"I'm—not—quite—sure—I—understand ! "

"I'm transferring the Purcell-Flood holdings to you. That's why I bought them."

"So I'll—— ? "

"You'll be on the Board of Directors. It will really be ' Purcell-*Flood*,' this time ! "

". . . Ring that bell for Agnes, will you ? "

She lifted her hand to his, which lay on her shoulder ; the pair of them looked down on the big, looping signature which stood, to one at least, for generations of Floods.

"By Jesus, I *will* write another book !—if," said Aldebaran soberly, "I ever have time."